MURDER IN A SMALL TOWN

A.J. HARRIS

Copy Editor and Typesetter: Vince Font
Cover design by Judith S. Designs & Creativity
Published by Glass Spider Publishing
www.glassspiderpublishing.com

To my loving wife, Yetta, who has been a constant source of understanding and encouragement for over three decades, nine novels, many short stories, and four radio broadcasts. She has calmed my moments of anxiety, such as computer crashes. This novel, like those that preceded it, would not have come to fruition without her diligence and forbearance.

ACKNOWLEDGMENTS

The following people were extremely helpful in providing suggestions, information, and technical data. Bob Baum, Bill Blundell, Paul Burri, Joan Marks, Kathie Marshall. To my editor and publisher, Vince Font of Glass Spider Publishing, with much gratitude, and Judith San Nicolas Villalonga for the tantalizing book cover.

–A.J. Harris

CHAPTER 1

Zacharius Mayhew Schwartzenpfeffer, a name I was saddled with but vowed to change as soon as I graduated from the Chicago School of Pharmacy in 1940. From that point on, I would be known as Zach M. Black. Along with my name change, I was eager to change my lifestyle and leave the big city with its grime, political corruption, and crime rate. In short, I wanted to live in a small town where big-city problems didn't exist and people moved at a slower pace. At least that's what I hoped for when I read an ad in my pharmaceutical journal: "Wanted: Pharmacist for Newbury, Wisconsin, population 9,650. Famous for dairy farms, cheeses, and small breweries. Excellent remuneration and benefits."

My school mentor, learning of my proposed move, warned me that the cow-town of Newbury was a haven for red-necked conservatives and that I had to be wary about mouthing off my liberal biases. Coming from a family of socially progressive thinkers—my father taught

Civics and my mother American History in the local high school—I was thoroughly entrenched in a liberal background.

Despite my mentor's warning, I answered the ad, took the North Shore Commuter for a three-hour ride, and detrained at a depot right out of a Norman Rockwell painting. I walked two blocks to the corner of Grant Avenue and Lincoln Street, the busiest intersection with the town's only electric traffic signal. This southwest corner was the location of the drugstore—a Victorian Age structure, dark, almost foreboding, with the ancient healer's globes of red and green liquid displayed in the window.

The cornerstone of the drugstore read: "Est. 1892 Prop. Samuel L. Withers."

People on the street smiled and said hello, which was my earliest indication of the townsfolk's friendliness—something to which I was unaccustomed.

Greeting me in the store was the owner, Earl J. Withers, an elderly man who limped toward me, and a much younger woman at his side who introduced herself as Irma, Mrs. Withers. She spoke with an eastern seaboard intonation and smiled brightly as she gazed into my eyes. She hooked her arm around mine and with constant chatter escorted me through the store to the pharmacy at the rear.

Her familiarity embarrassed me. I glanced at her

husband, wondering what he thought of her chummy closeness toward me. I tried to act casually as I looked about the well-stocked store with its abundant health products, household goods, cosmetics, and a lunch counter with a brass-foot rail, swivel seats, and porcelain-handled fountain dispensers.

Irma dominated my interview, which had little to do with my training as a pharmacist but more about my social life. She asked about my dating, my plans for marriage, and expressed interest in knowing how I spent my evenings. I thought she might have an eye affliction because she winked at me a few times.

My primary duty was to relieve Mr. Withers, who complained of rheumatism, lumbago, and chronic catarrh. Although I sympathized, I wanted to get to practical matters such as my hours and salary. Having settled on a salary which frankly was more than I had expected and given a temporary room with a cot behind the store, I started my job immediately with little time for adjustment. I could get a toothbrush and toothpaste off the shelf, even a pair of Jockey shorts and undershirts until I could retrieve my stuff from Chicago.

I slipped into one of Mr. Withers' small, ill-fitting white jackets and assumed my responsibilities, which were fine except that I was almost hidden from public view behind the elevated pharmacy counter, which prevented opportunities for socializing with customers.

After a week, I found the work to be easy, although it required more hours than I had imagined. Small annoyances arose from trying to decipher inscrutable scribblings on prescriptions from the town's three doctors and the occasional cry for help at the soda fountain during the lunch hour.

My salary allowed for renting three rooms in a boardinghouse and purchasing things I could not have afforded before. At age twenty-six, I was the owner of a new Plymouth coupe bought on an installment plan. It was one of the last cars made before the factory converted to manufacturing tanks for WWII preparedness. My wardrobe consisted of two suits, two sport jackets, and four pairs of slacks plus an adequate supply of shirts, shoes, and ties. My ideas for merchandising made a considerable difference in the store's profits, and my status as a professional was firmly established as customers came in asking for me by name.

After several months, I settled easily into community life with one wonderful bonus. My working hours left little time for outside socializing, which wasn't altogether bad since my need for certain outlets like sexual gratification were met splendidly by the drugstore owner's wife, Irma, whose own sexual desires seemed insatiable. Our covert and frequent liaisons caused me some concern—not about unwanted pregnancy, since I had a bountiful supply of prophylactics—but a fear of being discovered. That thought niggled at my pleasure every time I experienced a burst of fulfillment.

Irma Withers, a zaftig twenty-eight-year-old, latched on to me shortly after I arrived. We soon enjoyed clandestine meetings in the storage room behind the store where we would lie on large cases of toilet tissue or Kotex. Her repertoire, a virtual cornucopia of sexual treats, left me at times seeking relief. However, her chronic cough concerned me since I was sure old man Withers would hear her and catch us *in flagrante*.

I asked, "Have you seen a doctor about your cough?"

"My husband concocted a cough syrup that helps . . . but the only medicine I need is loving. My husband is limp . . . useless. You can understand that, can't you?" Her frank discussions made me uneasy but didn't seem to bother her.

She would use post-coital time as a sort of confessional—an emotional release perhaps to justify infidelity. I imagined myself in the role of a psychiatrist giving practical treatments, or at the very least a priest in a confessional listening while she engaged in languorous fellatio. During one of those sessions, I learned how six years ago she had snagged the then sixty-eight-year-old Withers shortly after his wife, Bertha, died.

Irma had met Withers through her cousin at an Elks social. A whirlwind romance led to marriage one month later. A wedding photo in Withers' office revealed a svelte bride at least twenty pounds lighter and a smiling groom who could have been mistaken for her father. Withers had not aged well.

Now thinner and completely bald, Withers took on a cadaverous appearance and moved with a shuffling gait. In recent months he asked me for injections of testosterone to satisfy Irma's demands, so he claimed.

One morning, following an injection which I had given him the night before, Earl (the name he preferred) came to the drugstore looking more haggard than usual. He asked to examine a vial of testosterone. I took one out of a box and handed it to him. He held it to the light, squinted, and read the small white lettering on the brown glass.

"Says here the dosage is 100 mg/ml, but the damn stuff seems less potent than it used to be." He returned the vial to me, then continued, "I could get it off two to three times a week, now I'm lucky to get it off once a month—even then, it's a goddamn struggle. Worst part is Irma doesn't understand. I think she still sees me as a young stud pawing the ground, snorting, ready to put that stiff pecker into . . . well, what's the use?" He looked down, then faced me squarely. "You don't have trouble getting it up, do you?"

I avoided looking at him and continued filling a prescription. "No, I have no trouble, at least not yet." Affixing a label to a bottle, I stopped, eager to change the subject. "Earl, I've been here for a year, and I've not had a raise . . ."

"Hold on there, Sonny, don't be so impatient. When you started here, I promised to turn the store over to you since I expected to retire soon. That promise still holds. You can have this place for what it's worth, that is, dollar for dollar on the merchandise, and your rent will apply to the purchase price. I can't think of a sweeter deal than that—unless you want me to throw Irma into the bargain." He laughed. "Well, maybe not . . . she wouldn't be agreeable to that sort of thing."

Withers cackled, thinking he was clever. I figured old Earl was too late with that part of the offer. Irma had already dealt herself a winning hand in that game.

* * *

Our intimacies were becoming less secretive. Irma flirted openly and spent more time with me in the prescription compartment. Although she helped by labeling and placing supplies on shelves, she purposely got in my way, wanting attention. I feared that old man Withers, suspecting our affair, might do something crazy like shoot me during one of our orgies. He kept a gun in his desk drawer, a 9mm S&W revolver, which he proudly showed me a few times. One day, at his insistence and my reluctance, I handled it, aimed it at an imaginary target, and without pulling the trigger, yelled, "Pow!" Both of us jumped. He never showed me the gun again.

As time went on, Earl's thinking became erratic. He revealed a paranoia and muttered about that damned socialist in the White House while praising Hitler for his racial-extermination madness. I found it difficult to be near him when he began his demented tirades.

In this town of conservative ninnies, a cuckold like Withers might be deemed justified in killing a rival if a case were to come to court. Besides, Withers would be favored since he was native-born and a stalwart on the board of city directors.

His admiration for Hitler did not sit well with Eddie Polanski, the soda fountain operator—or soda jerk, as Withers called him. Eddie had lost family in the Nazi invasion of Poland during the terrible airstrikes when fleeing civilians, including women and children, were mowed down mercilessly.

I would help during the lunch-hour rush when Eddie scrambled to prepare salads, sandwiches, and drinks. I watched in amazement as he deftly cut meats, cheeses, fruits, and vegetables with a long knife he honed frequently.

On one occasion, Withers walked by as Eddie was slicing a cucumber. When Withers passed, Eddie scowled and said, "See this knife? I could castrate that old sonofabitch, but what good would that do? His nuts are probably dry as dust. Better I should slit his throat."

"Why do you stay here?" I asked.

He sighed. "Because the old bastard owns that rundown shack we live in, and the rent is cheap. I already made a lot of repairs on it and never got paid." He looked around before continuing, "Besides, I can cop some food at the end of the day, and that's a big savings. My wife, Wanda, brings in a few bucks with her sewing, so we get along."

"Couldn't you do the same thing elsewhere?"

"I keep thinking about it . . . maybe go to Detroit, get a job in one of those war-machine factories." He spoke softly, "If that old bastard calls me a dumb Polack one more time or pinches Wanda's ass like he's done, I'll kill him." He fingered the edge of the knife blade before putting it down.

"If you do that, Eddie, they'll give you the chair or put you away for life. You're smarter than that."

Withers returned to the soda fountain. "You boys better speed it up. Some of the customers are waiting for their orders." He looked at a ham and cheese on rye and said, "Polanski, don't put so many potato chips on that plate. The more chips you give 'em, the less they'll want a piece of pie or slice of cake. Use your head. Don't act like a dumb Pol—" He stopped when Eddie shot him a threatening glance. Withers looked toward the prescription counter and said, "There's a customer waiting for a prescription. I'd better take care of her."

Eddie leaned toward me and whispered, "It's a good thing that bastard left. I was tempted to do something I could have been sorry for."

Seated on the end stool at the soda fountain, Irma, with legs crossed, showing much of her lower thighs, munched on an egg salad sandwich from a plate heaping with potato chips, coleslaw, and a dill pickle. As Withers ambled toward her, he cast a scornful glance. "You don't need all that food. You're putting too much fat on your behind."

I watched as Irma replaced the remaining sandwich on her plate, picked up the pickle, bit into it with a crunching sound, and tossed a baleful glance at Withers. "Try saying something nice, or are you unable to do that like a few other things you can't do?" She pushed her plate aside, slid off the stool, placed her hands on her hips, and went nose-to-nose with Earl, who sneered.

"You are a miserable, ungrateful whore," he said as he craned his thin neck toward Irma.

In a stunning move, she slapped the unsuspecting Earl across the face with a force that sounded throughout the store. He stumbled backward, knocking over a display of hernia trusses that landed in a loopy pattern on his head. He laid dazed on the floor, feeling his reddened cheek and adjusting his upper denture that slipped forward.

Mumbling curses, he got up and slowly walked to the pharmacy station without looking back.

CHAPTER 2

I learned from Irma that Earl and his first wife, Bertha, who had no children, directed their energies to improving the drugstore. They had replaced wooden floorboards with white octagonal vinyl tiles and smaller black tiles at the entrance that spelled "Withers Drug Emporium."

Earl had retained some of the features of the original establishment: suspended globes in the window filled with red and green liquid to signify the ancient healing arts. Awnings with green and white stripes created a distinctive landmark, a place where housewives could gossip over Cokes and high schoolers could indulge in sodas, sundaes, or banana splits.

Dark-stained oak cabinets with glass doors displayed old apothecary jars with labels written in Latin: nostrums, elixirs, purgatives, and appetite stimulants or suppressants. Contraceptives and condoms stored below the pharmacist's counter were requested by men or teenagers in near whispers.

Toxic substances like arsenic and strychnine were stored in a locked cabinet under the counter; a skull and crossbones were drawn on the door. Strong pain killers—opiates, codeine, and Demerol—were locked in another cabinet.

Withers, to his credit, initiated modern merchandising techniques that allowed customers to take products off shelves and carry them to a cashier. For all his business acumen, I was appalled when he dispensed medical advice to customers. That had to be a source of irritation or worse to the town's doctors, but Withers, the only pharmacist in town, was tolerated, albeit grudgingly.

Irma boasted on more than one occasion that she had filled Earl with a sense of youthful well-being after their marriage six years ago, while he confessed to me that he had not experienced such pleasurable sensations since his honeymoon forty years ago with Bertha. Being intimate with Irma, I had no reason to doubt that. Irma's gay spirit and sexual abandon had lessened the old man's infirmities until two years ago when his disabilities worsened and his disposition soured, leaving the corners of his mouth in a constant downturn.

Irma worked in the drugstore until she felt the need to get away from the confining and, as she would say, boring cow-town atmosphere. She would escape to Madison or take a few days off and go to Chicago on a shopping spree at Marshall Field's and Carson Pirie Scott & Co. Not that she needed more clothes—just the freedom of getting away.

She complained to me that Earl demanded to know why she found it necessary to spend two or more days in Chicago staying at luxury hotels like the Bismarck or the Palmer House that cost at least fifty dollars a day, which included food and services. When he began accusing her of entertaining a gigolo, she told him she would have but just didn't have the time. He would grumble and walk away.

She insisted that he hire a pharmacist to help and eventually replace him, but he was reluctant to acknowledge his disability, even though his symptoms worsened. To appease her, he ran ads in pharmacy journals and newspapers, but few responded. Those who did demanded too much money and benefits. Irma said he threatened to close the store and walk away, but she knew he was incapable of surviving without his cherished drugstore. He complained he needed the income. Irma pooh-poohed that notion, saying he was rich as Rockefeller but tight as a tick.

She continued, "One day Earl's back pain became so severe that even standing caused him to agonize. She demanded that he place an ad clearly stating the drugstore was to be sold under attractive conditions to a progressive-thinking pharmacist. The ad went on to describe the town and the potential for great success."

That was the ad that had caught my attention.

In addition to Eddie Polanski at the soda/lunch counter, there were other employees, including high school students doing part-time work. An employee of long standing, Mavis Johnson, tended the cosmetics counter, but she had taken on a position of much greater importance. She made purchases for general merchandise, paid bills, and kept the ledger for profits and expenses.

She was the mother of a seventeen-year-old son and had been working at the drugstore for eighteen years. I was impressed with her efficiency but put off by her aloofness. We seldom spoke, but I admired her, a woman in her thirties who maintained a slim figure and dressed smartly. She had a pleasant but not beautiful face and wore her hair like Bette Davis.

I never learned whether she had been married, divorced, or widowed, and she never volunteered that information. I thought her position of responsibility was unusual: she had a key to the store, arrived first in the mornings to turn on lights, check thermostats, and give orders to Walt Mason, the handyman. She parked her year-old Chrysler sedan in a designated parking space behind the drugstore and carried a leather case containing ledgers in which she entered the previous day's receipts and expenses.

Irma and Mavis kept an arm's-length relationship. My assessment of their association was that of a stew simmering just below the boiling point.

On a typical day, Earl would limp into the drugstore berating, cursing, and complaining about inefficiencies and creating an atmosphere of tension, but he never reproached Mavis. If he didn't smile at her, at least he didn't embarrass her.

While filling a prescription one afternoon, I looked into the store and saw a handsome young man in a neatly fitted uniform with a Sam Brown belt, visor hat, shoulder braid, and white gloves. Mavis, with a rare smile, hurried to his side, then brought him to my station. "Mr. Black, this is my son, Charles. He's a captain in the ROTC." The young man removed his right glove and shook my hand firmly.

"You're about the best-decorated soldier I've ever seen with as many decorations as a four-star general." I pointed to one colorful medal. "What did you do to win that?"

He tucked in his chin and looked down. "That's an expert rifleman's award."

We exchanged pleasantries until Earl approached; he thrust his left hand on the young man's right shoulder and pumped his right hand. I excused myself and left the threesome chatting like old friends.

*　　*　　*

Walter Mason, the seventy-four-year-old handyman, showed little or no deference toward Earl, or for that matter anyone else. When he saw Earl in the mornings he rarely greeted him with anything more than a grunt, then he would go about mopping or moving boxes from the storage area to the front on orders from Mavis.

I asked Irma about Walter (no one called him Mr. Mason). She motioned for me to sit because her story would be lengthy. She said his background was tragic, then she lit a cigarette, puffed, and began by saying, "He and Earl had been boyhood chums through grammar and high school. Walter won a scholarship to MIT and graduated with honors as a civil engineer. On a New Year's Eve, Walter, who had been living in New York City and working in a prestigious engineering firm, came back to visit family and friends here in Newbury. Of course, he partied with his old friend Earl. Both men, in their mid-twenties, dated local girls for the New Year's Eve celebration, and all had been drinking. A light drizzle earlier in the evening turned icy on the highway as the temperature dropped below freezing. Despite hazardous road conditions, Earl insisted on driving to another bar even though Walter opposed the idea.

"They argued, but since it was Earl's car, he drove. They left a bar at about 2:00 a.m. and planned to drive to another bar at the edge of town. The car skidded all over the road, causing the highway police to pull Earl over. Instead of stopping, Earl sped, and the police gave chase.

"Earl failed to negotiate a turn and the car struck a utility pole, crumpled like tin foil, and burst into flames. One of the girls flew out; her head struck a boulder and she was killed instantly. The other girl sustained fractures of both legs and pelvis. Walter lay on the road unconscious with second- and third-degree burns on his face and hands. When he opened his eyes a week later in the hospital, he had no recollection of what had happened, but worse than that he was unable to talk or recognize family members or friends. He was sent to the Neuro-Psychiatric Hospital in Marquette for further treatment and remained there for several months in rehabilitation. He was unable to remember anything prior to the accident."

CHAPTER 3

Irma continued her story: "Earl suffered from multiple spinal and rib fractures plus injuries to his left knee, requiring surgery. He remained flat on his back for weeks, then wore a back brace for months. The doc said the knee would never be normal, and it never was. The deformity left him with a limp. When his friend Walter recovered sufficiently to walk and talk well enough, Earl gave him a job."

"Is that why Walter works here as a handyman?" I asked. "He seems to know who Earl is now."

"He's been told about the accident a number of times, and I think by now he knows what happened. It's possible that he'll always hate Earl, and yet he understands enough to be grateful to Earl for his job. It's one of those love/hate things, I guess." Irma lit another cigarette and took a long drag. "With all his employees, Earl has a hell of a weekly payout, even though the drugstore makes good money."

I wanted to remind her of those clothes-buying excursions she took that must have cost Earl a bundle.

Irma, a cigarette hanging from the corner of her mouth, arms folded across her ample bosom, said, "Don't worry about that old miser, he owns a lot of property in this town, in fact, in the whole county—inherited from his old man. He owns a bunch of shacks like the one Eddie Polanski lives in, plus acres of farmland his father bought cheap during the Great Depression."

"I've noticed he's given Mavis a lot of responsibility. She orders merchandise and displays it as well as doing the payroll and the books."

Irma stubbed her cigarette in an ashtray. "That uppity bitch better never let me catch her handling anything else of his, or I'll slit her throat."

I was sorry I mentioned her name.

Irma continued, "I wanted Earl to get rid of her long ago, but he insists on her staying. Says she's worth her weight in gold. She's efficient and all that, but she's like a goddamned sphinx—says nothing to me but toadies up to Earl. A real kiss-ass. I just don't trust her. Know what I mean?"

"She must be paid well . . . dresses smartly and drives an upscale car," I said.

"Yeah, and that ain't all. You met her kid; he goes to East Lynn, an exclusive school for boys. Tuition there goes through the roof."

"Maybe she has outside income."

"Either that or my stupid husband is paying her big-time for a blow job now and then. If I ever caught them, it'd be too damn bad for her."

I said nothing but thought she obviously overlooked her involvement with me.

She continued, "Now that I have you, I don't need his limp old . . . in fact, I can't stand to have him touch me anymore—but you can, any time." She held me tightly and pressed her pelvis against mine.

At that moment, the door opened. I froze. Earl stood and stared at us. An awkward moment followed as I tried to think of an explanation for our closeness. Irma released me, looked at Earl, and said, "Zach has something in his eye. I'm trying to get it out."

"Uh-huh," Earl said, "and is it necessary for him to be squeezing your behind at the same time?"

"Really? I hadn't noticed," she said.

Grimacing, Earl turned to leave, then slammed the door behind him.

Embarrassed and ashamed, I pushed her hand away as I felt heat rising in my neck and head.

Irma put her hand to her mouth to suppress giggling. She kissed me and pinched my cheek. "Oh, don't worry," she said. "Nothing will happen. He needs you, and he can't afford to divorce me; he doesn't want to lose his precious money in a divorce settlement."

"Seems to me his solution would be to get rid of both of us," I said.

She pursed her lips and looked at me slyly. "Not unless we get rid of *him* first."

CHAPTER 4

At 7:30 a.m., the sight of two patrol cars in front of the drugstore gave me a few extra cardiac beats. The cold October wind blew leaves in eddies, adding to the chilling sense of dread. A police officer stood at the entrance of the store holding a billy club, tapping it against the palm of his other hand.

"Sorry, I can't let you in. The coroner and Chief Morgan are in there with the body. I have orders to . . ."

I knew I heard him, but maybe I was mistaken. "What? What body? What're you talking about?" I looked over his shoulder. Suddenly, my legs felt rubbery and my arms shot out against the wall for support.

"You okay?" the officer asked.

I regained equilibrium but remained confused and agitated. "Listen, I got to get in there. This is my drugstore. I got to see what's going on."

"I'm sorry . . ."

I pushed his arm away; he didn't resist, and I hurried

toward the pharmacist's station where the only light shone in the darkened store. Indistinct talking became clearer as I neared the druggist's quarters. Two men talking stood with their backs toward me. The man I assumed to be the coroner, Amos Finder, turned to look at me. His brow furrowed until I identified myself to him and to Jack Morgan, Chief of Police. Finder moved aside, allowing a full view of Earl's corpse lying face-up on the floor next to his desk. His S&W revolver lay in his right hand.

A hideous distortion of his facial features made him almost unrecognizable. From the wound in his forehead, rivulets of dry blood formed on his right cheek and chin. Blue/black rings around his eyes seemed to forecast the hollow eye orbits in a skull. An irregular corona of dark-red blood on the floor encircled his head, and his glazed eyes stared blankly. His upper denture had slipped down, adding to the grotesque death mask. I was overcome with nausea. The coroner moved a chair closer to me and ordered me to sit and place my head between my knees. I took a few deep breaths and hoped I wouldn't vomit.

I recalled so many things in the recent past. I was grateful to Earl for the opportunity he gave me. He was never unkind to me . . . even though he may have suspected my relationship with his wife. I never wished him dead. The operation of the store now depended on me. Jeezus, I didn't know if I could handle that. But why not? I had been running the pharmacy department for over a year, and the store ran well.

"Looks like suicide—plain and simple," the coroner said. The chief of police nodded.

I knelt over Earl's head to examine the bullet entrance wound above the bridge of his nose. "Mind if I turn his head?"

The coroner shrugged. "Be my guest. The photographer took all the exposures he needed." The police chief made no objections.

When I turned the head, I could see the ragged exit site of the bullet behind the head, meaning the bullet had been fired from a higher level and its trajectory arched downward. I looked at the coroner. "Suicide?"

The pot-bellied coroner tugged at his suspenders. He shook his head and in a patronizing manner said, "Well, now, look here." He pointed to Earl's right hand. "You can see he's holding a revolver. Smell the gun. It's just been fired." He smiled smarmy-like. "You got any other notions?"

I was not about to criticize this puffed-up pol whose appointment as coroner required no expertise. If he chose, he could ignore anything I said; he could order the body hauled to the morgue for autopsy or not, and the case would be signed off.

This was where my social and professional skills would be tested. Rather than answer his question directly, I asked, "Who called in the murder—uh, sorry, I meant his death, and how long has he been dead?"

Finder hesitated. He pulled at his suspenders and began slowly. "Been dead for several hours—sometime between midnight and 4:00 a.m., I'd say."

Chief Morgan took over. "Mavis Johnson called in when she opened the store at seven. We got the call from Ben Simon, the detective, he's assigned to the case. I came right over. Let me tell you, that gal Mavis was having the damnedest hysterical fit I ever did see. Judas Priest, does she usually carry on like that? Simon got her out of here. Took her to the station for questioning—a good thing, too." Chief Morgan looked at me. "Tell me about that queer old duck, the guy with the scarred face who was pushing a mop around when we came in."

I told him briefly what I knew about Walt Mason, but I omitted any comments about his relationship with Earl.

The chief listened, nodded slowly, then said, "Simon can grill him later. Well, I think we got all the information we need here." Two men in dark suits arrived. One held a folded stretcher upright. "Take him away, boys. Be sure he's concealed from those busybodies with their noses against the window," the chief said. He looked at me. "You're not planning to leave town, are you? Ben Simon will want to talk to you."

Where did he think I would be going? The question annoyed the hell out of me. "I'm not going anywhere.

I've got a drugstore to run."

The corpse left an irregular pool of dark, syrupy blood on the floor and a pattern of red dots on the baseboard and lower wall. The smell of death had already permeated the room.

Walt, moving slowly, began mopping the floor with water and Lysol. The wall clock read 8:45. I checked phone messages for prescription requests that might have come in during the night. I reached for my white jacket, then wiped the pill board with alcohol.

Irma had already made funeral arrangements and plans for an all-out wake-type celebration. Her initial response to the murder was a loud moan and crying as her shoulders heaved. She brought a hankie to her eyes, but I wasn't sure she blotted any tears. Mavis, on the other hand, would be incapable of anything but mourning for only God knew how long.

A short, broad-shouldered man in an old trench coat and a misshapen fedora with its brim turned up in front walked toward me. He looked from side to side as though sizing up the place. At my counter, he flashed a badge and in unvarnished Brooklynese said, "I'm Lieutenant Simon from the Newbury Police Department. You're Mr. Black?"

"Yes."

"I want to talk to you."

People started coming into the store, and this guy's

loud, abrasive manner annoyed me. I didn't want him here, but I knew he had to question me. "Lieutenant, I'm busy, can this wait?"

"Uh-uh. This can't wait. Your customers will understand. Put up a sign saying you'll be back at ten o'clock. We can talk here or go down to the station— your choice. I want to know all about your relationship with the deceased, his wife, associates, anyone who didn't like him."

His wife? What the hell? Did he know about my relationship with Irma? Going to the police station might be better.

"You can ride with me, Black."

"Call me Zach."

"Fine, call me Lieutenant—or Ben, or whatever."

I got into his mud-spattered, dented '37 Ford coupe that reeked of cigarette smoke . . . a kind of permanent stink enmeshed in the fibers of upholstery. The open ashtray spilled over.

I looked at his bulldog profile. "You're not native to these parts, are you?"

CHAPTER 5

His brow wrinkled; he gave me a knowing smile. "You got that right, Kiddo. My accent gave me away, right? Always does. Brooklyn, New York. C.C.N.Y. Criminology and Law Enforcement, class of '30."

I gave him my bona fides before we reached the police station with its gold-leaf lettering on the door window that read "Newbury Police Department." He walked in front of me with a proprietary air; threw a two-finger salute to a hefty, fortyish woman in uniform seated behind a counter. "Two cups of java to my office. Thanks, Baby Doll."

Simon's office, a 12x12-foot room, stank of cigarette smoke like his car. Several framed certificates barely relieved the depressing grayness of the walls. He sat at his desk and directed me to a chair opposite him. He leaned back, pulled out a cigarette, then offered me the pack, which I refused. "Tell me about yourself," he said. "What brought you to this bucolic corner of paradise?" He seemed pleased with his phraseology.

I gave him a brief personal history and watched as he pulled the ashtray toward him, stubbed the remains of one cigarette, then reached for another. He continued, "With old man Withers gone, you become owner of the drugstore, right?"

How the hell did he know? "Yes, but I'm responsible to the estate for the merchandise and all outstanding debts."

"Uh-huh, and the estate now belongs to Mrs. Withers—Irma. Of course, if you were to marry her . . ."

I interrupted. "Lieutenant, what are you driving at?"

He appeared cagey and calculating, knowing a great deal before this interrogation started. His sneaking manner was as welcoming as a fart in a confessional.

He ignored my question and went on with his own. "What were you doing and where were you doing it last night?"

Trying to be civil was becoming difficult, but I tried. "I was home."

"Can anyone verify that?"

"No, dammit, I was alone. What's this all about? Are you trying to involve me in Withers' death? The coroner said his death was a suicide."

Simon's eyes grew small; he blew a plume above my head then stared at me. "Do you think it was suicide?" He flicked his cigarette ash and waited for my answer.

"No, I don't think it was suicide."

CHAPTER 6

Tilted back in his chair, Simon's fingers were intertwined behind his head. "You don't think it was suicide? Why not?"

"For one thing, Withers was clutching the pistol after he supposedly shot himself. You know that never could have happened. His arms would have fallen outward . . . he would have lost holding control . . . anything in his hands would have dropped."

Simon sat up. "Go on."

"Try taking your gun, without ammo, of course, and pulling the trigger at a point above the bridge of your nose." Simon listened but made no effort to go through the motions. I continued, "More than that, why would Withers go through contortions when he could have put the gun to his temple?"

Simon poked his inner cheek with his tongue and nodded, then said mockingly, "Okay, what else, Sherlock Holmes?"

"There's the blood-spatter, the stippling on the lower wall and baseboard that would indicate an arcing trajectory from a point on the forehead to a point of exit on the lower skull. The murderer stood in front of Withers. There was a good chance he knew his killer. After Withers hit the floor, the murderer put the weapon in Withers' hand and curled his fingers around it."

Simon rubbed his chin then pointed his finger at me. "I like the way you think, Kiddo. In fact, that was my conclusion, but there are a few facts you don't know."

The woman officer appeared at the door with two cups of coffee. Simon waved her forward. I looked at my watch and thought about the people needing prescriptions filled, the luncheon crowd wanting food, and Eddie Polanski sweating, trying to fill orders.

"Simon, can we continue this another time?"

"Okay, Kiddo, just one more question. What is your relationship with the women in the store? Are you—what's the polite word?—intimate? Yeah, that's it, intimate. I'm referring to that Johnson woman and the widow, Irma Withers." He folded his arms across his chest, tilted his head, and watched me closely.

I sat up. "What the hell does that have to do with anything?" I was annoyed and wary that he could be building a case against me. "If you're planning to involve me in this murder, you're wasting time, and I resent it."

"Relax, Kiddo. I ask questions because that's my job.

All you've got to do is answer truthfully. If I think you're giving me bullshit, I'll come down on your ass so hard you'll beg for mercy."

"Don't threaten me, Simon. I can have an attorney charge you with harassment and—"

He cut me off. "Big deal! If I think you need to be grilled further—"

I stopped him. "I'd appreciate a ride back now."

"Alright, alright," Simon yelled to the lady officer to drive me back.

Officer Mary Beth Schultz, a plump, motherly type, got behind the wheel of the squad car. I sat beside her and suddenly the front compartment felt cramped. She turned to look at me after starting the engine. "Don't feel bad about getting your butt chewed out by Ben, that's just his M.O. A lot of people don't like his in-your-face tactics and his smart-alecky talk. I guess you can take the man out of the Bronx, but you can't take the Bronx out of the man." She seemed pleased with her cliché and elbowed me.

"Of course," she continued, "he's awfully conscientious. He'll go after a suspect like a hound dog and just won't quit. Know what I mean? Besides, this is only the second such death around here in over eight years."

I wasn't much for a one-sided conversation, but I listened politely as she droned on.

"Underneath his gruff talk and all, he's a good man. As for me, being a widow with grown children, I wouldn't mind if he gave me a tumble." She laughed and again poked my ribs. "I hinted as much to him, but he just doesn't seem interested. Maybe that's because he's of the Hebrew persuasion, and I'm Protestant, actually a Luddite, not practicing, of course, and besides, the differences wouldn't bother me. Would that bother you?"

I could have told her that her constant prattling was enough to discourage any man, but I said nothing.

She continued, "He's determined to solve all crimes and lock up every perp. I swear, it's a passion with him." She nudged me again. "He could give me a little of that passion, and I'd give it right back."

I was beginning to think people confided in me because I appeared interested or didn't rebut gossipy talk. She stopped in front of the drugstore. When I opened the car door, I got one last word from Mary Beth, "Don't worry, Zach, Ben will find the perp. He always does."

CHAPTER 7

Irma deposited the usual assortment of mail on my desk: bills, advertisements, and vacation entreaties. One brochure caught my eye. It announced in bold type the annual pharmacy convention to be held at the Mark Hopkins in San Francisco. Irma, at my side, became excited.

"Oh, Zach, wouldn't it be wild to go to Frisco for a few days—the two of us in that swanky hotel, strolling around like important people, shopping in those wonderful stores and eating all the abalone, lobster, and crab we want?"

"Hold on. We're supposed to be in a period of mourning, remember? And there's an investigation going on. Sorry, your idea is tacky—"

"No! Listen to me, Zach. The convention doesn't start for a month. We can start planning now. The only good times we've had around here is when we fadoodled on that cramped cot or on those boxes in the back room.

That wasn't exactly elegant, Sweetheart, it wasn't even comfortable. We're free now. The old man is gone—kaput." She embraced me and sang out, "I want to lie in a big bed with a bouncy mattress and soft pillows, have breakfast brought to me; reach over and touch you. We owe that to ourselves."

Her need to constantly indulge herself left little room for anything else. Whenever I resisted, she carried on by nagging, leading at times to tantrums. Truth is, and I'm reluctant to admit it, she was right some of the time. The more I thought about it, this wild idea about getting away was beginning to sound less crazy. I could get locum tenens for a week or more. There were always retired pharmacists who would accept an interim of work. I'd notify Ben Simon that I'd be gone; he could get in touch with me anywhere, but I didn't know why he would. Anyway, we'd be gone for only a short time, and that I hoped would mollify Irma. I had not been to San Francisco in years, and the thought of seeing some of my old classmates would be a kick.

*   *   *

I lay spread-eagle, exhausted on the bed, recovering from the uphill climb to the hotel and three hours of lectures. I don't know why I had to challenge myself, but I vowed not to walk up that hill again. I fell into a deep sleep until I was awakened by a moist kiss, then a raucous greeting by Irma, who rattled off her shopping experiences at I. Magnin, Macy's, and Gump's.

"Get up, sleepyhead! I want to model my gorgeous clothes for you."

She hurried to unwrap boxes piled next to me on the bed. With no pretense at modesty, she disrobed, then slipped into a slinky, low-cut red evening gown with sequins and sauntered like a model with one hand on a hip and moistening her lips with her tongue.

I made the expected sounds of approval that brought her running to my side to kiss me again. "Oh, Zach, I knew you'd love it. It's a copy from a famous French couturier. How'd you like the way I pronounced that?"

"Irma, the gown is beautiful, but when are you going to wear it in Newbury?"

"I thought about that. We can start by throwing a few parties and inviting those stiff-necked socialites, the ones who inherited money from their grandpas who started by making beer in their barns or pulling tits on cows to make butter and cheese."

"I think the proper word is *teats*."

"Whatever."

I got off the bed, yawned and stretched, then stood behind her after she removed the gown. I embraced her waist and nuzzled her neck. She sighed and fell limp in my arms. "Oh, Zach, I love when you do that."

A sharp rapping on the door disrupted our idyllic moment. I scrambled for my pants; Irma ran into the washroom. I shouted, "Who's there?" No reply. Someone tried the knob. I waited several seconds, then repeated, "Who's there?" Still no answer. I looked around the room for something I could use as a weapon. The closet next to the door had an ironing board and an iron. I grabbed the iron in my right hand, held my breath, then turned the knob with my left hand and with a jerk opened the door wide. I stood with the iron over my head—no one was there. I stepped into the hall and looked in both directions—no one.

Irma poked her head out of the washroom. "Who was it, and what are you doing with that iron?"

I wasn't sure what I was doing with the iron. I was reacting to the fear of being exposed in an affair that could ruin my career. That sounded stupid when I thought about it, but people in that hidebound community of ours would have talked.

Irma started to laugh. "Zach, relax. Someone just knocked at the wrong door. Put that iron away." Still in bra and panties, she placed her arms around me and smiled with covetous eyes. "You look like a little boy when you get angry or frightened." Her tongue explored mine as she held me firmly. She looked into my eyes and said in a smoky whisper, "I'd like to have your baby."

"Let's put that thought on the back burner. Some

think we're suspects in Earl's murder. Getting married would only jack up their suspicions. The last thing we need is Ben Simon dogging our footsteps, watching our every move, checking our bank statements. Wouldn't surprise me if he tracked us here."

"You don't think he'd follow us here, do you?"

I shrugged. "The guy's like a leech when he thinks he's on to something."

"Well, don't worry, Sweetheart. I can handle Ben Simon."

Another knock on the door. I wasn't about to waste a second this time and ran to the door, yanked it open. A stocky woman in a gray uniform looked frightened and backed away, striking her cleaning cart. In a meek voice she said, "Can I make up your room?"

"No! No! Not yet, thank you. I've got to wash up, get dressed . . ." I didn't know whether she understood me as I began to close the door and reach for the "Do Not Disturb" sign. Irma was enjoying the scene. "Getting back to our conversation," I said, "what did you mean when you said you could handle Ben Simon? Jeezus, don't tell me you've had a dalliance with him, too."

"Dalliance? Oh, I love that word, Zach. Do you mean did I sleep with him?" She giggled. "Of course not." A few seconds passed, then she said, "But I know him pretty darn good."

"I'm not going to explore the meaning of *that*. Let's get

dressed, grab a cable car, and find a seafood restaurant."

"I'd like to go to Chinatown for some dim sum, turtle soup, chow fun—things we can't get in that cow-town of ours."

She often complained about Newbury, its provincialism, its lack of amenities like fine dining or fashionable clothing stores. Being in the sophisticated milieu of downtown San Francisco stimulated her craving to explore and buy things. I had often wondered how a young, attractive girl from New York City wound up in the pastoral outreaches of mid-America. If I had questioned her in the past, I didn't remember her response.

*   *   *

The dim interior of the Kow Loon restaurant with its fragrances of Chinese herbs stimulated my appetite. In the five-minute wait for a table, my eyes adjusted to the diminished light, and I could make out a fully occupied bar to our right.

We followed the unsmiling maître d' to a maroon vinyl booth with a Chinese lantern above and wallpaper with recurring scenes of pagodas and two white-faced maidens in kimonos carrying umbrellas while crossing an arched bridge. Irma sipped a whiskey sour, set the glass down, then reached for my hands. "Zach, I'm so happy.

I want to live with you for the rest of my life. Do you love me as much as I love you?"

I didn't know whether it was the drink that made her maudlin and gushy, but I was relieved when our food arrived and I didn't have to answer. I began to have gnawing doubts about our relationship. Was she the woman I wanted as a wife? Okay, she was attractive with her yellow, almost white peroxide-dyed hair, her ample bosom, and her narrow waist cinched by a corset. Sexually, she was the most satisfying woman I had ever known, although I really hadn't known other women as intimately. She had plenty street smarts, and yet . . .

The waiter handed me a folded slip of paper with a handwritten note. "Meet me alone in your hotel lobby 7:30 tonight. Important." Irma grabbed the note and read it.

I called after the waiter who was walking away. "Hey! Who gave this to you?" He turned around and shrugged. I wasn't sure he understood. I pointed to the slip of paper and formed the words with my lips.

He nodded. "Man, at bar."

I stood. "Where? Is he there now?"

"No. He go out."

CHAPTER 8

I looked at my watch: 6:55. Irma held my arm as we sat on the sofa in our room. "Zach, stop fidgeting. The note could have been written by a classmate just wanting to get together, but if it's a woman, I'll . . ."

"Whoever wrote this had nothing congenial in mind."

"Who would even know you're here? You made your own travel arrangements, just as I did." She paused; put her hand to her mouth. "Oops. I did tell Lucy, my hairdresser, that I was going to Frisco . . ."

"Fine. You might just as well have taken out a full-page ad in the newspaper."

"Oh, Zach, I'm sorry."

"Screw it. What's done is done."

* * *

At 7:15, I was ready to leave the room when Irma rushed to my side. "You're not going without me," she said. "I'm not sitting here alone while some tomato invites you to sample her goodies."

"Calm down. To begin, that note was written by a man. Look at the writing. Besides, it says I'm to be in the lobby *alone*."

Irma's jaw came forward, her eyes narrowed. I expected unpleasantness, and it came fast.

"Listen, no more bullshit. I'm going with you whether she likes it or not." Irma held the doorknob.

"If he sees you, he might walk away." I tried to keep my voice down, although I emphasized the *he* rather than the *she*.

Her hostility diminished somewhat even though she retained a scowl. "Alright, but I'm still going with you. I'll watch from a distance so she won't know we're together. I'm not going to let any smartass cookie tempt you."

"You referred to her as a tomato before."

"Whatever. When I get through with her, she'll be ready for the trash can."

We walked out of an elevator into the spacious lobby. Twelve minutes to spare. Irma sat on a club chair next to a magazine rack. She held a magazine in her lap but watched me as I tried to appear interested in a wall painting. Actually, I was eyeing every man coming through the entrance and the elevators.

A man about forty years of age sat in a club chair smoking a cigar, reading the *San Francisco Chronicle*. As I watched him, he caught my eye, then looked away. I approached him, pulled out a pack of Chesterfields, and asked for a light. He reached into his jacket pocket, handed me a book of matches, then returned to his newspaper.

I lit my cigarette, thanked him, handed the matches back, and expected him to say something. When he said nothing, I initiated conversation. "Didn't I see you at the restaurant this afternoon? Kow Loon?"

He shook his head. "Not me. Chinese stuff gives me the runs—gas and belching . . . nails me to the crapper for hours . . ."

I was hearing more than I wanted and excused myself. More people arriving walked to the registration desk, mostly couples, some families. One man walked toward the center of the lobby and looked around. He wore a tan Burberry trench coat and a stylish fedora with a brim that concealed much of his face. He looked suspicious, a stereotype out of a Dashiell Hammett novel, or was it F. Scott Fitzgerald? He looked like someone capable of sending that note.

I stood in front of him and introduced myself. "Hi, I'm Zach Black." He extended his hand and shook mine vigorously.

"Arthur Randall McLeish, senior fellow at Cambridge, Ancient Greek Anthology. Have we met?" The guy spoke with a clipped, cultured English accent.

"I—I don't think so." I began to feel foolish; my face felt warm.

He continued, "Well, it's sporting of you to introduce yourself to a stranger and make him feel welcome. You Americans are marvelous at hospitality. Something we British should strive to develop."

I spent the next several minutes trying to extricate myself from a stupid blunder. We exchanged professional cards, and I made insipid comments about meeting again. I disliked lying, saying things that were insincere. Wait a minute . . . who was I kidding? Didn't I sign the register as Mr. and Mrs. Black? Truth was, we were masquerading as a married couple, even though . . .

Irma sidled up to me, smiling, a Cheshire cat squeezing my arm. She pointed to her watch. "7:55. Maybe Madame X decided not to come after all."

"It's not a madame. It's a man."

Irma stopped suddenly, held my arm tightly, her body stiffened as she stared at a figure coming toward us. "Oh, my God!" she cried.

CHAPTER 9

Ben Simon came through the entrance and walked wearily toward us. He mopped his brow with a handkerchief and breathed heavily as he spoke, "I called to tell you I'd be late. Guess you already left your room. Christ, I'm worn out. I climbed that goddamned hill to get here." He glanced around. "Let's find a place to sit before I fall down." Looking at Irma, he said, "I wanted to talk to Zach alone, but since you're here, you might as well hear what I have to say."

I didn't know whether to be cordial and shake his hand or let him know I was pissed. I settled for the latter. "Did you send that note to me in the restaurant?"

He plopped into a padded leather chair that whooshed as he settled into it; he closed his eyes and nodded.

I became angrier. "Why the damned cloak and dagger crap? Why didn't you come to our table and just talk to us directly? And how did you find us, and why the hell are you dogging us?"

We sat around a cocktail table. I remained resentful of this guy who intruded on our time. Simon got the attention of a bellboy and asked for a bottle of fizzy water. He turned to me. "My note said I wanted to talk to you alone. I thought I'd spare Irma some unpleasant news, at least for a while."

The bellboy returned with a bottle of Italian sparkling water and set it down on a tray with a bucket of ice cubes and three glasses. Simon placed two quarters on the tray and told the boy to keep the change.

The bellboy looked at the quarters, then at Simon. "I'm sorry, sir, that'll be one dollar."

Seeing Simon about to explode, I interceded. "Put that on my tab and keep fifty cents as a tip. I'll sign for that."

Simon put the quarters back in his pocket. "You can afford it, Black, now that you're a rich druggist." He poured a glass of the carbonated water, took a long gulp, belched, and said, "That's better." He looked at the empty glass. "You charge only a nickel for that in your store, but your customers aren't the Mark Hopkins type." He sat back. "Now, I'll tell you why I'm here."

"You better have a damned good reason," I said. "Who's paying for your trip? The department must have a surplus from parking fines and police charity drives."

"I'm here on my own. Vacation time. My money."

"Good for you," I said. "So, how did you find us?"

"You booked your airfare and hotel room with Stella

at the Newbury Travel Service. I checked with her."

Irma turned toward me. "I thought you made your own arrangements."

"I did. I asked Stella not to say anything to anyone. So much for confidentiality." I looked at Simon. "But why did you follow us here? What was so dammed important that you had to travel across the country? Don't tell me you couldn't resist going to Haight and Ashbury for a few porno thrills." My attempt at being clever and nasty was ignored.

"Two sets of fingerprints were found on old man Withers' revolver." He looked at me and tilted his head. *Did he think I was about to make a confession?*

My gut tightened, I felt warm, my heart pounded. "You found my fingerprints on the gun, right?"

Simon closed his eyes and nodded. "That's right, Kiddo." He sat forward. "When you applied to pharmacy school six years ago, your prints were taken as routine for entrance and were sent to the FBI in Washington. Experts compared the prints to those found on the gun, and voila! Only thing is, we were stymied for a while because the moniker in the D.C. files was one long handle—Schwartzengooper or something like that."

"Schwartzenpfeffer was my original name. Yeah, I remember picking up that revolver. Earl insisted that I hold it; he was proud of it. I know that sounds fishy, but that's the truth. Besides, what reason would I have for killing him? Sure, there were times when he was a pain in the ass but not so bad that I'd kill him."

"Uh-huh. That may be," Simon said. "But Withers really had no intention of turning that store over to you while he was alive, did he?"

"Hold on!" I couldn't get the words out fast enough. I sat on the edge of my chair and pointed at Simon. "Earl told me just before he was murdered that he was going to leave the store to me. Irma was there. She heard him say it. She can vouch for me."

"Really?" His cynical tone irritated the hell out of me. Arguing would have been useless.

Acting like a grand vizier, Simon reached for a cigarette, lit it, and blew smoke over my head. In that moment, I detested him even more.

"Of course," he continued, "Irma isn't totally off my list since she inherits a passel of shanties and farming acreage . . . all of which brings in a bundle every month."

"Look, Simon, you're sticking your nose into our personal affairs. What gives you the right to ask—"

"Murder gives me every right, Kiddo. I ask questions of anyone who benefits from a victim's death." He flicked ash off his cigarette. "I don't stop until I get the answers I want."

"Good for you. I still don't know why you had to come one thousand miles to tell us what you could have told us in Newbury."

Simon stubbed his cigarette in an ashtray and got close enough for me to see the hairs in his nose. "I'll tell you why, Kiddo. You didn't volunteer the fact that you applied for a passport three weeks ago and had Irma do the same. That raised a red flag. Made me think you were planning a trip, maybe to a country with no extradition laws, like Cuba or Morocco or some other damn place, taking a plane or boat out of Frisco."

"That's about the dumbest thing I've heard yet. Why the hell would I give up everything?"

He wouldn't allow me to finish. "I'll tell you why, Mr. Smartass—to escape a murder rap, that's why. Taking a powder to avoid prosecution . . . it's been done before." He sat back in his chair; his fingers intertwined over his abdomen. "Why did you apply for a passport?"

"If you must know, I thought we'd fly up to Canada or down to South America for a few days, extend our holiday, do some exploring, get to know one another better."

He looked at us. "You still have exploring to do on one another?"

I ignored his comment. "If I thought you'd be following us around, I would have suggested that you get a passport too."

"Very funny," he said.

"Since you were so concerned about us leaving the country, why didn't you notify the San Francisco police to keep an eye on us?"

"That crossed my mind. Problem is, they've got their own troubles, and besides, I've got a vested interest . . ." He trailed off and stopped.

I was intrigued. "What do you mean *vested interest?*"

He hesitated, looked around the lobby, his lower lip protruded. I figured this was the dramatic pause before a revealing comment. He glared at me, then at Irma. "If I brought both of you in as confessed killers, my stock would skyrocket and I'd get Chief Morgan's job. My story would be front-page reading in the Madison papers— maybe picked up by the INS and who knows?"

"Would you really think of leaving Newbury?" Irma asked as though she cared about this guy who could have been the prototypical compulsive, neurotic, anal personality described in every abnormal psychology text.

I held up an imaginary newspaper and said, "I can just see it now: 'Detective foils killers' plans to leave country.' Not a bad news item, Simon, but let me tell you. If you charge us with Withers' death, I'll return the favor and sue you for false arrest, defamation of character, harassment, and anything else my attorney can throw at you. Why the hell would you even think of charging us?"

"Enough with the histrionics, Kiddo. You both had a potful to gain with Withers' death. Irma inherits his estate: his mansion, every shack, every acre of farmland, and every mom-and-pop store on Lincoln Street." He turned his attention to me. "And you get to keep the drugstore, even though Irma is your landlord. Now that's a cozy arrangement, I'd say."

Simon, spouting all this, really irked me. "How the hell do you know these things, and what gives you the right . . .?"

"Hold on," he interrupted. "We're talking small town, remember? You don't get to keep your precious secrets very long. Just so happens, Withers' attorney, Arnie Teasdale, and me are buddies. We work cases together, play handball now and then, sometimes grab a hot dog or burger at Jennie's Café."

"Great. So much for client-attorney confidentiality."

Irma yawned, stood, and said she was going to have a cocktail in the bar and didn't need our company. Simon watched as she sashayed away in her slinky new sheath. I knew he was going to make comments as soon as she was out of hearing, and he didn't waste time. "Did I tell you about the time she came into Earl's life? She was a twenty-two-year-old kid, a beauty who brought nothing but her New York City street smarts with her. I introduced her to Earl . . . recently widowed. When she saw this old guy with a prune-like face and a nose with a hairy wart limping toward her, she said, 'Nothing doing.' I took her aside for a few minutes to explain that if she were to marry him, she'd live like Mrs. Rockefeller, and as his widow she would be the richest gal west of

Brooklyn. She took three minutes to consider, then agreed. She demanded a prenuptial arrangement and had a local attorney draw it up. Old Earl couldn't sign it fast enough since he was so damned eager to get his prong into her. If he had to, he would have run naked down Lincoln Street with a pink bow tied to it."

"Let's get back to the issue at hand," I said. "How did you expect to keep us from leaving the country?"

He reached into his inner jacket pocket and pulled out a folded official-looking paper. "I've got a restraining order signed by a judge. It prevents you from leaving the states without permission of the court."

I knew Simon was blowing smoke. My patience with this guy hit zero. I brought my shoulders back to stand a full three inches taller than him. "Listen, Javert, let's get something straight. We're heading back to Newbury at the end of this week. You can harangue us there and continue your conspiracy theories like the one-trick pony I think you are. I'll have Eddie Polanski concoct a sundae especially for you sprinkled liberally with nuts."

"Very funny."

"Right. And so are you."

CHAPTER 10

Clearly, I was a suspect in Earl Withers' murder since my fingerprints were on the handle of the so-called suicide gun. Irma came under suspicion because she was sole heir to his large estate.

Ben Simon knew all that and could have hauled us in then and there for questioning. I saw myself sitting in that miserable excuse for a police station. Of course, I would call a defense attorney from Madison. Simon had to know I was innocent since I really had nothing to gain financially by Earl's death. I tried to get into Simon's head. He might be thinking Withers' death would leave me free to marry Irma, who would inherit his fortune. God knew that wasn't true.

Coming here to San Francisco with Irma had to be one of the most stupid things I could have done, but I did it and now there would be hell to pay. Attending the pharmacy convention wasn't worth this aggravation, but I enjoyed seeing a few old friends. We didn't need to hide our relationship by running away. People back home must have known we were shacking up. Irma made no secret of it and probably would have used a bullhorn to announce it if I hadn't stopped her. She had no sensitivity about such matters and didn't care or understand the reasons for being discreet.

I thought about the whirlwind events of the last two years. To begin, when I arrived in Newbury, I was a virgin. That's right. I had never slept with a woman—not that I didn't want to. I thought about sex every time I saw a pretty girl or one not so pretty. I lived through nocturnal emissions for years and sometimes spontaneous ones during the day.

When I arrived at Withers' drugstore, Irma encompassed me and almost immediately introduced me to the worldly delights of adulthood. My pent-up sexuality exploded and recurred frequently. We acted like dogs in heat, mounting clandestinely after and during store hours. Irma had been sexually deprived by the waning ability of her aging husband and latched onto me with insatiable hunger. Of course, I'll admit, I was more than a willing partner.

Maybe too much of a good thing had begun to lessen my appetite, and I felt the need to back off. But it was more than that. Other than her ability to satisfy my carnal instincts, I found her to be shallow and lacking in cultural interests. Worse, she had become a persistent nag. Oh, she was clever about practical matters and her business sense was good, although she spent money on herself freely. Legitimate theatre, good books, museums, and the political arena meant little to her.

Lying in bed after intercourse, smoking cigarettes, then reaching out to each other was the extent of our relationship. I endured reluctantly her retelling of movie magazine and gossip column tidbits. When I suggested going to Madison or Milwaukee for a cultural event, such as a symphonic concert or lecture, she would refuse unless she was given time to shop in an upscale women's store. My efforts at playing Pygmalion were futile. After a while, I asked myself, "Who am I kidding?"

Her speech, like Ben Simon's, had an irritating nasal quality. Some of the locals asked if she were foreign-born. She was four years older than I, not that age difference was important, but it finally occurred to me that the cultural gap might be too wide for long-term compatibility.

Like I said, our sexual needs were well met, at least mine were initially; hers might never have been. I vowed to do the best I could, but quite frankly I began experiencing too many restive moments. I finally realized that she might be too coarse, too self-centered, to be accepted by my family.

Another problem with our relationship was that soon she would become my landlady. If I didn't toe the line, she could toss me out on my butt. I hated to think of starting over again. Was I letting my pecker decide what course to take? Down, boy.

*   *   *

We started packing for the flight back to Midway Airport in Chicago. From there, we'd catch a single-engine flight to Madison, where our car was parked. Irma, in her panties, gave me a coquettish glance as she was about to put on her bra. She knew I delighted in standing behind her, embracing her magnificent breasts and playfully touching her nipples. She would bring her head back and murmur delightfully, then turn around and invite me to suckle as she'd reach for my crotch. The whole cycle of foreplay leading to intercourse would start again.

As we lay lethargic after frenzied activity, Irma would prop her head on my chest and ask plaintively, "Are you getting tired of me, Zach? Do I still please you?"

"More than you know. I'll sleep well on the plane."

*   *   *

Our seats in first class allowed unlimited drinking, and we took advantage of that. After our second scotches, our conversation became less inhibited, if that were at all possible with Irma. In the semi-recumbent position, I turned toward her and said, "Did you kill Earl?"

Despite her boozy condition she became instantly alert, sat up, and said angrily, "What the hell are you talking about?"

"Calm down—just asking."

"Just asking? You've got a hell of a nerve! Here I thought I was protecting *you* because *you* got rid of Earl to marry me."

I, too, had enough scotch to speak without constraint. "Sorry to disappoint you, Dearie. Killing is not my game. Now that you've mentioned marriage, I think you ought to know . . ."

The stewardess leaned toward us and asked if we would like refills.

"Yes, yes," I said, preferring to be drunk while talking to Irma.

Smarting from our conversation, Irma pushed her glass past me toward the stewardess. "Hit me again, Sweetie." After the stewardess refilled her glass and moved forward, Irma bolted upright to continue her tirade. "Of all the ungrateful, stinking pill pushers, you turned out to be a real scum bag—yeah, a real shit."

I squeezed her thigh to inflict just enough discomfort to shut her up. She gave a yelp as I put my forefinger to my lips and tried to change the subject. "Your carping has turned your hair roots black. Be sure to use more peroxide with your next washing."

She put her hands to her head quickly, then reached for a hand mirror in her purse. After studying her hair color, she looked at me. "I think you're a damn liar. You're the one who could have killed Earl." Her eyes narrowed. "Jeezus, to think I might have been sleeping with a murderer." She paused long enough to launch another volley. "You act so dammed innocent, well, you don't fool me."

"I never intended to." Either she was innocent, or she was an exquisitely accomplished liar. Had I been taken in by Jezebel or Medusa? I should have played my cards better. No, if I were smart, I'd leave this game altogether . . . whoa, not so fast. Leave now, and the cops will be all over me. Why in the hell did I ever permit myself to get involved?

CHAPTER 11

Mavis Johnson returned to the drugstore with renewed energy, moving like an automaton doing things in a precise manner. I had the erroneous impression that Earl's death was going to drive her into a severe depression. Truth is, she did not appear to be sad, although she wasn't altogether happy.

I invited her to lunch at one of the three tables adjacent to the soda fountain. She thanked me but demurred, saying she really could not eat because she had little appetite after Earl's death. "Some of my clothes are actually loose now," she said with a weak smile. "I find that I'm using more rouge because I'm so pale. Forgive me for carrying on like this. It's just that I can't believe he's gone." She turned away and reached for Kleenex in her purse.

"Mavis, I'd like to help. Why don't you share your thoughts about him with me?"

She twisted the Kleenex in her lap and avoided looking

at me when she said, "I—I don't know where to start."

"Start at the beginning. When did you start working for him?"

"My aunt knew Earl from years back and convinced him to hire me part-time while I was still in high school. After working for him a short time, I became engaged to Larry and we married soon after. Larry and I struggled until he developed his law practice."

She paused, smiled weakly. "Earl and Bertha Withers became Larry's clients, and we were grateful. We bought a home in an upscale area, Cedar Heights Village, with two mortgages until Earl purchased them and made our payments much easier. They were a good deal older, of course, but we became close and invited them to our home for dinners, barbecues, birthday parties . . . occasions like that."

"So, you knew them quite well."

"Yes. They were childless, and I thought they regarded us as their children. Earl—that is, Mr. Withers—was forever bringing us gifts. Some evenings he'd call to talk to Larry about his many properties. After he talked with Larry, he would insist on talking with me."

"Really? What did you talk about?"

"Little things, silly personal matters. Larry would get annoyed and tell me Earl was a lecherous old goat who wanted to seduce me."

"Was he right?"

She laughed before answering. "I was flattered by Earl's attentiveness since Larry had . . ." She stopped suddenly, then continued, "At times I felt isolated. Larry was consumed by his work, driven by his need to make money. I was not unhappy about our financial situation, but for Larry there was never enough."

Our sandwiches and soft drinks arrived, brought to our table by Eddie Polanski, who fussed needlessly over us. When he walked away, Mavis continued her story with animation, unlike the rigid persona she projected on the job. "One day, I received a phone call from the hotel in Madison where Larry was lecturing to a group of realtors. I had a dreadful premonition, and then I heard the policeman say that Larry had suffered a massive stroke. I'm not sure I heard anything that followed, but I do remember hearing him say that Larry fell at the speaker's platform and was rushed to the hospital."

She looked into her lap and hesitated before saying, "He never regained consciousness . . . remained in a vegetative state. I couldn't even say goodbye to him. During that terrible time, Mr. Withers became more attentive, more solicitous, and began to visit me frequently—without his wife."

"Do you think Mrs. Withers objected to her husband's infatuation with you?"

"I'm not sure she was aware. Poor thing had become confused, forgetful . . . suffered dementia. Then I learned

I was pregnant. My baby was going to be born, and my husband would not know it. I was in emotional turmoil . . . thrilled about having a baby, but . . ."

"You had your baby, a fine boy who is now a fine young man."

She nodded and smiled. "Larry lingered in a coma for over a month. I just couldn't let them turn off the life-support system. Fortunately, we had excellent hospital insurance, although that was about to run out."

"What was Withers' attitude toward you during that time?"

"Like I said, he remained solicitous. Maybe too much so. I'm almost embarrassed to tell you he offered to marry me before Larry died. I would have had to divorce Larry, but I couldn't do that."

"Would you have married Withers when your husband died?"

"Oh, no! Bertha was still alive and . . ."

"Could you see yourself married to Earl?"

"Shortly after Bertha died, Irma came on the scene. Earl was captivated with this trollop who threw herself at him." Mavis stopped suddenly, apologized, then reached out to touch my hand. "Please forgive me. I never should have said that. I had no right to."

"I understand. When you think about what happened, would you agree that Earl was as much to blame as Irma for their marriage?"

"Yes, yes, of course, but it's still difficult for me to accept. Earl had been so close to me—I meant to say close to *us*."

Mavis looked around as though fearful her remarks might have been overheard. "I don't want to say anything to provoke Irma," she said. "I feel so vulnerable now that Earl is gone."

"Irma doesn't decide your employment. This is my domain. I decide who works here." Maybe that was the reassurance Mavis needed. She patted the back of my hand, then squeezed it as she thanked me.

She tilted her head and smiled wistfully. "I've got to get back to my job, a job I love, and I want to leave a favorable impression on my new boss. Thank you again for listening to my tales of woe, and thank you for the sandwich. Mr. Black, you would have been a wonderful psychiatrist."

I watched as she walked away. She managed to fill her clothes like a svelte younger woman, maintaining a figure with firm buttocks and a provocative bust line. I could understand Earl's infatuation with her. Was it possible that . . .?

Irma suddenly appeared, sat down heavily next to me, and exclaimed for all to hear that she was exhausted from shopping.

"What'cha eating, Dearie?" She reached for my half-eaten sandwich and took a bite. She looked at the plate

Mavis left and saw the remnants of her sandwich and fries. "Who were you eating with?"

Her abrasive tone embarrassed me. I said softly, "I shared lunch with Mavis. We discussed business matters." I wouldn't dare tell her the truth.

"Business matters, huh? Let me warn you, Sweetheart. If I hear that you two are playing footsies, well, both of you will get shagged out of here so fast . . ."

"Keep it down, for Chrissake!" I picked up the plates and utensils.

"I meant what I said." Her reminder irked me, then to further annoy me, she said, "I'll see you tonight at my place at nine, right?"

"No!"

"What d'ya mean, no?" She stared at me, hands on her hips.

"I've got to get things ready for the accountant, and I've got to go over an order list for drugs and supplies."

"I can help you with that," she said.

Her clawing presence was smothering, and I resented it. "No, Irma, damn it, I don't need your company."

"Oh, listen to Mr. Uppity. Alright. Tomorrow night, then." She picked up her shopping bags and was about to leave.

"Tomorrow night is out. I have other matters to attend," I said.

She placed her bags on the floor and gave me an icy stare. "I see. Let me know when we can get together—then I'll decide if I have time for you."

CHAPTER 12

Eddie Polanski, wiping the luncheon counter after the noon rush, got my attention and motioned me to come over. "You gotta minute, Mr. Black?" (He always called me Mr. Black, never Zach.) "I need to talk to you about something important."

I sat on one of the counter stools as Eddie looked to either side then leaned forward and, in a voice just above a whisper, said, "That detective, Lieutenant Simon, he came to my house last night . . . scared the shit out of Wanda. He asked me questions about old man Withers that made me mad, like I was guilty of killing him. I told him I didn't even own a gun."

Eddie looked around again and continued to speak softly. "Actually, I do have a piece, but I wasn't gonna tell him. Fuck him and all those cops, anyway. They don't have to know, right?"

"Is the gun registered?" I asked.

He pulled back and swiped the counter again with a

rag. "I wouldn't know. I bought it from a hood years ago. I used it only twice to shoot rabbits. Anyway, I'm not using it to shoot people, unless they're shooting at me."

"If your gun isn't registered, you'd be in a lot of trouble if Simon finds out."

"Jeezus, you ain't gonna tell him, are you? If he finds out, he'll snatch it and I'll never get it back. More'n that, he'll charge me with possession of stolen . . ."

I didn't want to pursue the conversation and put up my hand to stop it. I was more interested in confronting him about the murder. I couldn't think of a polite, non-offensive way of asking him, so I broached the question directly. "Eddie, tell me, did you kill Mr. Withers?"

In an anguished voice, he said, "Aw c'mon, Mr. Black, you know me better'n that. I didn't shoot that old tightwad—but you know what? I ain't exactly sorry someone did."

Wanda, Eddie's wife, came into the drugstore, threw me a cursory greeting, then picked up a trash bag on the floor at the end of the counter. Eddie moved quickly and grabbed the bag from her and placed it under the counter. He didn't want her to take the bag while I was looking on. She excused herself and hurried out of the store.

Eddie had a sheepish grin and looked embarrassed as he attempted to divert my attention by asking if I would like a cup of coffee. "I'll brew some. Won't take but a minute, Mr. Black."

"Eddie, you know the store is mine now. You're not skimming off Mr. Withers' profits anymore. If you take food home, you'll be cheating me."

He reached out and held my wrist. "Mr. Black, I'd never do that. I got too much respect for you. You know that. I only take stuff that can't be used here . . . like an end piece of cheese and salami, day-old bread, broken crackers, bruised tomatoes—things like that."

I knew Eddie was loyal, but I had to be forthright. Withers paid him a minimum if not a shamefully low wage, and frankly, I could not understand why Eddie stayed on even though he had rationalized his decision to me earlier. I told him that we could hire a high school student to help at noon. We could run daily specials and offer free soda pop or coffee with sandwiches or salads.

Eddie nodded enthusiastically. "I like those ideas, Mr. Black, but they eat into profits, don't they?"

"We'll advertise in newspapers and on radio. The increased foot traffic will create more profits. To prove to you I'm confident in the direction we're heading, I'm going to increase your salary by twenty dollars a month."

Eddie's expression of gratitude changed when Ben Simon walked in with a toothpick in his mouth. He approached the counter, sat on a stool, faced Eddie, then swiveled around to look at me. He pushed up the brim of his fedora and said, "Well, well, what have we here?" He answered his own question. "Two prime suspects in the murder of old man Withers. You guys hatching a plot to take over all of Newbury?"

Eddie found no humor in Simon's remarks. Without a hint of cordiality, he asked, "Can I get you something, Lieutenant?"

"Yeah. Find me Withers' killer."

Eddie's jaw muscles alternately tightened and relaxed as he stared at the detective.

"Gimme a cup of java—black and hot, and one of those doughnuts with sprinkles." He reached for his wallet in his back pocket.

"Put your money away, Lieutenant," I said. "This is on the house. It's our small way of thanking you for your service."

"Don't try to impress me with your generosity. Bribing me with a ten-cent cup of coffee and a fifteen-cent doughnut isn't enough to get either of you off the hook." He dunked his doughnut, licked two fingers, then wiped his mouth and hands with a paper napkin, crumpled it, and threw it on his plate. He slid off the seat and looked at me. "You gotta minute? I want to discuss something with you. We can talk in my car."

Talking with Simon was never joyful; his superior attitude and accusatory tone always annoyed me.

"A few minutes in your car is all I can take." I sat in his coupe, grateful it had been cleared of cigarette butts and candy wrappers. The car had been washed and made

MURDER IN A SMALL TOWN

presentable on the outside, but the stink of stale cigarettes lingered inside. I wound down the window and breathed the outside air, hoping our conversation would be brief.

"How well do you know Eddie Polanski?" he asked.

"Enough to know he thinks you're harassing him about Withers' death."

"Too fucking bad about what he thinks of me. Let me ask you a few questions about him." He took a cigarette out of a pack and let it dangle from the corner of his mouth. "Do you know anything about his background?"

I shook my head. "I know he's been a hardworking employee for several years. From what he told me, he and Withers tolerated each other for the most part."

"What about the appearance of his face? Notice anything unusual?"

I thought for a moment. "A scar on the left side of his chin?"

"That's right. Anything else?"

"He's neat. His clothing is clean at the start of the day. He wears freshly laundered white cotton trousers, white shirt, black tie . . ."

"White shirt with long sleeves, right?"

I thought for a moment. "Yeah, that's right. Is that important?"

"His sleeves are never rolled up." Simon's comment must have had meaning which escaped me. He continued, "If you saw his arms, you would have seen jailhouse tattoos. Does that surprise you?"

I shrugged, not knowing how to respond. If he expected me to condemn Eddie, he would have been disappointed. "What's the story on him?" I asked.

Simon pushed in the cigarette lighter on the dash, lit his cigarette, and took a long drag, then exhaled a plume out the window. "About eighteen years ago, he hung around with a gang of New Jersey hoods. One day, those stupid punks entered the Fidelity Bank of Trenton with guns drawn, yelling like lunatics. It was their first bank heist, and it went wrong big-time. Two of the boys entered the bank. One was shot dead by a bank guard. The other boy killed the guard then ran out of the bank after grabbing a measly few bucks. Eddie was driving the getaway car. As soon as he heard that one of his buddies was killed, he jumped on the accelerator, lost control, and crashed into a truck. He ran from the scene, but the cops caught him and his buddy. Both were sent up the river. Polanski got only five years for aiding and abetting since it was his first offense, and he had a clever mouthpiece. His buddy got the chair."

"How did Eddie land up here in Newbury?"

"When he got out of prison, he had trouble getting a job. Nobody would hire an ex-con. His mother's brother, who worked on a dairy farm here, offered him a job feeding and milking cows. Eddie came here, but he hated it, wanted no part of it. When a job at Withers' drugstore opened, he jumped at the chance. Let me back up a minute. While working at the farm, he romanced one of the neighboring farmer's daughters. Got her pregnant but did the honorable thing. Married her after a shotgun was poked up his ass. Figuratively speaking, of course."

"Did Withers know about his background?"

"Sure, but since Eddie would work for cheap, he hired him."

"Why didn't Eddie go elsewhere?"

"I told you. He couldn't get a job anywhere because of his jailbird background. Besides, Withers gave him a home. Okay, a shack, but it was still a place where he and his wife could raise their kid. In addition, Withers gave him a beaten-up Model A. Think of it as a scaled-down version of the American dream."

"Seems to me those are reasons for Eddie to be grateful to Withers."

"On the surface, I would agree, but you gotta understand. He harbored a deep-seated hatred for Withers, who kept him under his thumb. Withers had no respect for Polanski and called him every low-class name he could think of. Then Withers did the most unforgivable thing." Simon paused and inhaled deeply on his cigarette before tossing it out the window.

"What unforgivable thing did Withers do?"

"He pinched Polanski's wife's ass. A torpedo like

Polanski could have exploded right then and there, and he might have killed Withers, and I'm not so sure he didn't do that later. Withers had that crazy notion of the obligation to the padrone with all the women who worked in the store or the wives of the male workers."

"How do you know all this, Simon?"

"In this burg, secrets don't remain secret for long. Besides, I've got spies, informers." He flashed a knowing grin, more like a smirk.

"What do you plan to do about Eddie?"

"You don't need to know."

I opened the car door to leave when Simon called out, "One more thing . . ."

His last-second comment grabbed me like a lasso, yanking me into a freeze. What the hell more did he need to tell me? I turned to look at him. "Alright, what else do you have to tell me?"

"Old man Withers was going to can Polanski. That's right. Give him the ax."

"When?"

"The day before Withers was killed."

CHAPTER 13

Someone had been informing Simon of goings-on in the drugstore, and the previously friendly environment had changed to one of awareness and suspicion.

I thought of all the possible spies, including the part-time help, and came up with zip, zero. Among the fulltime help, I couldn't imagine anyone acting as an informant. Not that it would make much difference since there could be nothing said relevant to Withers' murder, but the thought of someone sneaking reports to Lieutenant Simon made me uneasy. I considered it a betrayal of whatever small confidences we shared in the store.

* * *

When I had worked as an employee for Earl Withers, my hours were 8:00 a.m. to 5:00 p.m., but now as the owner I worked from 7:30 a.m. to closing, which was anytime between 8:00 p.m. and 9:00 p.m.—or until the last customer had been accommodated.

Beside my own eagerness to please every shopper, I had taken time to train the sales staff to be courteous and helpful, but the store's profits remained stagnant.

At 6:00 p.m., Mavis, who had put in ten-and-a-half hours, slipped into her coat, made some small rearrangements at the perfume counter, and bade me good night as she headed for the rear door leading to the parking lot.

I reached out as she was passing and touched her coat sleeve. "Mavis, may I have a word with you?"

She stopped. "Sure, Mr. Black, but forgive me, I can't stay long. My son is waiting for dinner."

"I was hoping we could talk about making changes in the store."

Her eyes brightened. "Oh, I'd like that. Why don't you come over this evening? We'll have time . . . no interruptions . . . maybe explore some new avenues." She looked at her watch. "How does nine o'clock sound?"

"Terrific. Can I bring a quart of ice cream? Or cupcakes? Something?"

"No, I'll furnish the dessert."

* * *

I felt somewhat uneasy as I got out of my car in front of her house. After all, she was a widow, not unattractive, and I carried a bouquet. Anyone seeing this might think . . . but who cared?

Mavis' home, on a tree-lined street, was a tidy brown-brick two-story structure with a lawn bordered by rose bushes in bloom. The neat condition of the grounds required considerable maintenance, but she had a son who probably helped. I pulled my shoulders back and walked to the entrance. The door had been varnished recently, and the brass handle was burnished to a high gloss.

Westminster chimes bonged when I pushed the doorbell. I felt the knot on my tie and jiggled it into place. The door opened to frame a backlighted Mavis, whose appearance startled me. She wore black silk pants, a white blouse, and a jeweled belt. In the store, her hair was always pulled back in a bun; now it cascaded around her shoulders. She extended her hand. A warm smile welcomed me, and the fragrance of her delicate perfume was intoxicating.

She thanked me profusely for the bouquet and led me to the living room where a tapestry of dazzling colors struck me. Modern wall paintings, antiques, and Oriental area rugs formed a mélange of eclectic but warm and interesting contrasts. All this and her appearance were such a departure from the way I saw her at the drugstore, and imagined her living a buttoned-up lifestyle.

"Do you like what you see, Mr. Black?"

"I like very much what I see, and for heaven's sake, drop the Mr. Black. Call me Zach." Truth is, I was awed by her appearance. Her low-cut blouse revealed a cleavage I had never seen or noticed before. I turned away quickly and hoped my gawking was not noticeable.

"Come," she said as she reached for my hand and directed me to the dining room where the table held the store's ledger, folders, and other business papers. "I've gone over the books and found to my surprise that our business since Earl's death has improved over eight percent."

"That sounds good—really good."

"It would be wonderful if our expenses hadn't increased by seven percent. So, you see, we're hardly more profitable."

"Any suggestions?"

"I thought of several things. We can compete more favorably with a grocery chain, like Kroger's, on certain items that will get shoppers' attentions."

I watched keenly as she sat across the table and pored over the ledger. She appeared different, a mature woman with good business sense and more beautiful than I had noticed previously. I could understand why old man Withers was taken with her. But I couldn't believe she would have reciprocated. Then I recalled that Psych 101 chapter on "Love and Emotional Attachments" between odd or seemingly dissimilar couples.

"Zach, are you listening?"

"Huh? Oh, yeah—just thinking."

She continued, "If we advertise weekly leaders such as popular household items, like Maxwell House or Hills Bros. Coffee, Lux or Camay soap and sell them below our cost, we can bring in customers."

"That doesn't sound too profitable."

"Yes, it would be. All we need to do is get customers into the store. Once they're in, they'll buy other items. Another ploy would be to give a credit of fifty cents for every five dollars spent."

"Did you ever suggest these things to Earl?"

"He wasn't interested in increased volume. Quite frankly, he wanted to slow down since he had the burden of looking after Bertha, nursing his own pains, and keeping an eye out for Walt Mason. Remember, Earl had income from his real estate holdings. Profits from the pharmacy were secondary. When Irma came along, he thought she'd be able to handle his needs—business and otherwise. As things turned out, she took care of his *otherwise*, but she had no business sense."

"He was quite fortunate to have you handling the drugstore business."

She looked up from the ledger and said, "Thanks for the compliment. Would you like to share a little liqueur, a Drambuie?"

"Sure, but tell me, I'm curious, where did you develop your retail skills?"

"Years ago, in night school. Classes in small business practices were given at the junior college taught by a handsome man who provided special insights into retail management. When he became too interested in managing me, I dropped the class, but I managed to learn a few techniques."

The Drambuie was having an effect on me, maybe both of us. I felt less inhibited and started saying things I'd never say when sober. I slouched in the chair and gazed at her. "I can hardly blame the instructor for saying flattering things to you."

She smiled wearily. "I might have been flattered if he weren't married with three children."

"I'm single and have no children—as far as I know." I laughed.

She reached over and patted the back of my hand. "That's in your favor, but I'm older than you. I have a son, and besides, you appear to be firmly attached to Irma, and vice versa."

I sat up. "I'll admit Irma and I got to know one another quite well, but we've grown apart. Our interests reached a fork in the road, so to speak."

"*Your* interests may have. I'm not sure hers have. Besides, she is still under suspicion for Mr. Withers' murder, and unless I'm mistaken, so are you. If you're seen as a couple, people might think you are co-conspirators in Earl's murder."

That angered me. "Do you think I killed him?"

She did not respond immediately.

"Wait a minute. Wait one damn minute. Answer my question, please. Do you believe I killed Withers?"

Mavis walked to the fireplace mantel, picked up a framed photo of her son, then turned to me. "No, I don't believe you killed him. How could I? Unfortunately, what I think won't influence Lieutenant Simon."

I stood beside her and looked at her son Charles' photo. "He's a handsome young man. Is he upstairs studying?"

"No. He's with his counselor tonight."

"Counselor? I don't understand."

Mavis placed the photo back on the mantel then turned to face me. "He acts out at times, becomes belligerent, breaks things. He sits and broods. His father's death has been difficult for him. His counselor, a psychologist, has been helpful, but it's been a long haul. Despite that, he's done well in his studies and loves the ROTC."

She picked up another framed picture on the mantel. "This was my husband, Larry."

The photo revealed a fiftyish, balding, bespectacled man with a double chin and a smile that impressed me as insincere. "And your own response to your husband's death—has that been very difficult?"

Mavis walked back to the table to pour herself more Drambuie and asked if I'd like a refill. I waved it off. She sipped and ran her tongue around her lips. "Larry and I didn't agree on everything. In fact, we agreed on very little. In the months before his death, we fought terribly, constantly."

"Fought? What about? If you don't mind my asking."

Her features hardened; there was bitterness in her voice. "Larry had a number of extramarital affairs and became less secretive about them. For me, that was unforgivable. He became terribly paranoid and accusatory. He accused me of having an affair with Earl Withers."

"His suspicions were unfounded, right?"

She placed her hands on her hips and looked at me scornfully but said nothing.

I wanted desperately to change the subject. I looked around the room. "You have beautiful antiques. Have you been collecting long?" I asked while admiring a large vase on a marble base in one corner.

She walked toward it and said, "That's a late nineteenth-century Sevres, fine French porcelain. Lovely, isn't it?"

I studied the figures on it then looked at Mavis, turned to the vase again, and glanced back. "The face on the topless nude resembles yours."

She smiled and ran her fingers lightly, affectionately over the vase. "I've been told that by the person who gave it to me. He said he couldn't resist buying it for that reason."

"An admirer? Was he referring only to your face?" I could thank the effects of the Drambuie for my bold questions.

Her smile was enigmatic.

"While you're wondering, I can tell you this: the gentleman presented me with a number of exquisite French, English, and Bavarian decorative pieces as well as most of the art hanging on the walls." She pointed to several framed and signed oil paintings.

"Is your benefactor anyone I know?"

At that moment a flash of lighting transformed the room to a ghostly white. A crack of thunder followed with prolonged and repeated explosive crashings and rumblings. Mavis grabbed and held me close as the lights flickered then went off. Her trembling body pressed close to mine, and I wrapped my arms around her. The sweet warmth and softness of her evoked a masculine response. I knew she had to be aware of it as she pulled me gently but eagerly toward the sofa.

* * *

The morning sun awakened me. I blinked, rubbed my eyes, then sat up, supported by my elbows. I looked around, disoriented, but slowly the surroundings and events of the prior evening began to register. My pants lay folded on the back of a chair, and my shoes and socks were aligned on the floor at the edge of the sofa—all too neatly for my doing. An afghan with a geometric pattern had covered me. The fragrance of brewing coffee and frying bacon forced me off the sofa. I looked toward the kitchen where Mavis in a flowered-pattern apron was setting the table.

She turned and called out, "That was quite a storm last light."

I smacked my cotton-dry tongue against my palate before speaking.

"That storm was the beginning of a wonderful evening," I said, then waited for her response.

"There's a robe on the chair, a new toothbrush, and clean towels in the washroom." She spoke matter-of-factly, as though I were a guest in a rooming house.

I slipped into the robe and ran my hand through my hair as I walked into the kitchen. "Good morning, Love." I leaned over to kiss her; she turned her head, and I found myself kissing an ear covered by strands of hair. I didn't understand this detached attitude after an evening of splendid lovemaking.

I took hold of her shoulders and stared into her eyes.

"Hey! What's going on? Last night meant nothing to you?"

Her eyes began to tear as she searched mine; her lips trembled as she put her arms around me and held me tightly. "Oh, Zach, if only you knew how much I loved you and wanted you. I hoped by some miracle you would love me too. As for last night, it was the most wonderful night of my life. If I could, I would lock you in this house and keep you as a prisoner—my own love slave."

"Well, that makes me feel better—I think. I'm not sure about the slave part. I was afraid you thought I was an under-performing jerk or something like that."

She laughed and with a handkerchief wiped away tears. "I've lived with someone who was abusive. Our rare moments of intimacy were for his gratification and gave me no pleasure. Since then, I've been fearful about entering into another relationship." She took my hand. "Come, let's eat then go to the drugstore. Even though it's Sunday and we start at ten, you have yet to wash up and . . ."

I held her in my arms and gazed into her hazel eyes that seemed to beg for understanding and patience. In just a few magnificent hours, I knew she was the woman I could live with forever. The breakfast table was beautifully prepared although my mind was still full of her and the pleasures of last night. Only the prospect of confronting Irma again darkened this moment. I hadn't seen Irma for three days and hoped she had taken a long trip; better yet, found a new lover.

CHAPTER 14

Having two women to love was glorious at first blush but created a niggling worry. The more I thought about it, the more distressed I became. I knew Mormons managed polygamous marriages, but for me, this situation was becoming untenable. Irma was anything but rational about our relationship. If she discovered my involvement with Mavis, she would go bananas and attack me verbally and physically, then order me out of my cherished drugstore. Would there be any point in fighting? I knew the adage: *Hell hath no fury like a woman spurned.* I understood that and dreaded the anticipated confrontation.

All morning I felt uneasy and tried to think of other things, such as bringing in another pharmacist and increasing sales. Although I was busy filling prescriptions, I kept visualizing Irma storming through the front door, casting a baleful eye at Mavis and walking with a determined stride toward my station to create a hellish scene. While counting pills on my board, I looked up to see an unwelcome figure entering the store. It was Ben Simon followed by Officer Mary Beth Schultz, who held her right hand on her hip holster like a movie lawman entering a western saloon. Both walked directly to my station, stopped, and looked up at me. Simon's dour expression could only mean unpleasantness.

He muttered, "Black, I need to talk to you."

"Up here, or down there?" I asked.

"Better come to the station."

"What? Listen, Simon, I've got a business to run, prescriptions to fill, and advice to give customers. What is so damn important that you can't tell me here?"

"Irma Withers is dead."

I must have paled as I clutched the edge of the counter. I took a deep breath, hoping to quell the vertigo that gripped me. I backed into a chair, sat down hard, and stared dumbfounded. Simon rushed toward me and, in an unusually solicitous manner, said, "Hey, Kiddo, you alright?"

I nodded slowly, then looked at him. "What did you say about Irma?"

Simon looked at Officer Schultz. "Get him something to drink."

Mavis and Eddie Polanski brushed past several customers who quickly gathered around the pharmacy station. Eddie held a glass of water and Mavis a damp towel. Their cloying attentiveness annoyed me, and I still had difficulty believing what Simon told me. I tried standing; my legs quivered, and I grabbed the arms of the chair.

"Sit down, Black," Simon said. He motioned Mavis to stand next to me. "I'll leave you in Mrs. Johnson's hands . . . don't move. I'll be back in a while." Officer Schultz started to follow him out.

"Wait, don't leave," I called out. "I want to know about Irma. I'll go to the station with you."

* * *

Simon's office was more depressing than I remembered it from my last visit. The single ceiling light must have put out all of thirty watts, which were absorbed by the institutional gray walls and darkly stained prison-made furniture.

Seated opposite Simon, I began to ask questions. He held up his hand.

"Hold it! You're in my bailiwick. I'm the one asking questions. When I'm through, you can ask."

"Simon, forget your goddamn protocol. Tell me about Irma. How did she die? Where? When? Tell me now, or I'm walking out of here."

"Just hold on to your tuchas. We found her in her bed. An open bottle of medicine on her nightstand. Coroner thinks she died yesterday. Neighbors reported finding a newspaper and milk bottle at her door late in the day. She always picked them up early. That's all I can tell you. Now, you start answering a few questions. When did you see her last?"

"I think it was three days ago at the drugstore."

"Was there anything unusual about her—her appearance, her manner?"

"She was coming down with a cold, a bad cough. I advised her to stay in bed, take aspirin and cough medicine."

"You hadn't seen her since?"

"No, I hadn't."

He was writing in his pocket-sized notebook. "Where were you last night?"

An uncomfortably warm sensation came over me, but I knew I had to answer truthfully. "I was with a friend."

Simon looked up. "Uh-huh. Who? Where? When?"

His damn patronizing "Uh-huh" irked me. I didn't want to involve Mavis, which led to a momentary delay in my answer.

Drumming his fingers on the desk, Simon said, "What part of who, when, and where don't you understand?"

I blurted, "Alright! I was with Mavis Johnson. We were discussing sales techniques . . . trying to make the store more profitable, things like that."

He waited for a further explanation. "And?"

"And what?"

"Where did you meet?"

"At her home." I'd have walked out if he'd said "Uh-huh" one more time.

With his pen poised, and in an impassive voice, he asked, "What time did you get there, and what time did you leave?"

I had an urge to tell him to go to hell, but I didn't. "You recall, we had a thunderstorm last night. Mavis thought I should stay until it subsided. I wouldn't have driven in that downpour anyway."

"So, what time did you get there, and what time did you leave?"

I knew he would persist, and that griped the hell out of me. "I got there about 9:00 p.m. Left this morning at 9:30."

Like the Oracle of Delphi, he said nothing, for which I was grateful until he looked up from his writing pad.

"That cough syrup you concocted for Irma—it had codeine—enough to . . .?"

I cut him off. "I didn't prescribe it. Earl Withers did, long before he was murdered. She had taken it before and knew how to use it. That, for damn sure, didn't kill her."

"That bottle went to toxicology in Madison this morning."

"Where have they taken the corpse?" I asked.

"Also to Madison. There's a real coroner there."

"Do you think I could examine Irma's room? Maybe look in her medicine cabinet?"

Simon sat back, folded his arms across his chest, and nodded. "Not a bad idea. Yeah, both of us tomorrow morning at eight. Are there toxic substances in the drugstore that could kill?"

"There are some in every drugstore. In mine, they're locked in a cabinet under my counter. No one—"

"Who, besides you, has a key to that cabinet?"

The question had never occurred to me until he asked. I said, "All of Earl's keys were on a key ring in my office. Come to think of it, Mavis might have a key since she had duplicate keys to everything else . . . front and back doors, registers, jewelry, and perfume display cases."

Simon put his notebook away and slid his pen onto his shirt pocket. His eyes locked onto mine; he came close so that his garlicky afternoon breath forced me to back away.

"Tell me about your relationship with Irma."

At that moment, Officer Schultz appeared in the doorway with two cups of coffee and set them down on Simon's desk. I thought she wanted to stay, but Simon motioned with his head for her to leave.

I continued, "Irma and I enjoyed a close relationship, you know that, but in the last few months our friendship cooled off." I didn't wait for Simon's snide comments, so I hurried along. "Maybe we had too much going on initially, and the flames of love . . ."

"Spare me the violins, Kiddo. I've heard that song before. Do me a favor. Don't make travel plans for Cuba or Ecuador." He stood. "See you tomorrow morning at the Withers' mansion."

*   *   *

I parked behind Simon's coupe and walked toward the entry of the Victorian mansion guarded by a slouching officer who straightened up at the sight of me. Simon, from a second-floor window, motioned me to come up. The house, about a hundred years old, retained an austere elegance with high ceilings and tall windows.

Every time I entered this landmark house, I admired the exquisite woodwork in the wainscoting, archways, and stairwell, all of which suggested constant care with aromatic wood preservatives and polish. Carpeting had been patched to maintain its original pattern. As I ascended the stairs, I appreciated the hand-carved newels with their twisted rope design and handrails with a patina created by years of usage.

On the second-floor landing, Simon walked with me toward a closed door and stopped momentarily. "This is her bedroom, but you probably know that," he said. "The door's closed. A guy from the coroner's office is taking prints and samples of whatever."

Simon led me to a settee in the wide hallway. He started to take a cigarette out of a pack, then hesitated and put it away.

"Black, you knew Irma. Did she have any health problems?"

"Nothing serious. Like I said, she had a scratchy throat . . . thought she was coming down with a cold."

"Is it possible she had a heart attack?"

"At her age? Not likely, but I'm not a doctor. Maybe an anaphylactic shock due to some drug she might have taken. But I don't know of any since I supplied all her medications. Except her cough syrup. Earl formulated that."

The bedroom door opened and the tech walked out with a small metal case. "The room is all yours," he said as he hurried down the stairs and out of the house.

I took a step into the room, looked around, and stopped. "Leave the windows closed for a moment," I called to Simon as he placed his hands on the window handles. "Smell anything?" I asked.

Simon sniffed and shrugged. "Yeah, maybe."

"Smell like burnt almonds?"

"How the hell would I know what burnt almonds smell like?"

I wasn't about to attempt a description, especially to a habitual smoker. I recognized the odor from my smell-identity class at pharmacy school. Some odors one never forgets.

"Well, what the hell smells like that?" Simon asked.

"Cyanide."

Simon froze. In a strained voice, he said, "That shit will kill you in zip time, right?" He shoved his hands into his pants pockets as though to avoid contamination. "Jeezus. Think she committed suicide?" He did not wait for my response. "Or was she poisoned?"

"I'd opt for the latter. Only a psychotic would choose to commit suicide like that. She loved being who she was, especially after she inherited Earl's wealth."

Simon hurried to open the windows. "The stink of that stuff doesn't kill, does it?"

"Not in dilute concentrations," I said.

He took a deep breath of outside air, blew it out, then took another. After rummaging through a chest of drawers and a standing wardrobe, he walked to the closet, opened the door, and turned on the ceiling light. I walked behind him and smelled the delicate perfume in the narrow room with garments hanging on either side—some still with sales tags. He shook his head. "She had a damn fortune in clothes. Spent the old man's money as though he printed it." He ran his hands along the clothes and talked to me over his shoulder. "What the hell does one do with all this shit?" He turned around. "This freakin' death chamber gives me the willies."

"Did you find any personal papers? A will, letters, anything of importance?" I asked.

"Not here, but I was talking to her lawyer the other day at Jennie's Café. He said he was putting Irma's estate in order, reviewing all her holdings left by old man Withers."

"Did she designate an heir or heirs in the event of her death? She must have relatives back east," I said.

Simon turned away and began muttering. I listened closely and thought he said, "She was orphaned as a child—became a ward of the state."

"How do you know all that, Simon?"

He walked toward the door, looked over his shoulder, and said, "I was her last living relative."

CHAPTER 15

"Don't stand there like a goddamn golem," Simon said. "You heard me right, she was my kid cousin, but people around here don't need to know."

"Wait a minute, wait one damn minute! You mean—"

He stopped me. "You wait before you go epileptic."

"I think you mean apoplectic."

"Whatever. Come to my office. We can talk there, and I can refer to some notes on her."

*   *   *

Irma's death left me depressed even though our relationship had tanked some weeks before her death. I knew our intimacy had to cool down, but I recalled those fun-filled times when we laughed together and thrilled to touching and exploring one another.

*   *   *

Simon pulled out a manila folder from a cabinet behind his desk. "I've got a few notes that might interest you."

I leaned forward in my chair, eager to hear what he had to say. He blinked as moisture filled his eyes. He cleared his throat. "My mother was Irma's mother's younger sister. Irma, an only child, lost her parents in a head-on collision when some drunken sonofabitch rammed their car. Irma was a kid, fifteen or so at the time. Fortunately, she wasn't with them at the time of the accident. She took the loss awfully hard. The kid was spoiled . . . treated like a princess . . . never knew the meaning of the word 'No.' My father died at an early age, which made Mother and me Irma's only relatives. We opened our home and hearts to her." He said softly, "Why wouldn't we?"

"Did she stay with you long?"

"Three years. Rebellious as hell. Caused my mother all kinds of frustration. Day after high school graduation, she took off like a scalded cat. Said she needed to get away, make money and find opportunities in a world of suckers and frauds. She had a shitty outlook on the world. Never had to lift a finger to make a red cent. Why she had that attitude, I don't know. I always treated her like a kid sister. Actually, we got along alright, but she was restless and resentful like a caged animal.

"Wasn't long until she discovered she could make big bucks doing whatever she did—more than she could doing legitimate work. When I heard she was pole dancing in a so-called gentlemen's club, I knew she was hanging out with scum, maybe doing drugs. I figured I'd better get her the hell out of there where I could keep an eye on her. She didn't want to come out here, so I went back to New York and convinced her she'd wind up in prison if she didn't change her M.O. fast. Only my personal friendship with the deputy prosecuting attorney saved her from the slammer."

Simon lit a cigarette, took a long pull, blew out smoke, and became contemplative.

"Hard to believe she left that easy money to come out here," I said.

"She made money, alright, but pissed it away . . . one step from begging for handouts. When I told her I knew a rich old guy—actually I called him an elderly gentleman who was recently widowed and lonesome—she showed some interest. I bought her plane ticket and sent a few bucks for decent clothes.

"Let me tell you, when she saw old man Withers for the first time, she did an about-face and started to run until I told her what he owned. She skidded and stopped in her tracks. She liked the idea of having domestics in a big home with a spacious lawn and flowers tended by a gardener, a car of her own, and a personal bank account.

All that was more than she could resist. Meanwhile, old man Withers, that horny bastard, couldn't wait to get into her."

"That explains that odd winter-springtime romance. Sounds like Withers was thinking through his gonads when he saw Irma," I said.

"Well, yes and no. He went along with a prenuptial agreement, which I insisted she have. It made her the sole heir to his fortune in case of his natural or accidental death. Nothing was said about murder. Who would even think of it? Arnie Teasdale, the attorney who drew up the papers, thinks he might be able to keep things out of probate by doing some finagling."

"I'm curious, Simon, wouldn't Irma have named you as her heir in a will?"

He lit another cigarette. "No. Not that she didn't want to, but Withers had other ideas."

"Meaning?"

"Withers, that crazy old bastard, had his attorney insert a clause stating that upon Irma's death the estate would go to Mavis Johnson or her issue in case of her death."

"Is that even legal?"

"Apparently, but I'm no lawyer."

"So, you're left with nothing for your trouble."

Simon shrugged. "I never wanted anything. Irma promised to buy me a new car. I told her to forget it. Why would I want a new car when my old Ford starts every morning? I know where to stash my cigarette butts and I can reach the dashboard lighter without taking my eyes off the road. The car fits like an old broad. Besides, if I drove a new car, people might think I'm on the take."

CHAPTER 16

Nothing I learned about Irma from Simon made me feel better. In fact, I felt sadder. Losing her parents when she was a youngster and marrying an infirm old man like Earl, who she really did not love, gave her no physical pleasure. Even those secretive moments we shared could not dispel her recurrent moments of depression.

Although we tired of one another, our early clandestine episodes of sexual abandon did not create emotional stability. We had too many differences: she was flighty, unable to conform or obey the simplest civil obligations like traffic rules. She disregarded speed limits, and when confronted by a policeman would make some outrageous excuse such as hurrying to the hospital to see a dying friend. When in fact she had no friends. Earl made generous contributions to the policemen's ball and extended other favors to civic causes that more than paid for Irma's indiscretions.

Old Earl accepted or ignored Irma's behavior for the first two years of their marriage, but he grew tired of bailing her out of jail when she punched a policeman or refused to accept a traffic ticket. I wondered if he knew about our sexual dalliances and no longer cared. Irma had become less discreet and may have taunted Earl by her flagrant wantonness. A divorce would have been costly, and the notoriety more than he wanted. Had Irma died before him, he would have been a prime suspect.

Arnie Teasdale, Earl's attorney, who also represented Irma, had formed a management company for her after Earl's murder. I wondered if he could have manipulated the books so that he would eventually control the holdings.

When I thought about it, the old man's will, according to Teasdale, stated that in the event of Irma's death, Mavis Johnson was to inherit his estate. How damned ironic. Yesterday Mavis was my employee and grateful to have a job; today, she owned the building in which my drugstore was located.

I was sure she'd give me a lease, maybe one in perpetuity, or at least a very long one. Would she increase my rent to discourage my tenancy? Why would she do that? I began to feel a trifle unsure somehow. We made love two weeks ago. She initiated it, although I certainly didn't resist. Since then, neither of us had spoken about it and went about our duties at the drugstore as though it never happened.

The only change in our relationship was the faint smile she offered when our paths crossed or when she needed an answer to a customer's question about medication. She maintained an aloofness that puzzled me.

At age thirty-nine, she was ten years older than I, but her face and body remained youthful. Her smile of perfect teeth, probably the result of orthodontic care, was film-star attractive. The nearness of her, breathing her perfume and recalling that night of romantic bliss, made her constantly desirable. Could she feel about me as I did about her? If so, why wasn't she more demonstrative?

Usually, I was the last to leave the store at about 9:00 p.m., but this night Mavis stayed late to restock cosmetics. I shut the lights in the pharmacy station and walked toward the front of the store where she was arranging a perfume display. A dim night-light outlined her silhouette as I walked behind her and put my arms around her waist.

She jumped. "Oh!" She turned around quickly. Her frightened look became a smile as she put her arms around my neck and gave me an open-mouthed kiss. Her tongue eagerly explored mine, and her pelvis pushed against me. She murmured that she loved me, missed my company, and hoped that I still loved her.

I asked why she acted distant and unresponsive in the

days after our last date. By way of apology, she explained that I might have needed time to mourn Irma's death.

I told her I appreciated her thoughtfulness, and since I had been as much at fault about not pursuing our relationship, I asked if I might invite her to dinner.

"You may, and I thank you for the invitation, but my cooking is better than any restaurant food within thirty miles of Newbury."

"I'm sure you're right, but I feel guilty since this is the second time I've been invited to your home. I'd like to reciprocate."

"Fine. You can provide the dessert."

"Dessert? Like what?"

She smiled coquettishly while she walked toward the rear door leading to the parking lot. "Follow my car," she said.

"Will your son be joining us?"

"He's having dinner with his aunt tonight and will be staying at her home overnight."

"Perfect."

* * *

Mavis took two porterhouse steaks out of the refrigerator, seasoned them with garlic and her assortment of herbs, sautéed onions, and mushrooms that filled the house with a magnificent fragrance. She tossed a Caesar salad with anchovies, but what impressed me more was her selection of wine: a 1937 Lafite Rothschild Bordeaux. The lady had class and first-rate knowledge about fine things. Her newly acquired wealth from the Withers estate was finding good use in procuring great wine. The meal I would describe as wonderfully tasty even though I hardly considered myself a gourmet. She was pleased that I left nothing but a bare bone and smiled when I sponged gravy with the remains of a croissant. I refused the dessert of French cheeses, which were simply beyond my gustatory sophistication.

I helped clear the table and walked into a well-organized kitchen.

"We'll stack the dishes," she said, "then we can sit in the living room and enjoy the rest of our wine. Besides, I want to talk with you. There's still so much I don't know about you." This woman fed my ego as though I were a grand pooh-bah—not a big-city kid who became a small-town pill counter.

Everything about her spelled elegance: smart clothing, costly antiques, oil paintings, and fine wines. I anticipated an evening of further pleasure as I remembered that stormy night with her three weeks ago. It was more wonderful than any I could recall . . . even those with Irma . . . God rest her soul and her insatiable libido.

Mavis sat opposite me on a sofa. Her shapely legs drew my attention again. She started the conversation by asking about my background: family, training, and political views, to which she had shown more than polite interest. I savored the wine and was sorry to see her pour the last ounce into my goblet.

After talking for more than thirty minutes, she directed the conversation to drugstore business—another topic I could discuss fondly. To be accurate, I asked for her opinions and suggestions. After all, she had been working there for over twenty years.

"Zach, you know I love working at the store, but if you don't mind my saying so, it needs updating desperately. It should be more modern, more customer-friendly. To begin, we've got to get rid of those ancient apothecary jars in the window. They are *so* passé." She could hardly catch her breath with excitement as she continued, "Aisles should be wider, and there should be overhead signs indicating product location."

She leaned forward, her elbows on her knees. "We make approximately fifty to over one hundred percent profit on cosmetic items. Let's display them in more attractive cases. I'd like also to suggest selling other high-profit items like wristwatches, earrings, bracelets, necklaces, things like that. You know, costume jewelry."

That made a lot of sense. I liked what she was saying, and thinking about it made me eager to make those changes. "Why don't we drive to the drugstore now? I'd like to visualize those things."

She leaped off the sofa. "Wonderful! I'll get my jacket."

CHAPTER 17

I parked in front of the store and thought more about Mavis' comments, though I hesitated about accepting all her suggestions and criticisms. Those red and green apothecary globes represented something historically significant and sentimental: they were symbols of the healing arts through the ages going back to ancient times, a welcoming sign to the sick and weary wayfarer. I agreed with her suggestion that the large storefront windows should be eliminated to make space for merchandise shelving inside. I understood the need for getting rid of the striped awnings that had served as landmarks for many years and sidewalk triangle boards— they too were passé.

I unlocked the front door then stepped aside to allow Mavis to enter. We were several feet into the darkened store when a blinding light was followed by a deafening explosion at the back that knocked us flat on our backs. A huge ball of fire shot upward, shards of glass and objects flew past like missiles peppering us. Sharp stinging and prickling occurred around my neck and face. I raised my head cautiously to look around. For several seconds, I remained disoriented. Heat and smoke began to choke me. I coughed uncontrollably; my eyes burned and teared.

I turned to see Mavis lying next to me, hands over her face.

"Are you alright?" My voice was hoarse and gravelly. Bloody cuts on her legs pierced her hose. My breathing became labored. My chest ached with each breath. I pulled myself up, struggled to my feet, reached over, grabbed her around the waist, and put her over my shoulder. Walking and carrying her blindly through the dense smoke, I struggled toward the front door. Anxiously, I reached for the doorknob and hoped it would be there. When I felt it, I grabbed it and flung the door open. I stumbled onto the sidewalk, coughing and gasping as black smoke and red flames engulfed the entire rear of the store. I set Mavis down against the car.

We stood by helplessly and watched as the roaring blaze increased in intensity, destroying the old tinder-dry structure. Bright embers floated above the flames. Time seemed interminable until we heard the wail of sirens. Relief and sorrow filled my head as fire engines rolled up and firemen hurried to their hoses. Like a nightmare of indescribable horror, I watched as my store was consumed by roaring flames.

Mavis, shaking, leaned against my car, removing fragments of glass and debris from her clothing and hair. She brushed off burnt and exploded particles from my clothing and ran her hands through my hair to remove other debris. We watched the firemen battle the blaze for about thirty minutes until the flames subsided then died. Tears streaked Mavis' soot-laden cheeks. We stood by in despondent silence when the battalion chief approached us while several firemen were still hacking through charred wood and separating ashes searching for hot spots.

The chief said, "Sorry for your loss, folks, but I'm glad you're alive." He looked at me. "Can you tell me what happened?"

I told him how we had stepped inside the store when an explosion took place and all hell broke loose. That was followed by a massive fire that seemed to start in the pharmacy section.

The chief listened, nodded, and then made a strange request. He asked me to show him my hands, palms up. After examining them, he asked me to turn them over and to spread my fingers. He bent forward and pulled my hands to his nose. I realized he was thinking I might be the arsonist. He examined our clothing and continued sniffing.

"Chief, you can't possibly think *we* . . ."

"We don't make assumptions unless we have good reason."

I became resentful. "Wait a minute. I thought we'd die when that explosion occurred. How could you even imagine . . .?"

He interrupted me. "We found an explosive device and an accelerant."

CHAPTER 18

We rode back to Mavis' home at about 1:00 a.m. in silence. Numb, bewildered, and exhausted. I had difficulty making sense of what had happened. Mavis, disheveled, sooty in torn clothes, invited me to shower and spend the rest of the morning with her, but I felt an urgent need to return to the devastation . . . to think about the loss and recovery. The pharmacy section was demolished; spoilage by smoke and water had destroyed over half the remaining shelf items, and the stench of burned wood, pharmaceuticals, and packaging pervaded the entire store.

A couple standing on the sidewalk approached, eager to talk, and began by saying they were sorry for me but equally concerned for themselves. They wondered where their prescriptions would be filled. I knew them and their continuing need for insulin and heart medication.

I assured them I'd fill their prescriptions even if I had

to drive to Kennesaw, forty miles north. In our small town, such acts of caring were commonplace, a holdover from a time when the sick and disabled relied on neighbors' goodwill.

My heart sank as I walked along the north side of the building toward the rear that was burned out; a gaping hole in the brick wall exposed charred beams threatening to collapse. I shuddered at the thought that if Mavis and I had walked another ten feet into the store we probably would have been blown to bits, and those bits would have been fried.

I stood in the parking lot at the rear where employees parked their cars in designated slots. Part of the lot closest to the building was filled with debris: broken bottles, scattered pills, capsules, and liquids among the ashes. I kicked some of the waste aside and noticed skid marks near Eddie Polanski's space. The marks suggested that someone had stomped on the accelerator to make a quick getaway.

A closer examination revealed broad tire marks, possibly by a pickup or a large car such as a Packard, Cadillac, or Lincoln. I knew Eddie drove a Model A Ford that had narrow tires. Walt Mason drove an old Dodge pickup, but he drove it slowly because of his impaired physical coordination. Besides, neither Eddie nor Mason could have been responsible for those skid marks. I'd have bet my life on that.

The cold early-morning wind whipped through my cotton sweater. I rubbed my arms and was about to leave when I felt a tap on my shoulder. My heart hammered as I spun around. It was Simon—welcome as a venomous snake. His sneer had to be the prelude to something detestable. It always was.

"Can't stay away from the arson, eh?" He lit a cigarette, inhaled, then exhaled a plume made bright by the light of a streetlamp. His question, as usual, was terse, snide, and accusatory. "Like what you see, Kiddo?"

I didn't answer but thought what kind of a smartass comment was that, and what was he alluding to?

He went on, "Fire like this ain't altogether bad."

He waited for me to comment, but I refused.

He looked at me sideways. "A guy could recover enough insurance money to rebuild a modern facility, replace a lot of worn-out crap." He spoke slowly, deliberately. "The other benefit would be the destruction of any evidence to Withers' murder."

I turned to face him. "Simon, you are one unmitigated, suspicious, and insulting sonofabitch. My livelihood has gone up in flames, Mavis and I almost lost our lives, and all you can do is make shitty remarks. You've got one hell of a nerve. Why don't you find the sonofabitch who did this?"

"Relax, Kiddo. My job is to suspect and hold accountable any character who gains by breaking the law.

What's more, I don't have to explain or apologize for anything I say. You got that? Furthermore, anyone who insults or demeans an officer of the law—"

"Can it, Simon. You're not talking to a greenhorn who got off the boat yesterday. You don't get to insult or threaten just because you've got a tin badge and a pea shooter."

"My, my, such big talk. You better hope I don't find anything connecting you to this fire. Before you mouth off anymore, tell me why you came out here again."

"Because I'm goddamned angry, that's why." I put my hand out to stop him from moving. "Before you step on these skid marks, look at them. Someone tried to make a fast getaway."

Simon bent over and studied the marks. "I'll need a picture of these tread marks before they disappear." He pulled a walkie-talkie out of his coat pocket, punched in a few numbers, and ordered someone to get a photographer immediately. He listened briefly, then snarled, "That's too fuckin' bad. No one signs on for a nine-to-five job on my watch. Tell him to get his ass out here now. That's an order."

*   *   *

Within forty-eight hours, the fire-damaged area had been cleared; the insurance adjusters assessed losses while an architect and contractor were planning reconstruction. The rebuilt store would be completely modern. An emporium for health and related items.

Mavis and I contributed our ideas to the design of the new building, which extended an extra twenty feet into the backyard. The term "related health items" covered a multitude of things such as food, clothing, and kitchen utensils, which would contribute to healthy living in an expanded version of the term.

After the store had been closed for two weeks, our crew returned to work around carpenters, electricians, plumbers, roofers, and bricklayers in frustrating conditions, which made tempers flare. Somehow, we managed. Emphasis was placed on getting the pharmacy in order as soon as possible. Throughout the ordeal, customers and employees had shown remarkable forbearance.

Mavis collected damaged goods and placed them on sale for pennies on the dollar.

*   *   *

Four months later, a completely magnificent store, quite an improvement over the last, served the needs of a growing clientele. A contemporary approach to advertising became routine. Women's hygiene and men's prophylactics were displayed in subtle and sophisticated photos. One photo revealed a smiling young couple embracing in a bedroom. The advertisement touted new and improved condoms and diaphragms, bearing the message: "For pleasure without the anxiety of contributing to an explosive population."

CHAPTER 19

The YMCA had converted two rooms in the old BPOE hall to handball courts used mainly by business and professional men. Arnie Teasdale, the lawyer, and I had been playing for about forty-five minutes and had worked up a sweat that discolored his tank top. He held up his gloved hand and said, "That's it for me. You're too damned good and too young for fair competition. I do better against Simon. He's an older cock and moves slower."

We walked off the court to a locker room that reminded me of my high school days when the room reeked from overactive sweat glands, odors to make one's eyes tear before antiperspirants and personal hygiene became a national obsession. There was no time for showering between classes, and only the liberal use of talcum powder poorly masked the stink.

Arnie Teasdale was a self-assured fifty-one-year-old six-footer with a florid complexion and wispy white hair combed from one side over a pink scalp. He stood with broad shoulders and a thick neck with glabrous folds that hung over a starched collar; an abdomen dipping below his belt indicated a gourmand's lifestyle.

His law office located in the heart of downtown Newbury occupied an entire building modernized with a glass brick front, which distinguished it from the conventional red and brown-brick establishments nearby. The sign on the door read: "Arnold R. Teasdale, Esq. Attorney at Law."

I followed him as he entered, then I stopped to stare in disbelief. The reception room could have been designed by an interior decorator for a Park Avenue office. Walnut veneer covered walls displaying paintings with bright splotches of color to create vivid patterns. The secretary's desk had an impressive side extension of some eight feet. Soft indirect lighting reinforced the atmosphere of quiet elegance. My shoes sank into cushioned carpeting as I stood observing the smartly styled leather and chrome furniture.

Teasdale's secretary, a thirty-something brunette with an hourglass figure, removed her glasses and stood smiling as we approached. Arnie made a half-turn, introducing me to Roxanne Holley. She extended her hand with well-manicured nails and a sizable emerald-cut diamond on her third finger. Such glitz, I thought, was rare in provincial Newbury.

A beauty mark on her chin fascinated me, and I stared too long.

"I'm pleased to meet you, Mr. Black, and for the future, please call me Roxy."

Arnie walked on, releasing his tie and removing his jacket. "Any important calls?" he asked.

"Two inquiries about that property on Grant Avenue," she said.

"If we get one more call on that lot, we'll jack up the price," he said.

Roxy hurried to assist him with his jacket, folded it over her arm, and followed him to his office to place it in a closet.

His spacious office was even more luxurious than the reception room. Out of the corner of my eye, I saw him pat Roxy's derriere. She turned, her eyebrows arched, then she smiled. I looked away quickly as she left the room and closed the door.

Arnie swiveled in his chair to reach behind him for two tumblers and a bottle of scotch on a minibar. He placed two cubes from an ice bucket in one glass and filled it half full of scotch.

I requested no ice and measured off an inch with my thumb and index finger. He raised his glass and proposed a toast: "Here's to continued prosperity, good health, and wonderful fucking." The last part of his toast defined the man—too crude to be my type. He took a long gulp, set his glass down forcibly, and patted his ample abdomen. "We can review Withers' file, and since most of the principals are gone, no one's privacy is going to be violated—well, hardly."

In the last five minutes, Arnie's status as a decent, honest professional had taken a 180-degree turn. He revealed a client's document while he engaged in lewd behavior. I didn't think of myself as a prig, and yet Teasdale's mannerisms were frankly detestable. My eyes searched the walls, which held at least a dozen certificates and diplomas, spurious proof of professional competence. One diploma caught my eye. When I focused upon it, it seemed inconceivable. How was it possible? I got off my chair and walked over to examine it . . . a law degree from Harvard University. My incredulous expression caught Arnie's eye.

"You thinking 'How are the mighty fallen'?" His smile had smugness all over it. "Yeah, you're seeing right. I'm a Harvard man complete with bragging rights . . . if I wanted to brag. And your next question should be: what am I doing in a backwater place like this? That's a story I'll tell only if I'm persuaded."

"Okay, I'm persuading."

He took another sip of scotch then leaned back in his chair; his fingers intertwined over his abdomen. "Law school wasn't difficult. Oh, it wasn't a cakewalk, but I had no real problems. I enjoyed verbal jousting with those old farts with their detachable collars and righteous mannerisms. I would challenge their stilted thinking and their interpretations of the legal and illegal. I seldom won an argument, but they respected me for being contentious. I managed to finish in the upper ten percent.

"I had offers to join prestigious firms, clerk for a Supreme Court Justice, Louis Brandeis. Can you believe that? I figured I had the world by the balls, but I lacked maturity to take advantage of those opportunities. Truth is, I was beginning to feel my oats . . . getting to like liquor, women, and worst of all, gambling. In short, I had succumbed to the treats of manhood without being able to handle them."

"This is beginning to sound like a B-movie."

"You could call it that. I found I had an aptitude for numbers . . . probabilities . . . made money figuring the odds on cards, dice, poker—any game of chance until casino management got wise and barred me from playing. At that point, I should have gone straight, but I was approached by two thugs from the Mafia who convinced me I could make big bucks working for them. That meant overseeing gambling, managing cat houses, and selling bootleg liquor. To make a long story short, it all fell apart, and I spent a year at Rikers. My law license was revoked, of course. Even the gal I was shacking up with dropped me. But while I was in prison, I got to thinking about how low I had fallen. Then, like a convert who suddenly sees the light, I swore I was going to live an honest, wholesome life." He paused for another swallow. "At least those were my intentions."

He continued, "A year after my release, I found the path back to respectability was like scaling Mount Everest with bare feet. I wanted desperately to get my license back. I was told that I would have to qualify again, which meant reviewing my law books, taking refresher courses, and attending lectures. I worked so damned hard at times, and I had doubts about whether it was all worth the effort. I sweated through orals and written exams and damned if I didn't ace them.

"In spite of all that, prestigious firms would have nothing to do with me. In fact, no self-respecting law office would have me, and that really pissed me off."

"How did you wind up here in Newbury?"

"After applying to a zillion firms with hat in hand and being turned down, I figured: fuck the big-city gonifs who judged me by my prison record. About the time I really felt discouraged, my aunt and uncle, with whom I kept in touch, ran a dairy farm out here—Sunny Brook Farms. They were getting old, infirm, couldn't manage the farm. Since I was their only eligible relative, they prevailed upon me. I came out with a buck and a half in my pocket, I swear it. I looked the place over and agreed to manage it. When I think about it, I had a hell of a nerve. There I was, a big-city know-it-all agreeing to take over a farm with thirty head of guernseys. The only cow I had ever seen was Elsie on billboards.

"Anyway, I managed the property as best I could, hired a couple of cowhands until I learned the ropes, then I increased the herd to fifty head. My aunt and uncle died within three years of my arrival. I sold the farm and stock to a dairy consortium for a nice piece of change and was eager to get back to practicing law."

"How did you establish a relationship with Earl Withers?"

"He came to me just after I started practicing. Poor bastard was in all kinds of legal trouble. Nonpayment of taxes. Lawsuits from tenants who complained of poorly maintained properties. He knew nothing about taking care of tenants or didn't give a damn about them. I managed to get him squared away, but I worked my ass off doing it. I placed pretty high fees on my work, and he agreed. Hell, he had no choice, but I didn't take my fees in cash."

"What do you mean?"

"Most of Withers' properties were to be held jointly by him and me."

"Wait a minute. Did you say Withers' properties were held jointly by you and him?"

"That's right. In lieu of legal fees, Earl agreed to give me, at my insistence, twenty percent of the value of the properties. He thought that was reasonable, and I accepted. Another part of that agreement gave me the first right of refusal for purchasing the rest of his holdings in the event of his death or his wife's death if she should succeed him."

I experienced a wave of confusion, almost vertigo, but I managed to retain my equilibrium; I swallowed hard. "I thought Earl left everything to Irma, and in the event of her death, all properties were to go to Mavis Johnson."

"That's hearsay, mere scuttlebutt. I know what the will states—I'm the one who wrote it. Mavis Johnson gets a few ramshackle parcels."

"This is all so different than what I had heard from Irma. Do you intend to buy Mavis' shares?"

Arnie's mouth skewed to the side as he chewed on his lower lip. "I'll buy her out if she agrees to a realistic price. Hell, some of those properties are shanties about to collapse . . . razing them would cost more than . . ."

A picture of deceit and avarice with possible murderous intent began to unfold. Was this a well-planned operation to acquire all the Withers estate? As I listened, I could see his plan emerging. A murder here and there would give him much of Newbury's important real estate. Suddenly, I felt a chill. An apparition was forming . . . a specter with Teasdale's grimacing face. A scheming, greedy, clawing creature. I wanted out of his office.

I made an excuse for leaving, saying I had to meet an

insurance adjuster. I walked to Jennie's Café for a cup of coffee and time to think about what I had just learned. I finished my coffee and reached for my wallet. After a few frantic moments, I remembered taking my wallet out to give Arnie my new business card. I must have set the wallet on his desk and become distracted.

I hurried back to his office, charged into Arnie's room, and stopped immediately. Seated at his desk, Arnie slouched back with a rapturous smile, his eyes closed. Roxy knelt before him, her head moving back and forth, buried in his crotch. I grabbed my wallet off the desk and flew out of the room before they discovered I was there.

CHAPTER 20

Arnie Teasdale had to be reckoned as a possible killer. There was no way he could escape suspicion because he had a lot to gain after Withers' and Irma's deaths, and he had enough venom to destroy any spoilers to his plans.

He knew the law and used it to finesse any questions or suspicions regarding property ownership, authenticity of wills, codicils, or statutes about inheritance. Catching him in legal malfeasance would require services of another lawyer, and since his machinations didn't involve me directly, I shouldn't be concerned, but I really was.

Ben Simon should have been looking into Teasdale's possible tampering, and I wondered why he hadn't. After all, Irma had been his cousin. Simon was too thorough not to have known about Teasdale's relationship with Withers . . . unless Simon had also been in on some scheme to defraud—but no, that was not likely. As miserable as Simon could be at times, he was a straight arrow, a letter-of-the-law guy who turned dark and menacing at the slightest legal infraction.

* * *

The insurance carrier finally agreed to permit rebuilding the pharmacy and rear section of the store. Meanwhile, the identity of the arsonist remained unsolved, despite the repeated interviews by Simon of every store employee. The insurance carrier detectives grilled me about possible enemies, malcontents whom I might have prepared the wrong medications or improper dosages resulting in the patient's death. I denied knowing of any dissatisfied customers or having received any complaints.

All employees volunteered to work overtime to put the store in functional if not finished order, especially the drug department. I could fill most prescriptions, which was my greatest concern. I was grateful to Mavis for her organizing leadership, which meant clearing away debris, ordering merchandise, stocking shelves, and getting rid of water-soaked and burned merchandise.

Eddie Polanski, conscientious and wiry, had his fountain ready for serving food and drink. I asked him, as well as other employees, to keep a record of overtime hours for compensation.

In addition to the physical labor of preparing the store,

Mavis continued to keep the books and in her efficient manner encouraged other employees to work under difficult reconstruction. She appeared tireless and determined. When I found a moment to watch her, I realized how attractive she was even in stressful moments. Her beauty was subtle, refined, and more engaging than I had realized. I thought I knew her well, but during this trying period she seemed even more involved, more committed. She stopped momentarily to survey the progress with her hands on her hips as she blew away a few strands of hair that fell across her face. I felt gratitude and longing.

After store hours, I sat down heavily on a cardboard case of napkins and watched as she wiped ash off cans of Dutch Girl cleanser and replaced them on a shelf. She stopped when she saw me watching her and gave me a brief smile. "Mr. Boss Man, you've put in only twelve hours. Do you think you're entitled to rest?"

Only the two of us remained in the store as I walked toward the panel of electrical switches and shut all but the night light. When I turned around, Mavis stood gazing into my eyes with a look that spelled desire. I took her in my arms and held her tightly; she became limp and leaned against me.

I hand-brushed strands of hair off her face and kissed her cheeks and lips. "Come, Love, you're exhausted and probably need food," I said. "I'm taking you to dinner at the Claremont. We'll share a bottle of wine, dine on lobster and steaks. How does that sound?"

She smiled wistfully. "No, no, Zach. Thank you. I'm much too tired. Forgive me. I'm going home to plop into bed. My son is at my sister-in-law's, so I'll have an undisturbed rest, and oh, boy, I sure need it."

"You might fall asleep while driving. Let me take you home. Leave your car in our lot."

She shook her head. "You're wonderfully considerate, but that only poses problems for the morning. How do I get to work?"

"I'll come by to pick you up."

She didn't argue.

In the passenger seat, she nodded, her head fell gently on my shoulder. When I stopped at her home, she awakened, looked about and smiled, then reached for my arm. "Thank you, Zach."

"I'll fetch you to the door."

Despite her protests, I put my arm around her waist and walked her to the entrance.

She held my arm as we stepped into the foyer. I was about to release her when she said, "Wait, come inside, we'll have a nightcap and—"

"I shouldn't."

"But you must." She sounded adamant. "Sit on the sofa—read the paper. I'm going to freshen up. Be down in a few minutes."

I fell into the sofa, leaned back, and closed my eyes. When I opened them, I saw Mavis in a white peignoir, an angelic vision seeming to float down the stairs.

She took my hand in hers and walked toward the dining room table. "We'll have a glass of wine and some brie. I have a jar of Beluga caviar that I planned to serve on a special occasion, but we're more deserving of it."

Brie and caviar were new to me, and under other circumstances I might have rejected them, but being with Mavis made the introduction of these exotic foods exciting. The cabernet gave me a warm sensation, and the cheese and caviar on my palate were intriguing. Mavis, sitting across the table with her peignoir draped loosely, revealed an enticing cleavage made more noticeable by a delicate necklace that hung just above the divide.

I had a sudden urge to take her in my arms and make love to her and hoped she had similar desires. Her conversation, however, was sobering, and the way she pulled the peignoir around her dispelled any notion of intimacy.

"Zach, I've been thinking about our expenses and trying to figure ways to lower costs and increase profitability."

Suddenly food, drink, and amour became less important. "Okay, tell me what you're thinking."

"For one, there's Walt Mason."

"Walt Mason?"

"Yes, he's really non-essential. He's been on the payroll because Earl had a strong sense of obligation—guilt, I suppose, after causing that accident years ago, but you have no need to keep him employed. Besides, he reached retirement age long ago."

I breathed a heavy sigh. "I just can't fire Walt. I don't have the heart to tell him he's no longer . . ."

"You don't have to. I can do that. I can do that tomorrow morning."

"No, no! Give me time to think. I don't want anyone doing my dirty work." I looked at her, hoping she'd understand. I wasn't sure I could penetrate her shield of practical thinking, but I needed to explain. "If I'd been working and never missed a day in—what is it, thirty years? Then got sacked? I'd be mortified. Absolutely furious."

She reached out and touched my hand. "But we're talking about eliminating non-essential expenses. You simply can't be a sentimental patsy in business."

I looked away. "I know, I know. Give me a chance to talk to the man. Let him know I appreciate his contribution to the business after all these years. Come to think of it, I never have talked with him . . . never gave him the courtesy . . ."

Mavis sat back in her chair, pulled the peignoir again more snuggly around her as her expression turned dour. "Good luck trying to get that zombie to talk. Maybe you should be the one to talk to him. Every time I approach him, he stares at me with a blank expression and gives me the creeps."

Mavis' dispassionate approach to problem-solving could be hurtful. I had to think before taking action. She seemed to lack empathy, that which my mother called the "milk of human kindness." When I thought about those occasions when we made love, she did not linger afterward but moved quickly to the bathroom to reassemble, then made no mention of the pleasure I thought we shared. It was as though the intimacy had never happened. I didn't expect a standing ovation for my performance, but I didn't appreciate her ignoring it altogether.

"Now, if you'll excuse me, Dear, I'm going to bed," she said.

I kissed her cheek as she slipped out of my embrace, walked upstairs, and didn't look back.

CHAPTER 21

The following morning, Mavis went directly to the cosmetics display case to restock it while Walt Mason busied himself filling shelves with paper products: napkins, Kleenex, and toilet tissue. I found it difficult to understand how those two could work without conversation. I wasn't exactly talkative, but the silence between those people was eerie. Maybe Mavis was right. The time had come for Walt to retire.

I was on a mission to get Walt to say something, anything, when I greeted him. I blocked his path as he made his way to the stock area in back of the store. He attempted to walk around me, but I stepped in front of him. "How are you, Walt?" I spoke loudly. "Are you finding all the merchandise you need?"

He grunted, looked at the floor, and started to sway, attempting to get around me.

"Answer me, Walt. Are you finding everything you need?"

An unintelligible grunt accompanied a nod.

"Walt, I know you can talk. I've heard you and Earl yakking many times. Why don't you talk with me—or with Mavis?"

He shrugged, his eyes cast on the floor.

"I'm going to visit with you after work today at your home. There are things we must discuss. We've got to talk." I planned to give him a final payment plus a bonus and spare him the embarrassment of saying goodbye to the staff since I had determined that he was simply shy and withdrawn.

He surprised me when he nodded, then walked around me—still without a word.

*   *   *

I followed his old Dodge sedan converted to a pickup. It was hardly a showpiece but apparently functioned well enough with its worn wooden bed, side rails, dented body, and fenders, Walt's mechanical equivalent of his broken body.

He drove to the outskirts of Newbury, a twenty-minute ride, then turned onto a narrow, winding dirt path that would barely allow passage of one vehicle. Tall pines and poplars lined the rutted way for about a quarter mile until a white clapboard bungalow with green shutters came into view.

Walt got out of his vehicle and waited until I walked toward him. I saw a change in his expression. His constant frowning at the drugstore had disappeared; he seemed relaxed, the angry facial lines all but faded as he turned to me. "Darleen Anne is home. Her car is here."

A well-maintained 1933 Terraplane coupe was parked under an overhang. Walt walked up three wooden stairs with the aid of handrails; his gait, while not sprightly, had improved considerably from his shuffling in the drugstore.

He opened the door and called out, "Darleen Anne, we've got a visitor." His voice, loud and clear, came as a surprise. This grumpy, morose man suddenly came alive.

A smiling, petite woman wearing a flower-patterned apron came into the living room and extended her hand. Her gray curly hair, freckled face, and smooth olive skin contrasted with Walt's pale, scarred, and wrinkled complexion.

"In case you're wondering about this little lady, it's no secret, Darleen Anne is a mulatto. That's right. A Louisiana girl—white daddy and milk-chocolate momma who was a sort of mix herself. I guess Darleen Anne could be considered a quadroon. Sounds like a macaroon, and she's just as sweet." He smiled and pulled her in close. "We recently celebrated thirty years of marriage— well, common-law marriage—and have two of the loveliest daughters one could hope for. Well educated, married successful men, and damn wealthy by most standards. Our grandkids are more beautiful than you can imagine. Some are completely white, even blonde. Hell, color never made any difference to me. It's the ignoramuses, the yahoos who point fingers . . . well, what's the use? The ignorant will always be with us."

Walt's freedom of expression came as an amazing revelation, laying bare an intelligent and liberal bias.

Darleen Anne looked up at him. "Walt, darling, you've not introduced me to your friend."

She gushed when she learned who I was, and that embarrassed me. She insisted I stay for dinner. I demurred, but she remained persuasive, undermining my plan to talk with Walt briefly, thank him for his years of service, and hand him a bonus. All of that as a prelude to my firing him.

I looked around and commented on the warmth and comfort of their home.

Walt shook his head and countered, "Comfort, in this cracker box? Hah! This was the servants' quarters before the crash of '29. Our family lived in that Georgian monstrosity up on the hill, a hundred yards north of here. Dad lost everything in the Great Depression. Investments went belly-up . . . had to give up the big house and everything in it."

Darleen Anne had prepared a dazzling cornucopia of colorful dishes with tantalizing fragrances. The fried chicken was the tastiest I had ever had and was served with sides of ratatouille, collard greens, hominy grits, and other southern dishes which were unfamiliar to me. Her apple pie reminded me of my mother's and evoked a flood of happy memories. Notably absent were alcoholic beverages, and no explanations were given.

I had overeaten and almost succumbed to a stupor when Darleen Anne's voice jarred me into alertness. Her sweet southern patois was also sleep-inducing, but I was determined to be attentive and polite.

"Mr. Black, we are ever so obliged to you for Mr. Mason's employment—"

Walt cut her off. "Now, Darleen Anne, don't start in with that. You'll embarrass the man, for heaven's sake."

"Walter, dear, you know that's true." She faced me again. "Mr. Black, Walter looks forward to his job at the drugstore. It means so much to him. Our children insist on supplementing our income, which they can well afford, although Walter doesn't want them to . . . says that's not necessary. Truth is, between Walt's job and my occasional nursing calls, we manage. I worked three days last week at Milwaukee General and was paid quite well."

She patted Walt's hand and said, "That's where we met after that terrible accident twenty-eight years ago. Mr. Black, I'm sure you've been told about the accident." She shook her head. "Earl Withers drove on that icy highway and was responsible for that girl's death that also injured

Walt and himself. I will never forget that early morning when the ambulances brought both men in. Walt was close to death. But under all the bruises, broken bones, and brain damage, I thought he was so handsome. When he regained consciousness, he was gentle and grateful." She reached for his hand again. "I was assigned to his care and put in many extra hours. We fell in love, totally. His parents suspected that but of course would never have considered me a rightful mate for him, and certainly not as a daughter-in-law. That's alright. For thirty years, we've lived in sin—delightful, ever-loving sin." She smiled then turned her head upward and kissed his cheek. Walt lowered his head to conceal a smile.

I remained curious about the accident even though I had heard about it before. Walt excused himself and left the table to go to the restroom. I leaned across the table and in a subdued voice said, "You'll have to forgive me for asking, but did Walt ever say anything about wanting to get back at Earl for that accident? He had to be terribly resentful." I could have anticipated her response, but I had to ask to be sure.

"Oh, Mr. Black, Walt, despite anything you may think, is the sweetest, kindest man you could ever hope to know. To some, he may appear dull, mean, too quiet—but with me and children, he is gentle, understanding, and loving. He could never harm anyone. The very thought of that is ridiculous, shameful."

She continued, "Were you aware that Detective Simon had already asked Walt the same question? Well, he did, and Walt, I'm sorry to say, wasn't very cordial. Walt thought he was insulting and ordered him out of the house. I was terribly embarrassed. After Mr. Simon left, I told Walt that was ungentlemanly, but he only scoffed."

"Do you know if Walt is able to shoot a gun? Does he own one?"

She glanced toward the washroom then leaned toward me and in a hushed voice said, "Walt could shoot the eye out of a gnat at fifty feet—yessiree, no problem. He was an expert rifleman, a captain in the National Guard before that terrible accident. After the accident, he couldn't even hold a pistol, much less shoot one. But with his dogged determination, he became an expert shooter again. I couldn't keep him away from his gun. He set up a target in the woods and practiced for hours as though he had to prove something. He's passionate about guns. In fact, he has a remarkable collection dating back to the Revolutionary War, all types of pistols, revolvers, even blunderbusses and a shelf filled with marksmanship trophies."

Walt signaled his approach by his distinctive clomping gate and shouted, "You two hatching a plot to get me to leave my job?" He held the table edge to ease into his chair. "Hell, Mr. Black, if you can't afford my services, I'll work for nothing. You heard me. Look around. You can see we don't need much."

He was right, of course. The house had the feeling of dedicated owners. I would describe its décor as late American prairie with touches of skilled handiwork: crocheted throws, hook rugs, scrolled woodwork, and precise mitering.

"Come, I'll show you my collection of firearms, which I'm sure Darlene Anne has already mentioned." He moved more briskly than he ever had in the store. We walked in a narrow hall to a dark room. He switched on the light that transformed the room into a startling four-wall display of mounted guns: firearms restored to like-new condition and printed cards below each piece with names, dates, wars of involvement, firepower, and other data.

"Walt, this is amazing. Museum-quality restorations. Has Detective Simon seen this collection?"

"Sure, but the only thing he wanted to know was if any of my revolvers were missing, like that Colt .357 Withers used to commit suicide. You know, Simon must think I'm awfully simple, but I think he's simple." He continued, "Did you get that? I said he's simple, did you get that? Simon is simple, Simple Simon—now, that's a laugh."

I didn't think so, but I smiled agreeably. He led me out of the gun room and into the living room while Darleen Anne remained in the kitchen. For the first time in over two years, I was going to engage Walt in a man-to-man discussion. I would have appreciated a drink to take the edge off the encounter. I knew I had to couch my words so as not to offend.

"Walt, I knew the history of that terrible accident when you and Earl—"

"Mr. Black, talk plainly, what is it you want to tell me?"

"It occurs to me that your response to that terrible accident caused by Withers' bad judgment would have or should have made you justifiably angry." I wasn't sure how Walt would handle that. I watched as he chewed on his lower lip, brought his head forward, and stared at me.

"So, you want to know how I felt? Well, I'll tell you. When I came out of that coma, I wanted to kill that sonofabitch with my bare hands. That's right. I could have beaten him to a bloody pulp." He spoke slowly, choosing his words carefully. "I could have whacked him to death and spat on his miserable carcass." He remained quiet for a moment, and spoke quietly, "Well, that was long ago. My thinking has changed. I learned to live with the hand I got dealt." He paused, then said, "Maybe not completely . . . Oh, hell, don't get me started on that."

CHAPTER 22

Walt sat back in his chair, arms across his chest, as I reminded him of that accident thirty years ago. "I can appreciate how you felt about Withers. Have you had recurrent thoughts about killing him in later years?"

He looked at me as though I were demented, then glowered. "Mr. Black, weren't you listening to anything I said? Why in the world would I want him dead now? If I were going to kill him, I would have done that thirty years ago. Don't you think I knew he kept me on the payroll because he felt responsible? Hell, I knew he felt guilty for that stupid accident . . . killing that pretty young girl, Mary Jo Ainslee. Her family never did forgive him."

"Do you think anyone in her family would have wanted to kill him?"

"Huh? Why would they have waited almost thirty years to do that? Not likely, I'd say, unless a young hothead in the family decided to . . . but look, all that is far-fetched."

"Walt, Withers' death by a bullet to the head is far-fetched, yet it happened."

He gave no response.

"How did you feel when you learned about Withers' murder?"

Walt moved uneasily in his chair. "I didn't know what to think." He leaned forward again, placed his hands on his knees, and spoke softly. "Look, I'll level with you, Mr. Black, I never had a fondness for Earl after the accident. It left me crippled and robbed me of my profession as an engineer. But I was determined to survive, and Darleen Anne's love brought me around. I shed no tears for him. Don't get me wrong. I didn't jump for joy, either. His death left me with—what do you call it? Ambivalent feelings? Yeah, that's it, I guess, ambivalent feelings."

"There's something else I want to know, Walt. Why did you decide *not* to talk with me or Mavis? It's been over two years since I've taken over the pharmacy. That weird antisocial behavior of yours must be linked to something I know nothing about."

He cleared his throat. "To tell the truth, Mr. Black . . ."

"Call me Zach."

"Yes, sir, Zach. Earl and I got along. We talked to one another easily. There was no problem even after he married that loud-mouthed Jezebel, Irma. God knows I couldn't abide that woman, but I tried. I knew he was going to retire because he hired you, and you would have no need for me, so I resented and feared you. I figured if I kept my mouth shut and did my work, you might be less likely to fire me. I know now that might sound stupid, but that's what I thought. Can you understand that?"

"Well, I suppose I can, but what about your silent treatment of Mavis?"

He lowered his head. "That's a matter that goes back a long way. Withers made me promise never to say anything . . ." He stopped, shook his head, then said, "Sorry, I can't say anything more about that. Besides, I know you're sweet on Mavis, and I wouldn't want to say anything to hurt that relationship."

* * *

About to leave the Mason home, I thought about those two people who had been devoted to one another and carved a niche for themselves in a hostile environment. Walt's demeanor, his frank discussion, left me with almost no doubt about his innocence in Withers' murder. Yet, there remained a niggling uncertainty. I had been taken in before by people who had impressed me as being sincere then disappointed me later.

I recalled my father's advice: beware of one who professes friendship, then turns out to be your enemy. I was recalling Dad's clichés with greater appreciation.

I thanked Darleen Anne, kissed her cheek, and shook Walt's hand.

I stepped into the dark chilled air; a half-moon provided enough light for me to find my car parked about thirty feet from the house. On a hill about one hundred feet to the north were the deteriorating remains of the old Mason mansion—its dark empty windows like orbits in a skull—a morbid sight that took on the gloom of decadence, rot, and death.

Dry twigs snapped under my footsteps, and an owl's hoot startled me. I stopped, looked around, but saw nothing unusual. I started walking again. A low moaning came from behind. Was it the wind? I turned around quickly. Did something move? My pulse quickened, and I hurried.

I drove slowly. The car's headlights guided me through the dark, twisting path sheltered by a canopy of tree branches until I got onto the two-lane road back to Newbury. I was relieved to leave those eerie sights and sounds. I turned on the radio and dialed until I found static-free music that allowed me to think about my visit with the Masons. I was convinced there was no reason to fire Walt. Mavis would just have to tolerate him.

At 9:45 the road was devoid of traffic, and the only sounds were those from the radio and the hum of the heater. Few things were more enjoyable than the quiet freedom on a country road and the expanse of farmland on either side.

I glanced in the rearview mirror and saw something unusual—a vehicle without lights about a half mile behind me. I ignored it and maintained my speed at fifty-five, but the vehicle was coming up fast.

An explosion shattered my solitude. Flying glass bombarded my space and prickled the back of my head and neck. The car without lights whizzed past. I lost control momentarily and veered to the right, then to the left before I slammed on the brakes and skidded to a stop on the gravel shoulder. I sat paralyzed with fear. A stinging pain from my right ear brought my hand to it. My fingers were wet with blood. Shards of glass from the rear window lay on the passenger seat and on the floor. I held a handkerchief to my ear while the realization of what just happened came into sharper focus. Jeezus, someone just tried to kill me. What the hell was that all about? My hands shook, and I began to tremble all over.

I took a few deep breaths, hoping my shaking hands and thumping heart wouldn't keep me from driving. I still felt jittery as I started the engine and got back on the road, wondering if that sonofabitch would be lying in wait for me at the overpass. I ducked my head below the window, held my breath, and stomped on the accelerator, hoping the car would follow a straight line. I prayed a highway trooper would flag me down for speeding and escort me home. I felt relief as I raced beyond the overpass.

Finally, I reached the outskirts of town and headed directly for my garage, grateful no further catastrophes occurred.

CHAPTER 23

Lieutenant Simon grunted, an unlit cigar butt clamped in the corner of his mouth as he examined the blown-out rear window and the dinged metal around it. "Some cowboy with a shotgun peppered this pretty damn good." He looked at me. "You're lucky to be alive. Sonofabitch could have come up beside you and blown your head off." He walked around the car. "Let me get this straight: you just left that weirdo Mason's house . . . you were on the road for five minutes when you saw something speeding up from behind, and suddenly you're all shot up. You keep the car under control. Stop and look around, right? I don't suppose you got a license number or make on that car?"

"Simon, are you kidding? A guy is shooting at me on a dark road and you want to know if I got a license number or what kind of car it was? I've told you everything except that I almost crapped in my pants."

Simon regarded me quizzically. "What the hell were

you thinking when you went to that whacko's house? Didn't it occur to you that he could have put you away? For Chrissakes, the guy's a nut case. You should have known that."

"That was never my impression, and I wasn't worried about my safety with him. There were things I wanted to say to him I couldn't discuss in the drugstore. After talking with him and his wife, I'm convinced he didn't kill Earl Withers."

"Really? The guy convinces you that he's a choirboy, and you're ready to put him in a chorus. Kiddo, you are naïve. Let's think about what happened again. You visit the guy, he feeds you, shows you his gun collection, so you know he's an expert on firearms and a sharpshooter. You leave his house that's hidden where Moses lost his sandals, and as soon as you hit the road, you collect buckshot around your ears. You don't want to admit that Walt Mason is shooting at you? Well, I think he's the most likely bastard. He'd be number one on my shit list."

"I don't follow you. What reason would he have for killing me?"

"You think every crackpot is rational about killing? In their fucked-up minds, good reasons don't exist. Mason's gonna get more questions from me—maybe that woman he lives with, too."

"That woman happens to be his wife."

"Whatever. Wouldn't be the first time a guy and his

live-in decided to put out some joker's lights."

*   *   *

From my elevated perch in the pharmacist's section, I could see the entire store as well as traffic on the street. For the past month, Ben Simon had parked his car on the opposite side of the street and spent at least one hour a day surveying activity around the store. What he hoped to glean I couldn't guess, but Simon was, as Charlie Chan might say, "Inscrutable."

An elderly male customer got my attention when he spent several minutes studying the print on a small box then picked up another box and read the ingredients on it. He shuffled toward my station with both boxes.

"Can you tell me which one of these suppositories would be best? Do you have personal experience?"

I had learned in general merchandising class never to be flippant about urogenital or elimination problems. During that course there were opportunities for wisecracking, but for those students who continued with bathroom humor, the instructor would order them out of the room.

With sage concern, I said, "Either one of these preparations would get the job done."

He looked at me through thick glasses that magnified his tired eyes. I looked down at his head with wispy white hairs combed from one side to the other but failed to cover his pink scalp. His lined face showed evidence of years of sun and wind exposure. When he spoke, his ill-fitting dentures clacked.

"You seem decent enough," he said. "Not like that sonofabitch who owned this store for years. Can't tell you how many times I wished him dead. Not just dead, mind you, but a suffering, lingering, miserable death." He looked around, then continued, "Between you and me, he finally got what he deserved—just didn't get it soon enough."

"I'm sorry, I didn't get your name."

He placed the boxes on my counter, then extended his hand up to shake mine.

"Name is Bertrand Ainsley. People call me Bert, and I reckon a few other names, but not to my face. I haven't been in this store for many years. Not since that stupid bastard killed my daughter. She was beautiful, precious, full of life, just twenty years old. A day doesn't go by that I don't think about her—and that miserable sonofabitch who caused her death."

I knew he was referring to that terrible accident years ago when Earl Withers and Walt Mason celebrated a New Year's Eve with two young women. Withers' car skidded out of control and hit a utility pole, killing one girl and seriously injuring Walt Mason and Earl Withers. My heart went out to this bereaving father who mourned profoundly and needed to vent his sorrow to a willing listener.

I had several prescriptions to fill and had fallen behind in scheduling, but I couldn't be so callous as to ignore him. He continued in a raspy voice, "Withers was plain drunk when he drove that car." His reddening face hinted at a rising anger—a volcano about to erupt.

"That drunken sonofabitch got behind the wheel of that speeding Stutz his rich old man bought him and killed my daughter. Two-wheel mechanical brakes . . . a slick road and no way to stop . . . ignoramus should have been killed, not my angel."

Ainsley stopped, his eyes welled, his florid complexion subsided. I asked him to sit on a step stool in my section. "You're welcome to stay until you feel better." I gave him a glass of water and said, "If you don't mind, I'll work around you. I'm curious. You said very little about Walt Mason. What are your feeling toward him now?"

He looked up at me. "He got what he deserved. That head injury and those burn scars are his forever. He never should have allowed Withers to get behind the wheel."

I was reluctant to continue the conversation, a rehash of old, terribly sad events that resolved nothing and stirred resentment and hatred. I looked up from my pill-counting board and saw Ben Simon crossing the street to enter the store. He walked directly toward my station, giving Ainsley a cursory glance.

I was about to introduce Ainsley when Simon said, "I know Bert and his connection with Withers and Mason." He spoke out of the corner of his mouth. "Bert, you visiting the murder scene where you shot Withers in the head?"

Ainsley brought his stooped shoulders back as far as he could, then shook his forefinger at Simon. "Damn you. You have no right to accuse me of—"

Simon cut him off. "I have every right to question a suspect in a murder case. You had a strong reason for killing Withers. I never ruled you out."

"If you keep harassing me, I'll have Chief Morgan kick you off the force."

"Be my guest and get in line. You're still a suspect in my book."

Ainsley supported himself on a nearby shelf and stood, shaking.

"You are a stupid man, Simon. Why would I kill Withers thirty years after the accident?"

"I'll tell you why. Your vengeance festers. It grows like a goddamned cancer eating away at you, making you crazier, more vindictive."

Ainsley shouted in his high-pitched voice, "How dare you! You—you stupid Jew!"

I braced myself for an explosive response from Simon, but he surprised me. He pursed his lips, appearing to be unfazed. Perhaps he knew of the old man's emotional state and the early dementia responsible for his outburst.

"Do you deny owning a .357 revolver that's registered in Madison?"

Ainsley stammered; spittle formed at the corners of his mouth. "So what? I own three handguns. What does that prove? Besides, you already have the murder weapon, and it's not mine."

The noise level caused customers to glance our way. I became anxious about the mounting vitriol and interceded to remove both men from my section.

"You fellas will have to continue your discussion elsewhere, preferably out of my store."

Both left my station just as Walt Mason, carrying several boxes, walked in front of them. Ainsley said nothing and seemed to look through him while Walt, in his usual non-communitive way, passed without a word.

I wondered what went on in Walt's mind when he saw Ainsley. Did he feel shame, remorse, or guilt? His lack of emotion offered no clue.

With Ainsley's arrival, the list of suspects in Earl Withers' death grew, while Irma's death seemed to draw less attention. Somehow that seemed unfair, or maybe it was my skewed version of how things should have been.

I remained a suspect in Earl's and Irma's deaths, and I could only hope the actual murderer would be identified soon. The specter of circumstantial evidence began to intrude on my thoughts, but that attempt on my life while

I drove from Mason's home should have been enough to absolve me. Well, maybe not in Simon's mind.

I thought about seeking advice from attorney Arnie Teasdale, but he, too, was a murder suspect. I felt he might want me to appear responsible for those murders to deflect suspicion from himself. I was beginning to think like a paranoiac, but at least I was aware of that. One thing for sure, I'd need legal help before my world crashed down on me, with Simon savoring my incarceration.

CHAPTER 24

Almost a year had passed since Irma's death and two years since Earl's murder, and still no killer had been identified—although for sure, Simon regarded me as a likely suspect. He would make snide comments, such as, "You're spending a lot of time with the widow Johnson—maybe hatching a plot or two." He never said anything directly, such as accusing me of poisoning Irma, but he implied and not subtly that since Irma died, I was free to romance the widow.

I never denied keeping company with Mavis, who continued to amaze me with her savvy business acumen. But there existed a problem: those evenings of intimacy were being spaced farther apart, making me wonder if she held me off to increase my longing or whether she was trying to discourage me. Truth is, I thought she concealed things from me, making sure I would never be privy to her innermost thoughts.

Irma, by contrast, had spouted every thought, desire,

or dislike that came to her. Mavis remained circumspect, choosing her words carefully, thinking before she spoke.

Her invitation to dinner occurred about once a month and I gladly accepted, hoping the evening would conclude with shared intimacy. However, that did not always occur.

I recalled one evening when she had prepared my favorite dinner: prime rib, potatoes au gratin, and a bottle of Chateauneuf du Pape, which I brought. Her warm apple pie with cheddar cheese was the perfect ending. From across the table I marveled at her beauty: eyes of azure set off with enhanced lashes, a bow-shaped mouth, and a delicate nose. All her features appeared more beautiful by the glow of candlelight. The warmth of wine coursed through my body and stimulated a manly response.

I reached across the table to hold her hands; her eyes seemed to glisten, and in a moment of quiet expectancy, I asked if she would accept my proposal of marriage.

She slipped her hands out of mine as we heard the sound of the front door opening.

She called out, "Is that you, Charles?"

Her son looked in the dining room then without a word ran up the stairs and slammed his room door.

Mavis lowered her eyes, then looked at me. "Marrying me, Zach, comes with baggage I'm not certain you could handle." She arose and walked to the window, looking out into the darkness. With arms across her chest, she said nothing more, but her shoulders began to heave gently, and I knew she was attempting to suppress sobbing.

I walked toward her and placed my arms around her waist. "What are your concerns about Charles?" Before she could respond, I said, "He's a kid reacting to jealousy or fear. He may think you'll abandon him if you marry me and maybe love him less. I know and understand these things. I promise I will make every effort . . ."

She turned and faced me with a melancholy smile, placing her forefinger to my lips. "You don't have to say more, Zach. Thanks for being so understanding." She tilted her head. "That's why I love you. Now be good and go home. We can talk about your marriage proposal another time." She walked behind me, her hand on my back, gently guiding me to the door; she kissed me lightly on the lips and whispered, "Good night, Sweetheart."

Disappointed, I felt slighted when I got into my car, but to be fair, I knew Mavis had used good judgment in asking me to leave. My pretense at knowing about teenage issues and implying that I understood her son's problems was sheer hogwash. I knew little about adolescent angst, but I wanted desperately to make her feel better. I'm not sure I succeeded.

*   *   *

Reaching for a book on the nightstand, I allowed myself about fifteen minutes of reading, which proved to be excellent to induce sleep. But on this night, more than reading I thought about Mavis lying next to me, providing warmth and her yielding body. No book could compete with that. I closed my eyes, placed the book across my chest, and entered a world of fantasy. I was jarred into alertness by sirens that screamed as though coming through the walls. My heart hammered, I threw the covers off, ran to the window, and raised the shade.

Jeezus! Bright orange and yellow flames shot up from the engine of my car. In my house slippers, I grabbed my robe, dashed downstairs, yanked the door open, and yelled, "What's going on here?"

A fireman with an extinguisher ordered me to stand back while he squirted retardant on the engine. The fire hissed and the flames died as foam settled on the engine block, burying it in white goop.

"A neighbor called in," one of the firemen said. "You could have lost your car in another five minutes. As it is, there's a lot of damage to the wiring. The carburetor and its attachments look shot." The fireman with the extinguisher looked closely at the engine. With gloved hands he reached down and tugged at something that offered resistance. It yielded to his pulling, and he inspected it. He reached for a flashlight, brushing away ash and foam residue.

"I'll be damned," he said. "Looks like a timing device attached to a container of fluid." He sniffed it. "Smells like ether, highly flammable. Someone took the time and care to place this thing . . . knew what he was doing. Insurance adjuster would be interested. Might be a while before you get your car out of the shop. There'll be an arson investigation. Fire commissioner and insurance fraud investors will be at it."

Several neighbors who had gathered around left as the firemen and their truck pulled away. My wristwatch read 2:35 . . . a ghastly hour. My adrenaline titer kept me on full alert, and my senses remained sharp. The stench of burned rubber and oil lingered. An eerie quiet replaced the noise of recent activity. I could hear distant trucks on the highway while my eyes searched the street for suspicious characters. In the distance, I saw or imagined seeing someone lurking in the shadows, behind a tree or a parked car.

I squinted and was sure a figure moved between houses at the end of the block, but I was in a robe and house slippers, and the early-morning air gave me a chill. I wasn't about to investigate something that might not have existed.

I returned to bed and tossed and thought about the damned arson. This was the second. First the drugstore, now this. Some pyromaniac, some sonofabitch. But who and why?

I must have jumped a foot off the bed when the phone rang. Its piercing sound frightened and annoyed me.

"Hello! Who is this?" I looked at the clock on my nightstand: 7:35. I should have been grateful to whomever for getting me up. I was already an hour and a half late from my usual arising. "Who? Speak up!"

The voice filled me with loathing, but at this moment I was grateful to him for having awakened me. Whenever I heard Simon's voice, I expected trouble.

"Simon, how did you know what happened?"

With his usual laconic delivery, he said, "In this small town . . ."

"Okay, so who did it?" I asked.

"Don't know, but I've got my suspicions. You got any notion about the prick who might have done it? Anyone you tried to poison with one of your special prescriptions?"

"Go to hell!"

"Relax, Kiddo, only kidding. Need a ride? I can swing by in thirty minutes."

"Yeah, I'd appreciate that." I looked at the phone on its cradle and thought that Simon's good-neighbor offer might mask some devious intent.

CHAPTER 25

We rode less than a mile when Simon glanced at me. "I've got to tell you, Black, since you've come to town, we've had more murders, arsons . . . unholy happenings . . . what are you planning for Halloween?"

I refused to engage in a conversation that would only agitate me further and solve nothing, but I had to talk to him about my car, which angered and frustrated me. I blurted, "Why would anyone want to target me? What the hell have I done to deserve this shit? You've lived in this bucolic paradise long enough to know half the population. You must be aware of some morons capable of this."

Simon reached into his pocket for a toothpick and started chewing on it. "Yeah, I know about half the population well enough to know the crazies." He drove slowly, as though needing time to talk longer, while I was eager to get to the drugstore to arrange for a rental car.

"Are you going to question more suspects?" I asked. "Do you have someone in mind, some whacko capable of this? This destructive bullshit can't go on forever."

He didn't respond, but asked, "Can you spare another ten minutes?"

"I prefer not to. What do you have in mind?"

He swerved the car left onto a narrow, unpaved path with rutted wheel marks, minor craters, weed outcroppings, and tall brush on either side.

"Down this old passage is a deserted Menominee Indian encampment." He drove slowly, steering hard to the right then to the left to avoid chuckholes. "They lived here before their land was liberated by the great white settlers. Poor bastards were forced to yield to palefaces who offered them little or nothing for some of the richest soil in the country. But I don't want to get started on this tale of infamy. There's something I want you to see."

"Simon, I can't appreciate this history lesson. I've got to get to the drugstore and make arrangements for a car."

He ignored me as the car lurched and bounced, causing dust to rise to the level of the windows. "These goddamned holes are axle breakers," he said. "Hold on to your dentures."

We approached a clearing, a level area about a quarter size of a football field.

"This was once a village where Indians lived for hundreds of years. They farmed, hunted, enjoyed a rich cultural heritage, and passed it down through generations. They were the civilized, relatively peaceful people until the Europeans arrived."

Simon spoke with knowledge and sympathy about the plight of the Indians. Tribal names rolled off his tongue: Menominee, Sauk, Fox, Potawatomi, and Winnebago, as though they were friends or relatives.

My knowledge of Indian history was shamefully poor, but at this moment I felt irritated because of my eagerness to get to the drugstore. "Simon, I appreciate all this, but what does this have to do with the fire in my car?"

"See the opening in that mound over there?" He pointed to a black hole that appeared in a hillock partially covered with brush.

"Yeah, what about it?"

"The Indians used the cave as storage for fruits and vegetables to prevent spoilage."

Simon drove to within twenty feet of the opening. I felt a twinge of apprehension as Simon opened his door and kept an eye on the black hole.

I whispered, "You expecting a bear or wolf?"

Simon motioned for me to leave the car and put his finger to his lips. I closed the door noiselessly and walked behind him. He took a half-dozen steps, then stopped. He extended his arm backward to stop me and reached for his pistol, held it at his side, and advanced slowly.

Standing at the edge of the hole, he raised the pistol and fired a shot in the air. I jumped, and a flock of crows flew out of the brush creating a cacophony of cawing. Simon motioned for me to stay behind him as he crouched, poised like an animal about to spring. My heart thrummed against my rib cage as I anticipated a wild beast charging out of the cave.

The beast stumbled out, a frightened and bewildered, wiry, gray-bearded, bone-thin creature wearing a soiled sweatshirt, torn pants supported by a rope belt, and scuffed, lace-less shoes covering bare feet.

He blinked, placed his hands above his eyes to shield them from light, and swayed as though trying to find his balance.

Simon straightened, walked toward the disheveled man whose eyes bulged at the sight of us.

At arm's length, Simon said, "Goddamn, Oscar, when was last time you washed? You stink like a fresh load of shit. You are disgusting." He shook his head, then turned to me. "Zach, allow me to introduce Mr. Oscar Schmitz, also known to our security force as Oscar Wild. He's our pain-in-the-ass recluse, known for starting a few fires. A pyromaniac who has managed to escape prison too many times." He looked at the confused captive. "Isn't that right, Oscar?" The man began to pull away like a cornered creature, but Simon grabbed his sweatshirt.

"Look at me!" Simon yelled. "Did you set fire to Mr.

Black's car last night?"

Oscar shook his unruly hairy head and croaked, "No! No! I swear by all that's holy and sacred, on my dear-departed mother's soul, sanctified by our Savior, the Lord . . ."

Simon groused, "Spare us the churchy outpourings, you miserable sonofabitch. What have you got hidden in that rat's nest?"

Oscar blinked as he looked at Simon. "That which you call a rat's nest, sir, is my temporary living quarters until I find something a bit more suitable. As for the contents within my commodious abode, I have but a few select garments proffered by the generosity of the Salvation Army, plus a few comestibles salvaged from bins behind the A&P and Kroger's. I would gladly show you my worldly possessions if you release me."

Simon removed his hold on Oscar, then pointed his forefinger at him. "I'll tell you in no uncertain terms, if I find you setting another fire, I will not bother to arrest you, I will shoot to kill you on the spot. Do I make myself clear?"

Oscar hand-brushed his ragged sweatshirt sleeve where Simon held him, then raised his head and looked dismissively at Simon. "Sir, you will find that I am the epitome of civility, that my station sets a standard for the most rigid social demands of our fair community."

"Cut the bullshit, Oscar, just remember my warning,

and you can start improving the environment by taking a bath."

While walking back to Simon's car, I turned to see Oscar reentering his cave. I looked at Simon. "What was that all about?"

"That miserable creature is, among other things, an arsonist responsible for several fires, and in my book a prime suspect in your car fire. His M.O. includes burning trash barrels, tool sheds, tossing incendiary rags into wrecking yards, things like that. He's one sick sonofabitch who should be locked up permanently."

"He looks whacky, but he speaks as though he's had an education," I said.

Simon reached for a cigarette. "If I were charitable, I'd say he's a victim and a damn sad case, but I'm not charitable. He was the first child of a big-time beer producer here—Alpine Beer and Ale Company. He lived a privileged life as a kid, I was told, a poster boy for the company. Rode shotgun on the parade beer wagon pulled by draft horses down Lincoln Street during Oktoberfest. He did well in high school and went to the university at Madison for a year until all hell broke loose." Simon lit his cigarette and took a long drag.

"So, what happened to him?"

"Kid's behavior became erratic, self-destructive. They hustled him off to a shrink in Chicago who diagnosed him as schizophrenic with an atypical pattern. Whatever the hell that means. He took phenobarbital until he became zombie-like; got insulin shock therapy, then saw a guru who loaded him with herbs and snake-oil nostrums. Spent time in sanitariums here and abroad. Nothing helped."

"You seem to know a lot about him. What I don't understand is why you don't or didn't haul him in?"

"When I came to this town nine years ago, he was the subject of a lot of interest. I researched his past until the Schmitz family had Chief Morgan put a stop to my probing. I'd need a lot more time to tell you all I know about him. Suffice it to say I brought him in for questioning more times than . . . but why am I telling you all this? In short, he was set free every time I hauled him in. He was dismissed with not even a slap on the wrist. The guys upstairs always managed to let him go on some cooked-up shabby pretext. He would leave the jailhouse and get into a chauffeur-driven limo. Then, like a pig with a shit-eating grin, he'd wave to onlookers. Now, doesn't that frost your keester?"

"There's a lot I don't understand."

Simon rubbed his thumb and index finger together. "It's moola, wampum, donations to campaign funds for judges, prosecutors, contributions to police functions . . . anyway the Schmitz family could show gratitude. A fancy name for bribing."

"Wasn't there a public outcry?"

"Outcry? Hah! Newspapers, radio never carried the stories. Old man Schmitz threatened to pull his ads if his son's crimes were mentioned." Simon looked at me. "Don't shake your head, Kiddo, like this shit couldn't happen. You know damn well there's justice for the rich, and there's justice for everyone else."

"So, you're saying your hands were tied?"

Simon did not respond immediately, but his jaw muscles tensed and he stared ahead. His voice dropped an octave. "If I ever catch the sonofabitch in the act, I'll kill him—I swear it. One day he's going to start a fire that'll fry people."

"You think he's the one who set fire to my drugstore?"

"If I were a betting guy, I'd put money on it." He flicked ash off his cigarette and continued, "If I kill the sonofabitch, I'll lose my job—maybe go to prison. But know what? It'll be worth it."

CHAPTER 26

My relationship with Mavis didn't take off like a rocket, although I suspected she had feelings for me and eventually might become as fond of me as I of her. At her insistence, we pursued an affair that was discreet because of her concerns about her son's reaction to our relationship. She believed his fragile emotional state might suffer more if he thought her affair with me would diminish her love for him.

I could understand that, and yet, his insufferable personality was difficult to abide. Because of him, our clandestine catch-as-can lovemaking became frustrating and often unfulfilled.

On more than one occasion, I wanted to tell her that we should elope, but I knew she would not consent. She cautioned me to be patient and assured me that in time, everything would be fine. I didn't share her optimism.

*   *   *

The bedside clock read 12:10. I had been tossing for an hour; maybe too much coffee after dinner. I felt warm then cold, the mattress seemed lumpy, and the book I was reading became tiresome. I threw the blanket off and went to the medicine cabinet for a sleeping pill but found nothing for sleep. How could a pharmacist not have those pills in his cabinet? Unthinkable.

I decided to drive to the drugstore, grab a few barbiturates, and be done with it. People in our town retired early. Farmers rarely remained awake after the nine o'clock news. Streets were empty and clean after the sanitation crew had washed and brushed away debris, and the only sounds were the distant mournful cries of the Great Northern diesels.

Approaching the parking lot of the drugstore, I saw Walt's old Dodge pickup. I didn't recall seeing it when I left the store this evening. I parked next to it, then opened my car door and closed it quietly. The rear door of the store was closed but unlocked. I pushed it open slowly, stepped inside the darkness, and stopped when I saw a narrow beam of light directed on the cabinet of scheduled drugs.

Walt could be armed, and if I called out he might start shooting. My heartbeat drummed in my ears. I reached for a pen in my pocket and tossed it toward the middle of the store. It struck something tinny before falling to the floor.

"Who's there?" he shouted. His flashlight made wild movements. I stood motionless against the rear door. As my eyes adjusted to the darkness, I saw his listing figure and smelled his perspiration as he came closer.

"Hold it there, Walt!" I stepped in front of him and reached for the light switch. Frightened, he stood with his arms raised. Staring at me, he almost lost his balance as he took an unguarded step backward.

"Aw, jeez, Mr. Black. I never wanted—never expected you to be here."

I watched him closely but kept my distance. He appeared remorseful, disgraced. I had difficulty equating this scenario with the man I regarded as fiercely honest and forthright.

"Walt, what are you doing here?"

"Don't get mad, Mr. Black. I mean no harm. I'll pay for what I took. I know this looks bad, but it's not for me. It's for Darleen Anne. We ran out of her seizure medicine . . . gran mal. She must have phenobarbital, the only stuff that works. My fault for not keeping it on hand. She had a bad seizure tonight and might have another. They come in a chain."

"How many times have you done this?"

"This is the second time in all of six years, that's the truth. I've always had a key to the scheduled drug box. Withers gave it to me because he knew about her condition. I'll pay for the medication." He reached into his back pocket for his wallet and with shaking hands removed it as several papers and cards dropped onto the floor. He made a quick effort to retrieve and replace the contents.

"Put your wallet away, Walt."

"You're not going to report this, are you, Mr. Black?"

"No, of course not, but I think we should talk about something that needs to be said."

He looked at me apprehensively. I knew the look, and it filled me with shame as I broached the subject. I started hesitantly, awkwardly.

"Walt, I like you. I think you know that. I'm aware of your history. It hasn't been easy for you; you've worked hard. You're conscientious, but shouldn't you be thinking about retirement?"

Walt's chin dropped to his chest. He made no response, which made me feel worse.

"Look," I said, trying to change the mood, "you can come in on Fridays and stay until closing, then all day on Saturdays." I hoped the option would provide a modicum of relief.

He glanced at me, nodded, picked up his medication in a plastic vial, then said, "Sure, I'll think about it." He limped away slowly and closed the door quietly behind him.

I was sorry for having hurt him and wished I hadn't

mentioned retirement, but for two years I had listened to Mavis, who complained about his strange and distorted facial features and his silent manner which made him difficult to be around. Some customers may have been repulsed, but truth is, most people in the community tolerated his disfigurement and unfriendly personality.

As I bent over to take six capsules of Seconal from the cabinet, I noticed a corner of folded paper sticking out from under the counter. I bent down to pick it up. The edges were worn and yellow with age. It probably fell out of Walt's wallet when he dropped it.

Carefully, I unfolded the paper. It was a typewritten document on Earl Withers' stationery dated February 5, 1917, twenty-five years ago. The letter startled me. I reread it, then ran my fingers over the embossed notary public seal near the bottom. Stunned, I refolded the paper and put it in my pocket. Everything in my world was about to change—drastically.

CHAPTER 27

Another restless night. I must have gone over every word, imagined every dire consequence in the folded letter that fell out of Walt Mason's wallet. In less than three hundred words, Withers deeded the drugstore and building to Walt Mason upon Withers' death. Unbelievable. The alarm sounded at 6:30, and the cares of the evening seemed less troublesome in the light of day but still present.

In the drugstore at nine, I dialed Arnie Teasdale, Earl Withers' attorney. The singsong delivery of Arnie's secretary annoyed me. She spoke as if she had all the time in the world. "How may I be of assistance?"

"This is Zach Black. I need to see Mr. Teasdale—soon!"

"I'm sorry, Mr. Black, Mr. Teasdale has a very busy schedule. Can you tell me the nature of your problem?"

"When can he see me?"

Silence followed, then muffled sounds were heard in

the background. "Mr. Teasdale will be able to squeeze you in at 2:30. Is that suitable?"

"That'll have to do. Can you pull Mr. Withers' file?"

"I believe Mr. Withers' records are in a deceased client file in storage uptown. We wouldn't be able . . ."

"Get someone to pick them up before my appointment," I interrupted. I seldom made demands, but I had to assert myself with this person who seemed oblivious to the urgency in my voice.

*   *   *

"Mr. Teasdale can see you now." I followed his secretary, Roxy, who sashayed from the posh empty reception room to his office stinking of cigar smoke and scotch, which an ozone spray failed to mask. The opulent furnishings were too showy, and my cynicism led me to think that Arnie and his fancy office trimmings were a mere sham.

Arnie stood as I walked in. Reaching out to greet me, his lopsided smile, flushed complexion, and glazed eyes suggested recent imbibing.

"Zach, my boy, what can I do for you? Why the request for Withers' file? Do I detect some suspicion in my legal structuring?" He swayed slightly.

I shook his soft, sweaty hand and said, "I'd like some clarification on a matter that disturbs me. Disturbs the hell out of me."

He pointed to one of two chairs opposite his desk and pushed aside several manila folders. Leaning back in an oversized leather chair, he said, "Now, what can I do for you?"

I reached into my jacket pocket and pulled out the folded paper, a copy of the one that had fallen out of Walt Mason's wallet. I handed it to him. His brow wrinkled as he read it, then he leaned forward on his desk. "Is this an original?" he asked.

"That's a copy."

"I'll need the original."

I made no response.

"Alright, for the moment, it makes no difference," he said. "It's just that I want to verify the authenticity of the signature, the notary, the watermark on the paper—things like that in case anyone contests the legitimacy of this."

"Arnie, was anything said about the ownership of the drugstore in Earl Withers' will? Surely, he made mention of it. You told me months ago that Irma would inherit everything in the event of his death, and now . . ."

Arnie's complexion took on a deeper flush as he went through Withers' will, looking for details. He moistened his index finger on his tongue and flipped pages until he stopped. "It must be here somewhere." His eyes scanned one page, then the another as he shook his head slowly.

"I can't believe this," he said, then he fell silent.

"You can't believe what?" I asked.

"I've got to apologize, Zach. I don't see a specific reference to the drugstore. All the other properties . . ."

"What?" I stood and leaned over the desk, coming within inches of his head. "What do you mean there's no reference to the drugstore? You made me believe Irma was my new landlord, and now you tell me there is no reference to the disposition of the drugstore?"

Teasdale sat back; his double chin rested on his chest. He started talking hesitantly. "The will lists all properties owned by Withers. The buildings, lots, farmlands—but not the drugstore. It was my impression . . ."

"Goddamn it, Teasdale, you are incompetent! That's right, that's what I said. Were you drunk when you wrote this, or were you getting a hand or blow job that diverted your attention?"

"Zach, that's no way to talk to a friend."

"A friend? That's a laugh. You're a drunken sot who has no right to practice." I banged on his desk, which made his secretary run in.

"Is something wrong?" She looked at Teasdale, then at me.

"Send me a final bill," I shouted. "I'm closing my account here."

She nodded and left.

"Zach, don't be hasty. You may be attaching too much

importance to this trifling peccadillo."

"Trifling peccadillo? You use fancy words to cover up malfeasance. I think you're a bumbling lush who should be horsewhipped."

I left Teasdale's office infuriated, not knowing where to turn for a problem that needed an urgent solution. If Walt Mason was the legal owner of the pharmacy and the building, then so be it. I would deal with him face to face and be grateful I had never demeaned him.

When I thought about it, why didn't Walt tell me about his inherited ownership? Earl Withers had been dead for almost two years, and Irma collected rent from me until her death. Irma's estate owed Walt almost two years of rent. If Teasdale represented Withers' estate and subsequently Irma's, he would be held liable, but that was not my problem.

CHAPTER 28

The following day, I arrived at the store at my usual time, 7:30, and watched Mavis wiping the countertops of the jewelry and perfume cases. I stood behind her, placed my arms around her waist, and nuzzled her neck. She brought her head back, closed her eyes, and murmured, "How wonderful. Let's close the store and make love."

She turned around, placed her arms around my neck, and pulled my head toward her. An open-mouthed kiss with our tongues doing a tango was interrupted by Walt Mason carrying a case of mouthwash. He stopped, turned his head quickly after seeing us, and headed for the aisle with oral hygiene products.

Mavis pulled back, felt the bun on top of her head, then ran her hands along the sides of her skirt. With an arched brow, she said, "Zach, I thought you gave Walt a final notice. I didn't expect to see him here."

I shrugged. "I told him not to return except for the

weekends, and I thought he understood . . ."

"Do you want *me* to tell him?"

I pulled Mavis aside out of Walt's hearing range and whispered, "You may be shocked to learn that Walt Mason is the legal owner of this building, including the pharmacy."

Mavis stared at me; her head tilted as though she didn't comprehend. When the meaning of my words became clear, she put the back of her hand to her mouth and shook her head. "Zach, I can't believe that. I don't know what to say. This is the most outrageous thing—I just don't understand. Why would Earl leave the store to him and not to . . ."

Mavis looked around before saying, "Do you think Walt killed Earl?" Before I could respond, she continued, "Walt never really liked Earl. In fact, he detested him, and since Walt knew he would inherit all this after Earl's death—"

"Hold on, Mavis. You're talking about a tragedy that happened almost thirty years ago. Why would Walt wait all these years to kill Earl? Doesn't make sense."

Mavis pulled her shoulders back. "Darling, you are naïve. Walt's hatred for Earl festered with the passing years. There were times when the space between them was explosive with tension. Even I felt it."

"In all the time I was here, I never saw any signs of hostility between them. But then, I may not have been able to judge them well."

Mavis continued, "Earl Withers had been developing increasing physical as well as mental problems in the past several years. He showed signs of dementia. He became irascible, couldn't tolerate Walt's slowness, and began to berate him for the smallest things. Other problems cropped up. I knew he resented Walt's happy marriage, his children and grandkids. When Walt brought his grandkids to the store for ice cream cones or sundaes, Earl would get crazier. Another thing which you may not have been aware of: Earl had increasing resentment of Irma's infatuation with you."

"What did that have to do with his relationship with Walt?"

"He took out his frustrations on Walt."

"So, you're saying Withers was aware of Irma's affair with me?"

"You've got to be joking. Irma was as subtle as an alley cat in heat. Withers, even with dementia, would have had to be deaf, dumb, and blind not to be aware of that. The way you two carried on was shameful."

"As I see it, there were two people who would have benefited from Withers' death: Irma and Walt Mason. Irma's dead, so that leaves Walt as the most likely murderer. Agree?" I asked.

Mavis did not answer immediately. She shook her head. "Maybe, but what about Teasdale, Earl's attorney?

He's hardly kosher from what you've told me. He'd be capable of finagling Earl's will to make himself the beneficiary. And what about Mr. Ainsley, the father of the girl who was killed in that accident years ago?"

Mavis' questions increased my doubt, although I had thought about both of those men as possible suspects.

*   *   *

I watched Mavis as she polished the glass cases containing faux jewelry and wristwatches. She rearranged a few items then walked toward the soda fountain with her usual authoritarian bearing. Her appearance in a fitted dress emphasized her bosom, the roundness of her glutes stirred my imagination, disrupting my routine, and forced me to recount my pills. At the fountain, she cleared dishes off the counter then chided Eddie Polanski, reminding him to be more fastidious.

She stopped Walt Mason, who was carrying a box, and ordered him to fill some shelves. I watched her advise other employees to keep the store tidy and well stocked. Her skills made me feel grateful that she was the manager. As a bonus, we shared a bed, although not as frequently as I would have wanted. She doled out her favors sparingly, which I didn't understand. She seemed to enjoy those moments of intimacy as much as I had, but that was just the way she was. I didn't understand her entirely;

she remained unpredictable.

Looking up from the pill-counting board, I saw my nemesis, Ben Simon, wearing his wrinkled Burberry trench coat even though the temperature registered in the mid-60s. His fedora with the flipped-up brim gave him the distinctive aura of a Chicago hood.

He headed for the soda fountain, giving me a modicum of relief, even though I expected him to come over and talk with me after he finished his doughnut and coffee.

Since arriving in town almost three years ago, I had never felt completely at ease with him, and that damn shoulder holster of his appeared whenever his jacket opened. His unkempt appearance and casual manner made me think that if he had to shoot, the bullet might hit anything but its target, and that worried me.

I watched him wipe his mouth and hands, then toss a napkin on the plate and swivel off his stool. As I anticipated, he walked toward me with that little hitch in his gait . . . a physical disability or an affectation.

At that moment, Walt Mason appeared with a mop and pail where a customer dropped a bottle of ammonia below my pharmacy window. The spill covered a sizable area, and the intense odor permeated the rear of the store. Walt held out his hand to prevent Simon from stepping into the liquid.

I watched the small drama unfolding and enjoyed

Simon's frustration when he couldn't get closer to me.

From a distance, he yelled, "Black, I want to talk to you!"

I cupped my ear, brought my head forward, and pretended not to have heard. "Sorry, I can't hear you. Give me a few minutes to fill these prescriptions, and I'll be right with you."

Simon turned his back and walked away, but I felt no guilt since he always left me feeling dejected. Besides, if he had a strong reason for talking with me, he would be back.

*　　*　　*

At 9:00 p.m., Mavis locked the front door then walked toward the rear of the store. She would pass my station where I would wait to kiss her good night.

"Zach, is there a problem with the ladies' restroom?"

"Not that I'm aware. Why?"

"The door is locked."

"Maybe Walt is repairing the plumbing and locked the door. That's happened before. It's not a serious problem, I'm sure." I kissed Mavis, reminded her of our date for the weekend, and said good night.

The stillness following closing was a welcome respite from the day's constant activity, talking, and problem-solving. I enjoyed the moments of solitude and the leisure of thinking about things other than filling prescriptions. Truth is, I enjoyed talking to patients who had questions about medications or just wanted to socialize.

Some wanted to know if any progress had been made in solving the deaths of Earl and Irma Withers. Those questions were a major concern in our small town and provided for juicy gossip.

A single ceiling light in the darkened pharmacy provided enough light for me to clean up my counter with an alcohol sponge. While wiping, I became aware of a distant sound, a tapping. I stopped to listen; when it stopped, I continued cleaning until it started again. I set my sponge aside and stood motionless. The tapping stopped. I decided it was probably the heating or plumbing until I heard it again, more distinctly.

I began imagining weird things like the eerie sounds in Edgar Allan Poe's *Tell-Tale Heart* . . . sounds coming from behind the walls or under the floor. My heart began to pound, and I listened again, more curious than fearful. I walked with apprehension toward the women's restroom where the sounds seemed to emanate.

I tried the doorknob; it didn't turn. I put my ear to the door—nothing. I knocked. "Anyone there?"

I waited several seconds and was about to leave when I heard a muted "Help me." The plea came from a high-pitched voice that sounded like an elderly person. Whoever locked the door could not reach it.

I was going to break the door down when I remembered the keyring in my office. I hurried to pick it up. My hand trembled as I tried several keys that failed to work. Finally, one key engaged the tumblers, and the doorknob turned. I opened the door and my heart hammered.

An elderly woman lay on the floor between the commode and washbasin. Her pale face grimaced in pain; her left foot turned outward made me suspect a broken hip. I remembered that sign from my first aid class and the rules of treatment. The first rule was to resist the temptation to straighten the limb. The second was to keep the patient reassured and warm, and third, call the operator for assistance.

I made the call from my office then grabbed my jacket and placed it over her. From the linen section I took a towel, folded it, and placed it under her head. She attempted a smile and murmured, "Thank you."

I asked if I could call her family or friends and if she had driven to the store. I knew enough not to offer pain medication or sips of water because she might be going to surgery soon. I told her not to worry. All her treatment costs would be covered by my insurance.

As I leaned over her, she brought her hand to my face and patted my cheek. "Thank you, Mr. Black. I hoped you'd be as nice as people said you were." Then she said something afterward that puzzled me. "I'm grateful that you are so kind to Mavis."

The ambulance arrived with two young men: one with a stethoscope folded in his white jacket pocket, the other wheeled a stretcher. The doctor introduced himself, asked several questions, then he bent over to place a stethoscope on the patient's chest. When I asked if I could be of assistance, he shook his head since the washroom could not accommodate all of us and the stretcher.

I cringed at the sound of her shrieking then sobbing as she was lifted off the floor and placed on the stretcher. I followed them out to the ambulance. She reached out to me. "Thank you, Mr. Black."

"Yes, of course, Mrs. . . ." I didn't know her name.

In a small, constrained voice, she said, "Alice Brown."

The evening's events were emotionally exhausting, but I was grateful for the quiet that followed. I thought of what the elderly woman had said about my kindness to Mavis.

I knew the town had its gossips, but my relationship with Mavis was private—or so I thought.

CHAPTER 29

Allied casualties mounted as fighting in the European and Pacific theatres had been fierce and discouraging. I had been registered for the draft for over a month but heard nothing from the draft board. When several of the town's long-faced busybodies asked me why I wasn't in the service, I answered simply that I had yet to be called. And of course, that was the truth, but it probably didn't satisfy the gossips.

People needing medications expressed gratitude that I was available to fill prescriptions and offer what medical advice I could since two of the town's three doctors had been called into service. For many, getting an appointment with the one remaining doctor became difficult, and I was pleased to act as a surrogate medic, although I worried at times if my advice was being inaccurate or, God forbid, dangerous.

Mail deposited on my work counter one day consisted of the usual: advertisements from drug manufacturers, travelogues, clothing stores, etc. I discarded most of it, but the return address on one envelope caused a double-take and a few extra heartbeats. It was from the Office of General L. B. Hershey, Director U.S. Selective Service. I tore into it.

"Greetings:

You have been selected . . ."

I scanned the form letter, reread it, but the message remained clear. I was to report to the local draft board for further instructions on the date noted above. Despite the busyness in the store, I suddenly felt alone and overcome with momentary vertigo; I held onto the counter for balance. My whole world revolved around this store, and now it could be snatched from me. What would happen to it? Could I get a locum tenens? That might be difficult in these boonies; few professionals wanted to locate in the hinterlands.

I thought about my ROTC training in college. I really didn't mind it; in fact, I enjoyed the mindless routine and got a kick out of close-order drills. Putting on a smart uniform again would be like old times . . . but wait a minute. Better not glamorize military life because I really didn't know how miserable the real thing could be.

Leaving the pharmacy would be difficult, but maybe the store and I weren't as important to others as I had imagined. People would be able to get prescriptions filled by traveling thirty miles to Ashtonville. It could be simple as that, but there were the infirm who couldn't travel, and with gas rationing . . .

My turmoil subsided as Mavis approached with her warm smile and outstretched arms. She reached out and held my hands. "Thank you, Zach."

"For what?"

My phone rang, and Mavis started to slip away. I tried to grasp her hand but couldn't reach it. For the next several minutes, I was advising a patient about drug dosage. A customer stood at my counter wanting a prescription filled, and then another approached. The whole day passed that way, and I was unable to talk with Mavis.

*　　*　　*

The following morning I questioned Mavis why she had thanked me the day before.

"I meant to tell you, the woman who fell and broke her hip in the restroom, Mrs. Brown, is my aunt."

"Really?"

"Yes, she's a widow, my mother's younger sister. She said you treated her kindly . . . tried to comfort her. She's scheduled for surgery today."

"I don't know that I treated her especially kindly. I tried to make her comfortable until the ambulance arrived."

Mavis smiled. "She thinks she's a matchmaker. From what I told her about you, she decided you'd be an ideal husband for me."

"She's not alone there." I drew Mavis close and kissed her lips. She put her arms around me, gave me an open-mouthed kiss, then slid one hand along my inner thigh, creating an instant response. I backed away reluctantly. I had too much work for an unscheduled moment of pleasure in the storage room. Besides, I had come to prefer the comfort of a soft bed and the excitement of foreplay.

"Aha," she chided. "You don't trust yourself." She looked at me teasingly.

"Alright. How about getting married?" I asked.

"Not so fast, Bozo. You'll have to go through proper channels: an engagement period, an exquisite ring, and then a gala wedding . . ." She began to laugh, then walked away with an exaggerated sashay.

I couldn't be sure she was only kidding.

*　　*　　*

The local draft board met in a makeshift office in the abandoned Gold Medal Cheese factory. I had asked Ben Simon why the dilapidated building was chosen for the draft board. He said that old man Withers, who was head of the town's council, would not approve a bond issue for a community center. He was regarded as a stingy old buzzard who wouldn't approve any measure requiring an increase in taxes.

Two fellows older than I sat on wooden milk crates outside the closed door of the board's office. Indistinct voices floated out of the open transom above the office door. The forlorn-looking fellow next to me fidgeted with a worn straw hat between his knees.

He spoke without looking at me. "Hope they can see their way to giving me a deferment. Can't see my wife and daughters looking after our herd."

"They might give you an agriculture deferment," I said.

The office door opened and a young man with a red face stomped out. He looked at the three of us, stopped, and said, "Those bastards will fry your asses quicker'n you can give 'em your names. They couldn't even lift a Springfield '03, and they're deciding who goes to war. Ain't that a crock o' pig shit? Well, good luck."

"Next!" The call came from the office, and the twitchy fellow next to me crossed himself then walked into the office.

I began to feel pressure in my buttocks. I stood, stretched backward, rubbed my glutes, and looked around the barren building with its dusty wooden shelves and dirty windows laced with cobwebs. The odor of sour dairy, like old cheese, lingered. Maybe it wasn't cheese.

One of the fellows could have farted, or worse . . . reminiscent of Limburger.

The farmer emerged from the room with a broad smile and announced that he got a II-C deferment. He looked upward and said, "Thank you, Jesus." He gave me assurance. "Don't you worry. The Lord will look after you."

"Before or after my induction?"

Truth is, I no longer worried. Curious and expectant could better describe my feelings. Whatever that board of three wise men decided, I would accept. What options did I have? I had already imagined myself in uniform, marching in a splendid parade while a band played a Sousa march.

"Next!"

I walked into a barebones office stripped of everything and smelling of cigarette smoke. The walls showed light rectangular spaces where pictures or certificates had been removed. The periphery of the wooden floor had tack boards where carpeting had been pulled off. Dirty windows dimmed the sun's rays that revealed light blue-gray smoke that layered the air. Two ashtrays needed emptying.

The appearance of the three men seated at a wooden table with a stack of folders gave me a jolt. Smiling as though he had just won a Buick in a card game, Arnie Teasdale, the attorney with whom I had a recent falling out, leaned back on a card chair. He pulled on his suspenders and nodded as I had imagined Clarence Darrow in a courtroom scene—or was it Spencer Tracy?

Seated to Arnie's right, Mr. Bertrand Ainsley, the elderly man I had met in the drugstore, the father of the young woman killed almost thirty years ago in that car driven by Earl Withers, looked at me vapidly, as though I didn't exist. The man to Arnie's left glared at me from under bushy brows in a scowling pudgy face. I knew I had seen him before, but I couldn't identify him until he spoke in a screechy voice ordering me to sit down.

Jeezus, I remembered. He was the so-called coroner who examined Earl Withers' corpse and declared his death a suicide. When I challenged him, he became irate and let me know that it was his name that would appear on the death certificate and that his diagnosis was final.

Okay, so my fate was sealed. I figured these guys would ask me a few banal questions then rubber-stamp my papers, allowing me a two-week delay before shipping out. I could start my goodbyes and get my affairs in order. I thought about pleading for more time until I found a pharmacist to replace me or sell the drugstore outright even at a distressed price. But I was getting ahead of myself.

Arnie Teasdale spoke with my records in his hands. He pointed at them, then shook his head. I wanted to say something insulting, but I held back. I rose from my chair and stood erect, waiting to hear how they had classified me. My heart hammered with the expectation of doom, but I decided not to plea for a deferment. Screw these tinhorn martinets.

"Black, sit down and listen." Arnie sounded serious. "It's our considered opinion that you just don't measure up." He broke into a laugh and elbowed one of the men next to him. "We've decided to give you a II-A deferment on the basis of your importance to the community. We can't afford to have our farmers get sick just because they can't get medicine. We need you to keep them well, even if you have to die trying." He guffawed and again elbowed the men on either side, who did not share his laughter.

I said nothing but felt an enormous relief. Teasdale was going to speak further. After all, an attorney talks. That's what they do—talk, talk, talk. If I truly liked him, I would have given him a bear hug.

"Actually," he said, "a copy of your medical report indicated that you suffered from asthma as a child and had been diagnosed with juvenile rheumatoid arthritis."

I scratched my head, trying to remember those conditions since I'd never had a recurrence. I recalled vaguely learning about those things from my father years later, who said the doctor who made those diagnoses didn't know his ass from his elbow. Father's terse comments were often less than refined.

"I haven't had those symptoms in years," I said to the trio.

Teasdale leaned forward, stared at me, and cleared his throat as though he were about to deliver the Emancipation Proclamation. "Black, if you get an asthmatic attack on the battlefield you'll be a dead soldier, and even worse, responsible for the death of others. If you suffer an arthritic attack, Uncle Sam winds up responsible for all your treatment for the rest of your life. Let's face it. You're a bad military risk. Sorry, we don't need anyone with all your liabilities." He looked at me dismissively, pointed to the door, and yelled, "Next!"

CHAPTER 30

Sunday afternoon. I felt obliged to visit Alice Brown at the hospital and brought a bouquet of roses. I peeked into her room and found her sitting up in bed reading the *Ladies' Home Journal*. She smiled when she saw me. "Oh, Mr. Black, how thoughtful of you. What lovely flowers."

"You're feeling well?" I asked.

"I feel grand. No pain—well, very little. My problem is," she looked around, then whispered, "forgive me, it's constipation. You being a druggist know all about those things, and I feel I can trust you with my secrets." She rang for a nurse.

When the nurse left, Mrs. Brown leaned forward, grimaced with discomfort for a moment, then continued in a confidential tone. "I told Mavis to stop stalling and marry you. She's very capable, and when she fixes her mind to do something it'll get done, but she's very cautious. She'll come around in time. I'm sure both of you would get along just fine. Poor thing's been through a lot . . . deserves a real man who can love and respect her. Do you know what I mean?"

I nodded. "You say she's been through a lot. You're referring to the death of her husband?"

"Yes, and there's Charles, her son."

"Her marriage to Larry Johnson—was that troublesome?"

She looked around, straightened the edge of her blanket, then hesitated before saying, "I don't know how much Mavis has told you, and maybe I shouldn't be talking about such things, but if you're serious about coming into this family, you'll learn this sooner or later."

The nurse returned with the flowers in a vase then fluffed up Alice's pillow and asked if she were comfortable.

I hoped the nurse's conversation would be brief and Alice would remember what she was about to tell me. When the nurse left, I looked at Alice expectantly. "You were saying something about Mavis and Larry Johnson."

"I was?" Confusion crossed her face. "Oh, dear, perhaps I've said too much. I'm sorry. I feel so terribly tired, I . . ."

She fell asleep while talking. I tiptoed out of the room. Whatever she had to tell me could wait.

CHAPTER 31

Before facing the draft board, I was resigned to entering the military and prepared for it psychologically. When I learned of my deferment, I was thrilled. Later, I became dejected. They said I had a history of asthma and rheumatoid arthritis. Maybe I did as a kid, but . . . there had to be jobs in the army I could have handled without jeopardizing the safety of troops around me.

I couldn't even recall the last time I had an asthmatic or allergic attack until I remembered the evening Irma prepared a pork stew. Even thinking about it made me queasy. The meat had a peculiar gray appearance as it lay in a greasy sauce next to lumpy mashed potatoes, a pyramid of Brussels sprouts, and string beans too firm to chew. I steeled myself as I attempted to eat, but I started to gag. I ran to the washroom, hoping to subdue a vomiting reflex. I didn't succeed. My breath, which became wheezy, may have been the result of an allergic reaction or just plain nausea. When I returned to the table, Irma commented on my deathly pallor and unsteady gait. I requested a glass of Alka-Seltzer and apologized as I turned my head and belched into my napkin. Despite her pleading, I could not be persuaded to eat another morsel.

She never prepared a meal for me again. At my insistence, we ate at my place where I followed recipes and prepared dishes I enjoyed. She never objected to eating at my home and was always delighted when we traveled to Madison for dining.

Mavis, by contrast, had prepared gourmet meals, including *hors d'oeuvres*, magnificent entrees accompanied by proper wines, and exquisite desserts. One evening not long after my meeting with the draft board, after one of her lavish dinners and too much wine, I loosened my belt and fought the urge to fall asleep at the table. I had the same kind of reaction to overindulging following my mom's Thanksgiving and other sumptuous holiday meals. Mavis, seeing my discomfort, took my hand and led me to the sofa, had me lie down, and placed a decorative pillow beneath my head. After loosening my tie, she unbuttoned the top three buttons of my shirt then leaned over and kissed my forehead. When she removed my shoes and placed them on the floor, I reached for her arm, but she pulled away. "Rest while I clear the table and put things away," she said.

I must have slept thirty minutes or longer until the clatter of pots and pans invaded my unconsciousness. My wristwatch read 9:35. I sat up, placed my feet in my shoes, and looked toward the kitchen where Mavis was wiping the counter. She looked at me.

"The evening is delightful, Zach. Why don't you sit on the porch swing and enjoy the cool air? I'll join you in a moment."

The wooden-slat swing moved easily as I rocked and enjoyed the idyllic setting and my good fortune. The country sky glowed with millions of stars twinkling brightly. I closed my eyes and breathed deeply, swinging slowly. Only the creaking swing and chirping crickets disrupted the stillness of the night. A citronella candle in a yellow crazed-glass chimney kept mosquitoes from invading my space.

Fresh with reapplied lipstick and combed hair, Mavis smiled and sat at my side. I placed my arm around her and pulled her in. "You smell terrific," I said. (I knew immediately there had to be a better way of saying that.)

"Glad you like it. It's a new fragrance called Nuit d'Amour. The salesman gave me a sample vial. At five dollars an ounce, it should capture the heart of any bozo within sniffing range." She placed her forefinger high on her cleavage, indicating where she had dabbed the perfume.

When I leaned over and put my nose there, she said,

"Does that meet with your approval?"

I smiled. "Yes, ma'am. The fragrance and everything around it."

"Zach, behave and just enjoy this delightful evening."

Getting my mind off carnal thoughts wasn't easy since I had been thinking lasciviously for the past two hours. I peered at the forested area about a hundred yards beyond and became fascinated with its dark, dense atmosphere of mystery that could shelter unknown creatures. I looked at Mavis. "That forest—it doesn't bother you?"

She laughed. "You big-city dwellers have no notion of what goes on in God's country. Sure, there's wildlife out there: deer, fox, maybe a wolf, even a black bear, but they don't want any part of your world unless you intrude on theirs."

She couldn't convince me. "I just don't know. Forests can hide a lot of mischief . . . evil doings."

"You've been reading too many pulp magazines." She sprang up. "We need an after-dinner drink. I'll get some sherry."

The firmament revealed more heavenly bodies than I had ever seen in the big city. I could locate the Dippers and one or two other constellations and an occasional speeding meteor.

As I bent forward to lace up my shoes, I heard a distant cracking sound. The citronella-glass chimney exploded inches from my head. Jeezus! What the hell! Was someone trying to kill me? My right cheek prickled with tiny glass fragments. My hand came away from my cheek, bloody.

I dove off the swing onto the floor and crawled to the screen door, opened it, and moved crablike into the house.

"Mavis, turn off the lights!" My command came out in a hoarse whisper. "Get down on the floor! Someone just took a shot at me."

"Oh, my God! Are you hurt?"

"Nothing serious." In the darkness, I whispered, "I'll lock the porch door."

In a tremulous voice, she said, "I don't understand . . ."

"I don't either, but some sonofabitch wants me dead."

I reached for the phone on the kitchen counter by pulling on the cord and called Ben Simon's private number.

*　*　*

The twelve minutes we waited motionless on the floor in the darkened house seemed an eternity until Simon arrived. He strode in with a flashlight, reached for the wall switch, and turned on the lights.

He looked at us, shook his head, and without a trace of compassion or understanding said, "Black, how in the hell do you manage to get involved in every goddamn crime in this county? Don't bother to explain."

After I described what had happened, Simon walked to the porch and with a pocketknife dislodged the distorted bullet from the doorjamb. He held it to the light and turned it between his thumb and index finger, then placed it in a small bag and stuck it in his pocket. He pushed his fedora back on his head. "I've got two officers combing the woods with lights. Whoever did this is probably long gone by now."

We returned to the living room. He sat on the edge of an easy chair and pulled out a notepad.

"Let's start with you, Black. What time did you get here? Did you see anyone following you? Did you get any threatening phone calls or letters?" A small smile curled his lips. "Any angry husbands who . . ."

"Come off it, Simon. Some bastard wants me dead, and you're making jokes."

"Just answer my questions, Loverboy."

CHAPTER 32

Simon signaled his officers in the woods to come in. When the two officers and Simon left, the shooter remained at large, and our sense of security diminished. Simon said he'd post a man to watch the perimeter and assured us we would be safe. Mavis joined me on the sofa, reached for my hand, and rubbed my fingers nervously.

"Zach, this frightens me. You could have been killed."

"The sonofabitch had a scope. He was aiming at me— no doubt about it. Say, do I have competition from a jealous lover?" I hoped a little humor might relieve the tension.

My question hung in the air for a disturbing moment until she said, "This may sound silly, but my next-door neighbor, Helmut Gunz, has been overly attentive recently. He's a divorced tow truck operator I can't abide. I've refused his invitations to dinner, but that hasn't stopped him from bringing me bouquets and boxes of candy. I've run out of excuses to refuse him. When I told him I'm seeing someone, he wasn't put off and doubled his efforts."

"Would you like me to talk to him?"

She smiled, placed her hands around my neck, and kissed me. "Zach, you're my big and wonderful protector, but my boorish neighbor outweighs you by at least fifty pounds—much of it in his belly, but his arms are as thick as Popeye's. I guarantee he won't be cordial if you approach him."

I pulled up my right sleeve and flexed my muscles to show off my biceps. "Did I ever tell you I was co-captain of my high school wrestling team? Well, I was. Won every match in my weight division except for one in Peoria— guy outweighed me by ten pounds. Besides, I'm pretty fast on my feet. I can dodge, weave, and kick where it hurts. Size doesn't worry me." I stopped when my nervous chatter began to sound foolish. Who was I trying to convince?

We were still sitting on the sofa recounting the events of this crazy evening when another shot rang out. This one at close range. I dove off the sofa and pulled Mavis with me. We lay face down on the floor.

I whispered, "What the hell's going on? Is that sonofabitch back? Jeezus, are we going to be under siege all night?" I reached for Mavis' hand and held it firmly. "Don't move. I'm going to call Simon back." I crawled to the kitchen, pulled at the telephone cord until the phone fell to the floor.

As I started to dial, the front doorbell rang. I hoped it was the cop Simon assigned to watch this place. I scrambled to the door, opened it quickly, and stared. Sneering at me was a six-foot primate, unshaven, wearing a soiled T-shirt stretched across a potbelly and Levi's that looped below his waistline. His glazed eyes indicated alcoholic excess. He walked unsteadily toward me, and with his forefinger almost touched my nose. "So, you're the boyfriend, huh?" I backed away. He lumbered past me, then turned around and walked back. "Shit, man, Mavis can do better than you."

He reeked from a variety of stinks: beer and cigars, but most offensively, perspiration.

"Did I scare the shit out of you with that last shot? Heh, heh, bet I did. I seen somethin' move in the forest. I shot at it. Bet you ran for cover, eh, Mr. Pansy? Mavis needs a real man like me to protect her, not a wimp like you."

Mavis hurried to stand between us and faced Gunz, who grabbed her in a bear hug and forced his lips onto hers.

"Stop that!" she shouted and struggled to get out of his grasp.

"Aw, c'mon, Sweetie, just a little kiss. You know you love me."

I got behind him and tried to pry him away. "Let go of her, you slob!"

He released his grip and turned to face me. "Who you calling a slob?"

Before I could defend myself, he whacked me across the face with the back of his hand, sending me stumbling backward until I struck the wall. My left cheek seared. I put my hand to it—blood came from my lip.

Lurching like a gorilla, he came toward me and leaped clumsily forward. I jumped aside. His ham-sized fist struck the wall behind me with such force a painting fell, and glass shattered. His movements were telegraphic, so I could anticipate and avoid them. He rubbed his injured hand; his eyes turned fiery; sputum formed at the corners of his mouth. He grumbled, "Stand still, you fuckin' weasel. I'm going to kill you!"

Bobbing and weaving, I avoided his punches and watched his mounting frustration. My old wrestling moves returned; I felt less threatened. I knew I could wear down this ape by taunting him. It was my turn to be the aggressor. I kicked his left flank. When he turned, I kicked his right side. This went on for several minutes until he presented a full-frontal view: a slobbering bulldog face with a weary, unsteady stance. When his tired arms hung loosely, I brought my right arm back and with all my power buried a cannonball punch into his soft belly.

He doubled over with an "Oof." When his head and neck flexed forward, I brought my knee up and smashed his face. He jerked backward, then fell forward. Blood gushed from his nose and puddled onto the floor. Attempting to stand, he staggered and fell, knocking over two chairs, a side table, and lamp. With this disarray and spattered blood on the wall, floor, and carpeting, the living room looked like an abattoir.

Mavis, who had phoned the police, ran toward the moaning Gunz, handed him a towel for his bleeding nose, and gave me a washcloth.

The right corner of my upper lip swelled but no longer bled.

Simon charged into the room. "What the hell's going on since I saw you only an hour ago?"

"This ape got by the officers stationed outside and came into the house bragging about how he scared off someone in the forest with his shotgun. He grabbed Mavis, and I intervened. We got into it, that's all."

Simon looked at Gunz. "Okay, muscleman. Yeah, you with the bloody schnoz, you're coming down to the station." Simon had one of the officers put cuffs on him. "Time in the lockup should take some of the drunken stupidity out of you." Simon looked at Mavis. "You going to press charges, ma'am?"

"No, he's pathetically lonesome—tolerable when he's sober. Besides, he's a neighbor and . . ."

Simon cut her off. "Yeah, and a prime suspect in the attempted murder of Zach. Maybe one or two others."

"I'll press charges," I said.

Gunz, holding the bloody cloth to his nose as he was led out, looked over his shoulder and in a muffled nasal voice said, "I'll get you yet, you sonofabitch."

CHAPTER 33

"Sorry about the mess. I'll help clean up," I said.

"I should hope so. No one will convince me that this carnage was necessary."

My spirits took a dive. "Mavis, I don't understand you. I got into it with that slob because he was forcing himself on you, and I thought you were mad as hell."

"I was about to kick him in the crotch before you interfered."

"Before I interfered? Hell, next time just kick him. We could have avoided this damned chaos and spared me a fat lip."

Mavis picked up the picture with its shattered glass and broken frame. "It's a Whistler print...dark and depressing. I never cared for it, but it was a favorite of the one who gave it to me, so I hung it up to please him."

Aha, *him* again, the secret admirer I was warned not to ask about.

Passing her hand over the wall where Gunz had slammed his fist, she said, "My God, he actually cracked the wall. You're right, I should have kicked him in the groin. He could have broken your jaw if he landed that punch. Now I'll worry that he'll be looking for revenge."

"Not if I see him first." I touched my mouth gingerly. "Damn, my face smarts. My lip is swollen and numb."

"Zach, go home, get some rest. You'll be opening the store in a few hours . . ."

"And leave you alone while some moron with a high-powered rifle might be out there in the woods? Nothing doing. I'll sit on this easy chair with an ice pack on my face. You go upstairs and rest. I'll keep an eye on the forest."

"Are you sure you want to do that? I'd invite you to share my bed, but intimacy probably isn't on your mind."

"Intimacy with you is always on my mind—but you're right, not tonight."

She kissed me on my head before leaving.

* * *

I must have fallen asleep with my chin resting on my chest. I rotated my head, and my neck creaked. I smacked my tongue repeatedly against my Saharan palate. My Timex read 6:35, and the sun began to lighten the room. I heard no movement upstairs and thought I ought to check on Mavis.

I had never been upstairs, since all our intimate moments were in the luxury of her magnificent living room, and I didn't know which room was hers. I opened one door slowly and peered into a room darkened by closed venetian blinds. I was about to enter when Mavis, in a bathrobe, ran in front of me and closed the door. "Zach, this is Charles' bedroom!"

I backed off, hands in the air. "Hey, I'm sorry. I don't know my way around here. I thought I'd awaken you. Get you ready for opening the store."

"My bedroom is down the hall." Her voice became softer, apologetic. "Forgive me. I didn't mean to bite your head off. It's just that I try not to invade Charles' privacy or allow anyone else . . . his temperament is fragile and . . ."

"No need to explain, but when I opened his door, I saw a swastika on the wall."

Mavis gave me one of those consider-the-source shrugs, then explained, "He and his friends play a distorted version of cops-and-robbers they call Allies and Axis. Charles is the leader of the Allies. He captured the enemy flag. I know it's a morbid game, but they're only kids acting out."

"Uh-huh." Somehow her explanation sounded less than believable. I was thinking of something more sinister. "There are Nazi sympathizers in the community, and young people are being recruited—"

She cut me off. "For heaven's sake, don't make more of this than it deserves. These are kids who don't know diddly squat about the meaning of war."

"You may be right. However, I hope Ben Simon doesn't hear about the swastika. He's Jewish, you know, and anything that smacks of Hitler and the Nazis . . ."

She turned her back and headed downstairs. "All that shouldn't concern us. Come, we'll have juice, coffee, and toast, and you can tell me how ravishing I look even without makeup."

Her backside as she walked downstairs was, indeed, ravishing, but her disregard for the swastika made me uneasy. Any sign of Nazi influence made me uncomfortable. I knew from my course in Twentieth-Century American History that German-Americans during WWI had suffered hostility and ostracism. I couldn't be sure things would be better during this war.

Our townspeople were largely second and third-generation Germans, Scandinavians, and a few Belgians, Dutch, and Finns. Some recent German and Polish refugees kept a low profile, but everyone knew who they were. Most of them, except for Gunz and his ilk, proclaimed their patriotism by displaying American flags and bumper stickers that read "Death to the Axis, Buy War Bonds, Loose Lips Sink Ships" . . . slogans like that.

Banners with blue stars began appearing in windows,

along with a few gold stars. When I passed a gold star, I felt a twinge of sadness and guilt. Men my age were fighting and dying while I lived freely. On a cool day, I would turn up my collar and pull down my hat, hoping to conceal my identity.

Our town was thriving even though some items became rationed or unavailable. A large number of dairy products went to the armed forces, but our farmers managed to supply local housewives with sufficient butter and cheese at a higher than pre-war prices. We were down to one meat serving a week, but two butchers had enough beef, pork, and lamb for anyone willing to pay inflated prices. Housewives learned not to argue or complain about cost because butchers had other eager buyers.

I don't mean to imply that our townspeople were unpatriotic or greedy; breaking rules was unavoidable.

Fuel rationing put a crimp on auto travel, but we had A-ration cards that allowed increased gasoline purchasing, as doctors, nurses, and pharmacists who delivered medications had priority. I thought our town had more essential service drivers than most, and I was grateful for my A-rating.

I could drive Mavis to Madison to one of those better restaurants once or twice a month just for a change of venue; to get away from the limited menu of neighborhood eateries with their mock-meat dishes made of soybeans and mushrooms seasoned with onions, garlic, and chili powder. Some of our chefs had been drafted. Others moved out of the city to better-paying jobs.

*   *   *

At the Madison Grand Hotel, Mavis and I sat in an alcove with subdued lighting, a candle in a glass chimney, and a bottle of Chablis in an ice bucket. Danceable music came from a sextet of elderly men allowing me to exhibit my skills at the waltz, two-step, and fox-trot. Mavis followed beautifully and covered my missteps, taking the lead when necessary.

In the glow of candlelight, her face was beautiful; her eyes glistened, her smile bewitching. After a glass of wine, she became positively radiant. I reached for her hand and kissed the back of it.

Her shoeless toe moved slowly up and down my leg, causing me to fantasize. I'd yank everything off the table and do it right there. The fantasy stopped when she spoke. I didn't hear a word she said as she bent down, put on her shoe, and excused herself.

Her absence gave me time to cool my erotic desires. My meandering mind ultimately focused on all the possible murder suspects in the deaths of Earl Withers— that old cuckold and his wife, Irma, my former paramour.

I thought about them almost daily and tried to think who might have benefited from their deaths. Moreover, there were the attempts on my life and the arsonist who burned the drugstore and my car. Suspects began passing in an orderly file through my head. Now suspicions were emerging more clearly.

The one to benefit most from Withers' death would have been Irma, if one were to ignore Walt Mason's questionable legal claim on that note he carried in his wallet. Two factors ruled out Irma's involvement in the murder. Number one: Earl was shot in the middle of his forehead, which suggested murder by a professional hitman. Secondly: Irma knew nothing about firearms. Thirdly: she was out of town at the time of the murder. Of course, she could have hired someone, but I couldn't imagine her doing that. She wasn't clever enough to plan that well.

The other suspect, Walt Mason, was physically impaired but had a smoldering hatred for Withers since that terrible auto accident thirty years ago. Walt had suffered brain damage but could function as a handyman in the drugstore. He also had a collection of guns, and despite his physical disability, practiced shooting frequently. His wife, Darlene Ann, attested to his marksmanship.

Another suspect, Bertrand Ainsley, was the father of the girl killed in that auto accident. Yet, if he were guilty of killing Withers, why would he have waited thirty years? The other suspect, Attorney Arnie Teasdale, could have altered the terms of Earl and Irma Withers' wills to his benefit. He said he had already owned a percentage of Earl's properties, which he took in lieu of fees, but I knew he was eager to own more—legitimately or otherwise.

Irma's death continued to mystify and anger me. Okay, so I had lost my passion for her, and our relationship at best had been physical. It never could have been anything more than that. Our backgrounds and interests were miles apart, and the thrill of sexual gratification with her lost its luster.

Because of her tasteless antics, her lack of gentility, and her condescending attitude toward the locals, she could not adapt to small-town living. I thought of her as frightened and insecure, masquerading beneath a hard shell that failed to protect her from corrosive criticism. I had avoided making her aware of her shortcomings. In fact, I complimented her whenever possible.

Her young life never should have been snuffed out. Murder by poisoning—a vile, sadistic, reprehensible and cowardly act.

CHAPTER 34

If I were objective about Irma's murderer, I would have to consider Mavis, as painful as that seemed. The theory, I suppose, was crazy, and yet she could have gained the most since Withers willed property to her. I looked at my watch. Mavis had been gone almost thirty minutes. The waiter at his station raised his brow as though to ask what had happened to my date.

I shrugged and poured another glass of wine. The bottle would soon be empty, and I would be forced to surrender my car keys to Mavis since I was becoming blotto. My ability to focus clearly was fading, as were my libidinous plans for the evening.

Mavis returned and apologized for her prolonged absence. Preoccupied, she forced a smile and began to fidget with the wine goblet. Her cold hands reached for mine, and with teary eyes, she said, "Zach, forgive me, but I can't dine and enjoy the evening."

"Why? What's the trouble?"

"It's complicated, and I prefer not to talk about it here. Would you mind driving me home?"

The situation evoked a rapid transition to sobriety. A moment ago, the effects of wine had produced a state of euphoria, a feeling of freedom; a kind of floating-out-of-body sensation. Now a demanding situation whipped me into clear thinking. I signaled the waiter, gave an excuse, and peeled off a ten-spot, which he accepted gladly.

In the car, she held a handkerchief and dabbed her eyes and nose, saying nothing more than to thank me.

I could only speculate about her problem, but I wouldn't say anything that could have aggravated her. Maybe a little humor would be helpful.

"Did you learn you were pregnant?"

She smiled tolerantly and nudged my arm. "That would be a blessing since you would be the father."

"I won't accept fatherhood without a blood test."

She forced a smile. "Zach, I can't begin to tell you how grateful I am for your patience." She continued to twist a handkerchief in her lap.

"Don't tell me. Show me. No, wait . . . not while I'm driving."

With that, she chuckled. Whatever caused her misery seemed to have lost its sting. She breathed a sigh of relief as I placed my right hand on her thigh. She removed my hand and kissed it. "Thank you, Zach, for being you."

She made no mention of the dinner-date fiasco; she

would tell me in her own time. If I had learned anything about women, it was to back off if they were reluctant to discuss something.

*　　*　　*

Toward the end of the workday, I was cleaning up when my phone rang. A call at the closing hour usually portended a matter of urgency. Since there had been a shortage of doctors, house calls were no longer made except for the most dire cases. As a pharmacist, my function as a health-care provider took on a more meaningful role. My responsibilities increased, along with my liabilities. I hoped the caller did not have a fever of unknown origin or symptoms that defied me.

I picked up the phone. "Newbury Pharmacy. How can I help you?"

Several seconds passed before a male voice growled breathlessly, "Listen, Kiddo, I've got a sonofabitchin' back pain. Got something to help me? Maybe a mustard plaster . . . a shot of morphine—anything for this fuckin' misery? I can't even get up to piss. I'm scheduled to appear in court day after tomorrow and . . ."

I recognized Simon's voice, and there was no way I could ignore him. "Give me half an hour." I reached for an old, black cracked leather Gladstone bag left by Earl Withers that would serve as a doctor's kit. I filled it with pain medication, a mustard plaster, two corsets, and a heating pad.

* * *

Simon's unit was a recently built colonial style duplex just outside Newbury in an upper-middle-class development. I used the shiny brass knocker on the door. A distant gruff voice yelled, "The damned door's open!"

I stepped into a tidy, sparsely furnished living room that stank of cigarette smoke and found my way to a bedroom.

Simon lay propped up on two pillows, his knees flexed over several rolled blankets. Besides the cigarette stink, there were odors of camphor oil and rubbing alcohol. Simon's painful expression was more noticeable with a three-day-old gray-and-black stubble.

"Jeez, Zach, I hope to hell you can get me out of this sack. The pain comes like a bolt of lightning, a zinger that knocks the breath out of me. Wakes me up from a snooze. I'm afraid to sit on the crapper or take a leak."

"Show me where the pain is greatest." I helped Simon roll on his side while he complained in staccato gripes, invoking the Lord's name along with terms of excrement. He placed his index finger at the approximate point of the left sacroiliac joint.

"Simon, I'm going to give you an injection of Procaine,

a local anesthetic, which I'm not licensed to do. If you tell anyone, I'll deny it. So happens I've seen doctors do this during my clinical courses." I cleansed the skin with alcohol and injected the solution.

Simon lay still until he said, "When you gonna do it, Doc?"

My status had been elevated to the title of "Doc," and Simon's speech no longer blurted foul comments. "It's been done," I said and watched anxiously as he turned onto his back without complaint.

His brow furrowed as though he expected pain, then an expression of relief washed over his face. "Doc, the pain's gone. Jeezus, it's absolutely gone! You're a fuckin' genius."

Genius? I couldn't be sure my new title was meant to be flattering, but it was better than some things he had called me in the past. I had him sit on the edge of the bed, then assisted him in standing. He staggered momentarily; I held him until his vertigo passed, then I applied a corset and buckled it firmly.

"Jeez, I feel like a human being again." He ran his hands along the sides of the corset. "This ain't bad for my shape, either."

I left a bottle of non-narcotic pain tablets, closed the medical bag, and wrote out dosage instructions.

"Wait, don't leave, Zach. I haven't talked to a real person in three days. Stick around for a few minutes, will ya? Let's have a beer. I gotta discuss some things with you."

I'd never had a friendly chat with Simon because I thought he was incapable of civil discourse. His terse comments were usually snide. I figured I ought to take advantage of his high spirits to learn what he knew about the murders.

We walked slowly to the kitchen. Simon's gait was tentative; he reached out to the wall for balance. I sat at the table while he opened the refrigerator and pulled out two bottles of Pabst.

The clean and orderly home was so unlike Simon's usual slovenly appearance and that of his automobile, which was a rolling trashcan. "Simon, your place is immaculate. Everything sparkles."

He raised his bottle to click with mine. "Yeah, it's clean. You're wondering how a slob like me lives in a place like this? I'll tell you how. A gal comes in once a week to dust, mop up, do the laundry, even prepare a meal or two for the freezer."

"Think she would give me a day once a week?"

"I doubt it."

"Could I have her name? I'd call and ask . . ."

"Don't bother. Her name is Mary Beth Schultz."

"Why does that name sound familiar?" I asked.

"She's that zaftig dame in my front office. You met her. In fact, she chauffeured you once, as I recall."

I did remember her. A plump, pleasant gal who told me she'd hoped for a serious relationship with Simon. "Seems to me she'd be an ideal candidate for a permanent relationship with you."

He seemed to study the beer bottle in his hands, then leaned toward me to speak confidentially as though others could be listening. "To tell the truth, she's the one who caused my back pain. She kept demanding more, and like a damn fool I . . ."

"Hold on. I'm not sure I want to hear any more of that," I said.

Simon tossed his empty bottle into a wastebasket and reached for another in the fridge. He became more talkative without my encouragement.

He continued, "She's a sweet, caring gal. Mother of two kids. I don't know if I could be a father to two teenagers—besides, there are other issues."

"Obviously, you're physically compatible."

He stopped to chug-a-lug the rest of the beer, then slammed the bottle on the table and belched. "Listen, I'm an old cock who has no problem in that department—until this damn thing with my back. I was a stud before I had hair down there, and I've had my share of broads. I can't think of any I didn't enjoy."

Simon was on a roll, and I couldn't stop him. "Schultzie is well endowed. Being with her in bed is like bouncing on a bunch of balloons while your prong is getting massaged. Take it from me, that's gotta be like heaven. But, in all fairness, a skinny gal isn't bad either. You hit that bony pelvis and get right down to business. The result is good, either way."

I wasn't expecting a discourse on comparative anatomy, but I learned that Simon was not a reclusive bachelor who spent all his time trying to solve murders.

"Seems to me, Simon, you could do worse than making a commitment to Mary Beth Schultz. She'd look after you, and . . ."

Simon held up his hand to stop me. "Hold it right there, Kiddo. Like I said. It's none of your business. She has kids. More than that, her ex still lives around here, and he's a fuckin' animal who I might kill one day—unless he kills me first."

CHAPTER 35

My feelings of warmth and friendliness toward the community since my arrival four years ago had turned cold and menacing in the past several months.

The explosion and firebombing of the store was a heinous crime, but there was also the fire set to my car and the shooting while I sat on Mavis' back porch. Of course, there was also the highway shooting after I left Walt Mason's home. Someone wanted me dead. No getting away from that.

The murder of Earl Withers and the poisoning death of Irma remained unsolved. My luck might run out, and there wasn't a single solitary arrest, although several suspects were still around—one of them planning my death.

Had I overlooked someone? I must have. How many times had I tried to consider every possible suspect? Too many. Ben Simon must have felt frustration also, but his pride and determination would never allow him to admit that. He would say something like, "Kiddo, it's just a matter of time before the sonofabitch steps in his own shit and stumbles. When that happens, I'll nab him."

His words reflected the thinking of an East Coast tough who resented the thought of some cow-town yokel outwitting him. I'm sure his thinking did not exclude me as a suspect in the murders of Earl and Irma Withers.

*   *   *

Several early-morning coffee drinkers at the soda fountain were reading newspapers while waiting for Eddie Polanski to brew his special blend of coffee. Baked goods from Milwaukee consisted of a variety of sweet rolls, doughnuts, buns, and breads. Once or twice a week, I would treat myself to Eddie's special brew and a jelly-filled doughnut while chatting with Eddie and the customers.

On this day, Eddie was not at his station hurrying to serve breakfasts, but two youngsters hired for fountain service were scurrying to fill orders.

I sat at the counter and asked one of the beleaguered youngsters about Eddie.

"He couldn't come in, Mr. Black," the breathless girl said apologetically. She hand-brushed a few strands of hair off her sweaty face.

"That's all you can tell me?"

"Yes—yes, sir."

"Who called it in?"

"Wanda, Mrs. Polanski."

"What exactly did she say?"

"She said Eddie couldn't come in. He . . . he shot himself."

"He *what?* Where is he? Is he in the hospital?"

"She didn't say."

"Oh, for God's sake! Get her on the phone."

"The line's been busy for the last half hour."

I rushed to tell Mavis what I had just heard and told her I was going to Eddie's house to find out what was going on. I asked her to give the kids a hand at the fountain. She grabbed an apron and was tying the strings when I left.

"Zach, be careful, don't speed."

*   *   *

Eddie and Wanda lived in the old section of Newbury called Shanty Town, a name given by those who lived everywhere else. Originally, the shacks were put up to accommodate railroad gandy dancers. Most shacks had been dismantled when the rail tracks were completed, but a few shacks remained and were inhabited by transients, sharecroppers, and hunters. Earl Withers' grandfather

241

had bought the property from the railroad after the Civil War with the undocumented promise that he would develop the land. The improvement had never occurred because of the worldwide financial panic of 1873. I had learned all this from reading the town's history in our public library.

Eddie's home had numerous improvements and was in better shape than neighboring shanties. The windows and frames had been replaced; the entrance door glistened with a coat of varnish that smelled fresh.

Wanda opened the door after I knocked. She gasped when she saw me. She put her hand to her mouth; her eyes widened as she stepped back and moved to the side, bowing as though welcoming royalty. "Please come in, Mr. Black." She scurried to remove papers from the dining table and straightened chairs around it.

"Can I give you a glass of tea? A cup of coffee? Maybe a glass of beer?"

I waved away her offerings and looked around anxiously.

"You're looking for Eddie?"

"Yes. I was told he had a gunshot wound. Is he hurt badly?"

She hesitated, looked upward, mumbled incoherently, and made the sign of the cross over her chest. "Please, come with me." With quick steps she led me to a bedroom, an add-on, she explained, built by Eddie.

Dimly lit, the room smelled of camphor oil and iodine. Jesus hung morosely on a cross over Eddie's bed. He lay with his left leg propped up on pillows, his foot swathed in dishtowels. He smiled weakly as I approached, and in a voice above a whisper said, "Hello, Mr. Black." He extended his hand to shake mine. "I gotta apologize for not coming to work today."

Wanda brought in a chair for me, then left.

"What the hell happened, Eddie?"

"I was stupid—just plain stupid, that's all. I was cleaning my old S&W .38 when it went off—bang! Shot the tip right off my big toe. Blood spurted like a fountain. I tell ya. Wanda came running in screaming. She grabbed some dishtowels and covered my foot. Can you believe she picked up pieces of the toe off the floor and put 'em in a pickle jar? Want to see 'em?"

"No, thanks. But how did you manage to shoot your foot?"

"I was gonna check the barrel when the goddamned thing went off. It had a tricked-up hair-trigger."

"Did you call a doctor? Did you think about going to the hospital? This could become infected, lead to blood poisoning and death. You can't ignore it."

Eddie pouted, shook his head. "Mr. Black, I can't go to the hospital."

"Why not?"

"I'm an ex-con. I'm not supposed to own a gun.

Gunshot injuries are automatically reported. It's the law—you know that. They'll lock me up."

"Where'd you get the gun?"

He turned his head aside; his jaw muscles tightened; he said nothing.

"Answer me, where'd you get the gun?"

He blurted, "I don't remember. I got it a long time ago. What's the difference?"

"That's not acceptable. Again, where did you get it?"

Reluctantly, he said, "Some greaser. I gave him a fin and two sandwiches for it. I could never buy a gun legit."

"Why did you buy it?"

He looked around furtively as though someone could be listening.

"To protect myself. Look, I made a few enemies when I was in the tank. They fingered me for not going along with their drug deals. Those guys never forget, and when they get out, they'll look for me."

"Did you rat on them?"

"I didn't want to, I swear, but the screws put a lot of pressure on me. They made me an offer if I gave them names." He looked at his bandaged foot and spoke slowly. "Mr. Black, I couldn't take another month in that shithole . . . excuse my lingo. I wouldn't be here now if . . . well, you know."

"Did you kill Mr. Withers with that gun?"

His mouth dropped as he glared at me. "Aw c'mon,

Mr. Black, why would I do that?"

"Because you hated him."

"Well, yeah, but not so much that I'd kill him. If he was younger, I might have popped him after he pinched Wanda's butt. No one can do that but me. Right?"

"You'll have to surrender that gun. Why don't you give it—"

"To me!" an officious voice filled the room.

Eddie and I turned to see Simon at the doorway. His dour expression gave no hint of concern for Eddie's injury.

"Simon, what are you doing here?" I asked.

He ignored my question and kept his eye on Eddie. "Give me the gun, Polanski, and no bullshit excuses."

As Eddie turned his head away from Simon, his jaw muscles tightened and relaxed alternately.

"Hand it over, or we'll tear this place apart until we find it." He tapped his watch. "You have two minutes to decide."

Eddie brought his head forward. His fiery eyes glared at Simon. "What the hell do you want from me? I didn't shoot anyone. I shot myself. There's no goddamned crime in that, is there?"

"I want that gun for ballistics . . . determine whether a round shot from it matches the one that killed Withers."

Eddie's nostrils flared. "You're wasting your time."

"Wouldn't be the first time." Simon's laconic reply

matched his flat expression. He tapped his watch. "You have one minute."

"Alright! Alright!" Eddie sat up, supported by his elbows, and shouted, "Wanda, come here!"

A wide-eyed Wanda stood at the bedroom door, wiping her hands on an apron. "What's the matter?"

"Get the gun," Eddie said.

"Where is it?"

"On the bookshelf behind the Bible."

"Wait!" Simon shouted. "Don't touch it. Show me where it is and give me a dishtowel to wrap it in. I'll return it—the dishtowel, that is."

Eddie's voice was pleading as Simon walked away. "Are you going to arrest me? Put me back in the can?"

Without turning around, Simon said, "If your gun killed Withers, you can kiss your ass goodbye, 'cause it'll belong to us." He tossed a two-finger salute and left.

Eddie looked at me. "That sonofabitch could frame me. He never did like me. He's been looking for any excuse to put me away."

CHAPTER 36

The Blue Skies dining room, an upscale restaurant in Milwaukee, served French food—or their version of it—and imported wines. I ordered a vintage Bordeaux before our entrees and felt the comforting warmth in my gut after two sips.

Tilting her head and smiling coquettishly, Mavis reached across the table to hold my hands. Candlelight enhanced her beauty: a warm smile, the contour of her bosom, and the roundness of her arms were sexually stimulating. At that moment I wanted to be with her for the rest of my life, but especially that evening.

I knew little about Charles, her seventeen-year-old son who had psychological problems, but I was sure they could be ironed out after we married. Besides, he would soon be at the university taking courses in human behavior, philosophy, sociology, and maybe the history of Western civilization. Those studies might alter his skewed views of malignant governments and the sociopaths who presided over them.

"Mavis, I know you're reluctant to talk about your son's involvement with the Nazis, but I think we should discuss it—get it out in the open. We can't ignore the problem."

"Of course not."

"Reports out of Europe indicate mass killings—"

"Zach, I'm aware of all that, and I'm terribly ashamed. I wish you had never seen that awful swastika in his room." A pleading expression washed over her face as she said, "I'd be grateful to have a man confront and explain some things to him." Her eyes beseeched mine. "Could you do that?"

"I'm not sure I'm up to it. Tell me, how do you think all this started?"

Mavis drew in a breath. "For years Charles had to fend for himself while I was working, and his father was busy at . . ." She stopped suddenly, then continued, "Charles had to find his own friends, who unfortunately had strange interests.

"For the past year, I've been listening to him praise that damned Hitler and his maniacal ideas. When I think about that, I get so infuriated. Imagine murdering people because of their religious views. It's so terribly shameful and depressing." She looked to either side, then leaned forward and whispered, "Are there any Jewish people in Newbury?"

"There's our solitary detective, Lieutenant Ben Simon."

"Yes, but is there anyone else?"

"His cousin, the recently murdered Irma Withers."

She gasped. "Oh, my God! I didn't know that." She became pensive, her brow tented, she spoke quietly, "Do you think those crazy Nazis . . .?" She had difficulty completing her question.

Anticipating what she was about to ask, I said, "Simon knows every crime committed in this area in the last ten years and has a detailed dossier on every suspect."

She blanched while turning the stem of her wine goblet. Her voice quavered. "Do you think he suspects Charles?"

"I don't know. Besides, what would Charles' motive be?" As soon as I said that, I realized how stupid that sounded. As though any of those morons needed a reason for killing.

CHAPTER 37

When we left the restaurant, the conversation about Charles' involvement with the Nazi party created a niggling uneasiness for me, but I convinced myself that my relationship with Mavis could endure.

The cool breezes of the mid-September evening helped drive away my negative thoughts as we walked hand in hand, swinging our arms like children until we reached my car. I opened the passenger door for Mavis but noticed that something was not quite right.

The car listed toward the rear. The right rear tire was flat without enough residual air to drive to a service station. I bent down to examine the tire, complaining all the while as I ran my hand around the wall of a tire that had been purchased just two months ago when I bought a set of four.

Supplies of new tires had been curtailed since the start of the war, but our tire-supply store had several in stock at twice the cost of pre-war prices. *C'est la guerre.* Then I saw it—a clean-edged slit about four inches in the tire wall. A knife cut. I looked around . . . Some damned sonofabitch . . .

"Zach, this is terrible. Do you have a spare?" Mavis asked.

"There's a spare in the trunk with a jack and a lug wrench."

I started to remove my jacket when Mavis said, "Darling, I'll call Triple-A. There's no need to soil your clothes. Let's go back to the restaurant and call them. We can wait inside 'til they come."

The moment Mavis completed her call and thanked the maître d' for the use of the phone, a truck horn blasted in the parking lot. I opened the restaurant door to see a tall white cab-over-engine tow truck with a logo on its door displaying a G.I. helmet and below that, the name: Helmut Gunz, Owner Operator.

Perched on his high seat grinning with a grizzly stubble and a cigar butt in the corner of his mouth, Helmut leaned out the window and growled, "This is your lucky day, Mister Drug Dealer. I'll get you out of here in fifteen minutes. Got a spare?"

Mavis looked at her neighbor Helmut curiously. "How could you get here so quickly? I just called Triple-A . . ."

"This is my regular run. I drive around here at night. I know there's gonna be trouble. Always happens." He climbed down from his cab and walked to the rear of his truck.

"Wait a minute, Gunz. Everything is happening too fast. Are you with Triple-A?" I asked.

"Nah. I work faster as an independent. If you wanta wait a half hour or more, it's okay with me."

"How much do you charge?" Mavis asked.

Helmut scratched the back of his head as he pushed up the greasy rim of his baseball cap. "You being my neighbor and all, would fifteen dollars be too much?"

"Fifteen dollars is what I pay for yearly dues to Triple-A, and that entitles me to unlimited service. We'll wait for the Triple-A truck," I said.

Helmut grunted and spat. A glob of sputum landed on my right shoe.

I grabbed his shoulders and slammed him against his truck. "Listen, you miserable slob. You think I don't know your game? Slashing tires could land you in jail."

He wiped his mouth with the back of his hand and pushed my hands away. "You got no right to accuse me of anything . . . you got no proof." He rolled his shoulders forward, then climbed into his truck and sped off in a cloud of black exhaust.

I watched as the truck traveled about fifty yards to where the parking lot ended, then the truck turned in a tight arc and stopped to face us. The engine roared, the headlights shone brighter like the eyes of a monster preparing to strike.

Sure enough, in high gear, the truck surged toward us. I grabbed Mavis' hand, and we jumped between two parked cars. As the truck sped by, I glimpsed Helmut's ghoulish smile. His upright middle finger mocked us; his highway horns blasted like an angry beast.

Mavis shook her head. "I can't believe he did that."

"He's an insane sonofabitch capable of killing."

"I'll tell Simon what happened. The fact that Gunz is a Nazi sympathizer should give Simon greater incentive to burn his ass."

"Do you think Helmut has influenced your son? I mean, encouraging him to join the Bund?"

"I—I don't know. Now that you mentioned it, that sounds like a possibility. He has always been solicitous towards Charles. I encouraged the friendship, thinking it was more like an uncle-nephew type relationship. He could have been filling Charles' head with hateful propaganda."

"There is also the undeniable fact that Helmut would like to get to know you better."

"Zach, that man's appearance disgusts me, but he has been helpful when I need repairs around the house. If I thought he was responsible for Charles' involvement with the Nazis, I'd kill him, I swear it."

"Sure, sure. With your bare hands?"

Mavis pursed her lips, looked away, and was about to respond when the Triple-A tow truck pulled up.

CHAPTER 38

Keeping company with Mavis was not without its stormy moments, but life without those moments might have been too bland. Her moronic neighbor, Helmut Gunz, and her son's involvement with the Bund kept me off balance, and at times I plainly worried that one day the shit would hit the fan. I was absorbed in my thinking and pill counting when I looked up to see two black suits with fedoras and polished oxfords entering the store.

They walked with a purposeful stride—no smile, no emotion as they walked toward my station. I had seen the type before in movies, and I read about them in crime novels, but seeing them in front of me caused a few extra systoles.

"Mr. Black?" The slightly taller one opened his wallet to display a badge which I couldn't see closely. "I'm Jack Miller, FBI, and this is Peter Gottschalk, my partner. We're out of the Madison office." Both were clean-shaven, wearing white button-down oxford cloth collars and school-striped ties. Their suits were off-the-rack Sears' or J.C. Penney's better-label wear. I knew because they were my clothiers.

"How can I help you fellows?"

"We've been advised about the presence of a strong anti-American sentiment among some of the town's citizens . . . specifically, Nazi sympathizers who are guilty of aiding the enemy and engaging in seditious acts. As you know, those are treasonable acts punishable by imprisonment or death, depending upon the degree of involvement. Do you know or have you heard about any such persons?"

I swallowed hard, and my failure to respond immediately must have provoked Agent Gottschalk into saying, "If you give a false answer or withhold information, you'll be considered a co-conspirator . . ."

"Wait a minute! Back off. You sound more threatening than enemy propaganda. I won't answer questions without the presence of an attorney."

"There's no need to make a contentious case of this. All we want to know . . ."

He continued talking, but I wasn't listening. My head was swimming with images of a battalion of G.I.s with bayonets drawn, marching down Grand Avenue behind a troupe of forlorn out-of-step Nazi sympathizers with their swastika armbands and polished boots. The scene became vivid in my mind as people in the sidewalk crowd cheered the American soldiers and booed the Nazis. As I stared at the vanquished, I saw Mavis' son, Charles. His being there would break Mavis' heart.

"Mr. Black, do you hear me?" Agent Miller asked.

"Uh-huh, yes, sorry."

"Once more. Have you in the past or do you now know anyone who is associated with enemies of the United States, such as the Nazi party, or sympathetic to the Empire of Japan?"

The simple answer would be *no*, and I could get rid of these black suits, but ultimately, they would discover I had not been forthright. I had to do some fancy footwork, stepping cautiously in and out of a ring of truth. Did I know any Nazi sympathizers personally? No, not personally. I had seen Charles once in an ROTC uniform at the drugstore, but I didn't recall ever talking with him. If I never talked with him, how could I know him?

I rationalized my answer and would deal with conscience later. Besides, how could I face Mavis if I told these agents I knew her kid was a member of the Bund? I didn't want to risk losing Mavis' loyalty and love. "Sorry, fellas. Can't be of much help."

Agent Miller reached into his wallet, pulled out his card, and handed it to me. "If anything crosses your mind, give me a call."

"Sure thing. I'll do that."

While placing his wallet in his inner jacket pocket, Agent Miller said, "You familiar with a guy by the name of Helmut Gunz?"

Jeezus, just when I thought I absolved myself from any involvement, I'm tossed a ringer. I could feel a flush in my face, and my legs began to tremble. How much did they know? Were they playing games with me?

My voice strained into a higher pitch as I said, "Yes, I know the man." I stopped. I refused to embellish my answer, but I knew that would not satisfy him.

"How well do you know him?" Miller said.

"Fellas, I know you've got a job to do, but I'm running late, and I've got a dozen prescriptions to fill, some require compounding. People expect them to be filled . . ." I looked at the wall clock. ". . . within an hour or so."

"What time do you close?" Miller asked. "We're planning to stay in town overnight at the Newbury Inn—"

"Sorry, fellas," I said, "I promised my lady friend I'd take her to dinner tonight, and . . ."

Miller looked around then leaned toward me, and in a voice above a whisper, said, "Black, we can be cooperative up to a point, but then our cordiality vanishes. We'll make demands on you that will curl your hair. So, it behooves you to make time to answer the few questions we have."

Miller's steely eyes showed no compassion. Clearly, he suspected something and was not about to leave until his questions were answered. "Now, getting back to this Gunz character, what can you tell us about him?"

"He's a queer duck," I said. "A neighbor of one of our employees, Mrs. Mavis Johnson."

"Queer in what way?" Miller said.

This interrogation had all the earmarks of a profile study of my most disliked character. What did they expect me to say? That he was a slob who became offensive when he drank? That he shot his rifle at real or imaginary creatures in the forest or at me? That I suspected him of slashing my tire so he could replace it at an outlandish cost? That he might be responsible for screwing up the thinking of a young man into accepting Nazi propaganda?

Miller's piercing eyes waited for my response. "All I can give you is my general impressions of the man. I think he's obnoxious. I just don't like him, and I'm sure he doesn't like me. I would avoid him if we were walking toward one another."

"Have you had any disagreements? Has he ever said anything to make you think he was sympathetic to the Nazi cause?"

"To answer your first question, yes, we've had disagreements. As to your second question, I don't recall any specific references he made about Nazis."

Miller nodded. "Would it surprise you to learn that Gunz has been a flag-bearer at Bund meetings in Milwaukee? That he has a rap sheet for sexual abuses, using illegal substances, and committing petty thefts?"

"None of that surprises me."

"Thanks for your cooperation, Mr. Black. We'd appreciate your not mentioning our conversation." He tapped his index finger on his professional card and said, "If you can think of anything else that might be of interest, call me at this number."

CHAPTER 39

Simon's dour expression as he sipped coffee at the fountain hinted serious matters. He pushed up the front of his fedora and gestured to a limping Eddie for more coffee. No words were spoken in the communication.. Ballistics had no results yet on the bullet fired from Eddie's gun.

I had just filled three prescriptions, but before looking at the next I wanted to talk with Simon to learn what was happening in the community. I was eager for outside news since most of my day was spent at the drug station. I sat on a stool next to Simon as he read *The Capital Times*.

He shook his head and turned toward me. "Have you read what this bastard wrote about me?" He pointed to a column on the second page. "Listen to this: 'Unsolved murders in a small town reaches third year without solutions. The mysterious murders of druggist Earl Withers and his wife still baffle police in rural Newbury.' Can you believe this shit?" He bit into a doughnut then brushed his tie as sprinkles fell on it. He continued, "They have nothing better to write, so they rehash this old crap." He looked at me for comment. "Did you tell any reporters that you were baffled by these murders?"

"There's been no one here from any newspaper since the last murder."

"What gripes my ass is this reporter referring to me as the chief investigator who may be in over his head in attempting to solve these crimes. The goddamned nerve of some effete shithead who knows nothing about these murders or the community is mouthing off about my inability." Simon's mood warned me against saying anything construed as offensive.

Disrupting our conversation was the repetitive revving of a motorcycle. Employees and customers were annoyed and curious by the sound since motorcycles were a rare occurrence in Newbury.

All heads turned toward the entrance as a burly six-footer came through the door followed by a small woman wearing a red bandana. Both wore dark goggles, leather jackets, and trousers with chrome studs and western-style boots. The man carried a plastic German-style helmet and swaggered toward the fountain. He sat next to Ben Simon; his companion sat next to him.

Eddie approached them with his usual smile. "Can I help you folks?"

"Yeah." The stranger's coarse voice demanded, "Give

us two javas, and be sure the mugs are clean." He turned toward Simon. "You one of the locals?"

Simon glared at the biker. "You could say that."

"How's the grub here?"

"You some kind of traveling gourmet? Doing an evaluation for a cyclist's guide?" Simon asked.

The stranger stared at Simon. "You being clever, Buddy, or ain't I reading you right?"

"Read me any way you want. For your information, I don't like bikers who make annoying sounds with their stupid two-wheelers."

"Zatso? Maybe you'd like to do something about it, little man."

"Don't press me. For one thing, we have noise suppression laws in this town. Offenders can be fined ten dollars for the first offense, twenty-five dollars for a second offense, and jail time after that."

The stranger turned toward his companion and sneered. "Did you hear that, Babe? We committed an offense in this fine town. They don't like the sound of a revving Harley." He placed his helmet on the counter, infringing on Simon's space.

Simon looked at the helmet. "Where did you get a fake Nazi infantry helmet?"

"That's none of your freakin' business."

Simon turned away and ignored him.

The biker turned toward Simon. "You sound like a

nosy jerk. That profile of yours—you a rabbi? Your beak could get you in a heap of trouble, where I come from."

Simon's jaw muscles alternately tightened and relaxed, but he said nothing. Ordinarily, he would not linger over his coffee, but I thought he remained long enough to hear this boor's insults. Simon pursed his lips and moved his mug slowly away from the stranger's side.

Eddie brought the bikers their orders of fried eggs, bacon, fries, toast, and a tray of assorted jellies. Within ten minutes the biker had cleaned his plate but demanded a second helping of toast and washed that down with his third mug of coffee. Eddie presented the bill, which came to two dollars and fifty-eight cents for both servings.

The biker reached in his back pocket and brought out his wallet. He thumbed through it, then looked up at Eddie. "Sorry, amigo, I thought I had the scratch. I must have left my money in my other wallet. When I come out this way again, I'll pay and leave a good tip."

Eddie looked at him and said softly, "Sure—next time."

As the biker turned on the stool to leave, Simon grabbed his sleeve. "Hold on, buster. That's a cheap trick. Screwing a guy out of his earnings. You're a rotten sonofabitch."

"Hey, who you calling a rotten sonofabitch?"

"Sorry, I meant to say you're a rotten cheap sonofabitch."

The stranger threw a punch at Simon, who ducked like a professional boxer.

I jumped between them and held them off, hoping to avoid a fight that could have damaged the merchandise.

Simon flashed his badge fixed to his belt and pulled his jacket aside to reveal his holster.

"Whoa, Nelly!" the biker said in mock fright as he raised his hands. "Why didn't you say you were a lawman? Lucky for you, you got a badge and pistol. I would have beaten the shit out of you."

"I'll give you the opportunity."

Simon turned to the biker's companion. She moved off the stool and backed away. Simon said, "Can you drive that motorcycle?"

She hesitated. "Sure, if I had to. Why?"

Simon removed his shoulder holster and badge and handed them to me, then turned to the biker.

"Okay, big mouth, let's go into the parking lot and settle our differences. You're about four inches taller and about fifty pounds heavier than me. That should even the odds. Maybe give you a few advantage points that you'll need." He looked at me. "Black, bring a few bandages. This gorilla's gonna need them." Walking with his adversary to the parking lot, Simon said, "What the hell are you doing in our town, anyway?"

"None of your goddamned business."

"If you've come to cause trouble with your shitty Nazi

ideas, you've come to the wrong place. What's your name, Storm Trooper?"

"You don't need to know."

"You won't get your bike out of impound unless you give me your name, address, and state your business."

"My Harley, impounded? You're impounding my Harley?"

"That's right. You parked it in a no-parking area, and you violated the town's noise suppression law. Now, what's your name, and why are you here?"

After a moment of hesitation, the biker said, "Streicher, Konrad. That's Konrad with a K. Kommandant American Bund Mid-Central State Motorcycle Division."

"Long title, it'll be hard to fit on a tombstone. Just a word of warning: stay away from the parked cars. I don't want you falling and damaging any."

Employees and patrons, including Mavis and Eddie, formed an irregular ring in the parking area. Simon and Streicher removed their jackets. Streicher wore a tank top with a swastika and a skull with crossbones. On his right arm was a tattooed heart with a message of love to his mother. Simon rolled his shirt sleeves to his elbows.

Streicher's companion, visibly concerned, ran to his side. In an audible whisper, she said, "Are you crazy? Do you know what you're doing?"

He shoved her aside. "Go make side bets—give 'em

odds. I'm gonna finish off Abie here in less than a minute. No sweat." He turned his head, spat, rolled his shoulders, and glared as Simon moved sideways, sizing up his adversary; his hands were clenched, his eyes alert.

Streicher watched, his arms hanging loosely at his sides. He sneered. "Come on, little man, let's see what you can do."

I watched as both men sized up one another. Streicher, looking menacing, moved slowly while Simon jittered nervously. Even in the cool autumn air, beads of perspiration glistened on Streicher's forehead. His movements were slow, lumbering, but I knew if he got his massive arms around Simon, he could crush him, or if he struck him, the blow could be fatal.

Simon gauged his opponent carefully; he bobbed and weaved, then began to taunt. He motioned to Streicher. "Come on, big shot, let's see how fast you can move your fat ass."

Like a bull, Streicher snorted and came rushing at Simon. A collective gasp rose from the onlookers as Simon, like a matador, twisted and sidestepped while Streicher's clumsy momentum carried him headlong into a parked car. The onlookers were silenced after the crushing sound. With outstretched arms, Streicher attempted to hold on to the car; his fingers slipped as he turned around slowly, dazed; his eyes unfocused, he leaned against the car and slid down to the ground.

I rushed toward him. His ashen face revealed confusion. His sweating became profuse, his pulse barely perceptible. His eyes flickered as he moaned and clutched his chest. I knew the man was having a heart attack. The tattooed skulls on his arms seemed to smile ominously.

CHAPTER 40

I delivered drugs and supplies to our local hospital pharmacy when it ran short. I enjoyed visiting with nurses who participated in innocent flirtations and doctors who told ribald stories. Two patients were of interest to me, and I was eager to talk with them. Alice Brown, Mavis' aunt, was recovering from her hip fracture while Konrad Streicher, on the floor below, was receiving cardiac treatment, which consisted of six weeks of limited activity, bed rest, and medication.

Both patients had information I wanted. Streicher's visiting times were limited to two thirty-minute periods per day. I entered his room surreptitiously once, but he was asleep, and of course, I wouldn't disturb him. The following day, I brought a two-pound box of Whitman's samplers to the nursing station and asked the head nurse if I might visit with him for just a few minutes since I couldn't visit during the designated times.

The candy served as a less than subtle bribe, and I felt

no qualms about the subterfuge. I promised the nurse I would not engage in any arguing or give the patient any reason to become upset even though I knew he had suckered Eddie out of two meals. I wasn't the one who challenged him to the fistfight that preceded his heart attack.

Streicher's presence in Newbury bothered me. Maybe I had a naïve notion of our town as a kind of idyllic place where most people lived by the Good Book, despite the horrible murders of Earl and Irma Withers.

I was convinced that Streicher, arrogant and deceitful, was using our town as a hub to assemble a cadre of troublemakers working for the Nazis. Why would a member of the Nazis want to be in Newbury, anyway, and who was he going to meet? That swastika flag in Charles' room was the only symbol of Nazi presence I was aware of in our town. But there could have been other signs that escaped me.

I approached Streicher's' room, opened the door slowly, and saw him lying in a semi-recumbent position. He turned toward me and sneered.

In a gravelly voice, he said, "Well, if it ain't the pill pusher. D'ya come to collect the two bucks? I almost beat you out of it, buddy, and I would have if my ticker didn't start to fade."

I asked a few innocent questions about his condition before I said, "Streicher, why did you come to Newbury?

Don't tell me you were just passing through. I know better."

He glared at me. "Get lost. You don't know what the hell you're talking about—you and that fucking Lieutenant Simon."

"I'll tell you what I'm talking about. Simon went through the pouches on your motorcycle and . . ."

A nurse walked in, looked at me, and pointed to her watch. As soon as she left, I got closer to Streicher and said, "When you get out of here, you'll be hauled off to federal prison for spreading seditious literature. You can talk to the feds while you're in Leavenworth."

"That'll never happen, Mr. Dope Peddler, now fuck off."

"You think not? Listen, you and your Nazi ilk are going to prison for preaching enemy propaganda that includes overthrowing our government."

"Listen, jerk. I'm a citizen of the United States. I know my rights. The First Amendment gives me the right to free speech and assembly. The Fourth Amendment protects me from improper searches and seizures. That punk lieutenant had no right to invade my property."

Streicher knew enough about his rights to spout off guarantees provided by the Constitution, and that annoyed me. He was prepared to argue because he knew he would be challenged. "For your information, the rules during wartime supersede personal freedoms when the safety and welfare of U.S. citizens are compromised." That pronouncement sounded official to me even though I couldn't be sure of its accuracy. Hell, it had to be true.

Before the nurse returned to remind me again to leave, I leaned close to Streicher's ear. "Do you think Shicklgruber would permit you to speak against his tyranny? If you dared, you would be shot dead on the spot."

Streicher grimaced. "Get the hell out of here and leave me alone." He rang for the nurse.

"One more question, Streicher. Who is your contact in Newbury?"

He reddened; his eyes flashed. "Go to hell!"

The nursing supervisor appeared. "Mr. Black, leave. The patient needs rest."

I left the room and said to her, "We might all be better off if he had quiet and rest—the permanent kind."

*   *   *

Mavis' aunt, Alice Brown, occupied a bed on the floor above in the orthopedic ward where some patients were strung up on traction devices like giant erector sets. I watched as a nurse fluffed up Mrs. Brown's pillow then gave her medication and liquid from a glass with a straw. I remained at the door until the nurse left. A vase with fresh-cut flowers was on her bedside table. She smiled as

I walked toward her.

"Mr. Black, how nice to see you again. A box of candy? You are so thoughtful." She reached out to hold my hand. "Mavis said you were kind and gentle, and now I know she was right. I hope you can visit for a little while. People here are quite pleasant, but I treasure outside company."

Mrs. Brown recalled a generation of gracious and genteel people who lived in a world that seemed to spin more slowly, when there was time for greater civilities and courtesies. Perhaps I imagined all that. I hoped our conversation would yield more information than I gleaned during my last visit when she fell asleep while we talked.

"Beautiful flowers, Mrs. Brown. From a suitor?"

She laughed. "Heavens, no! An old widow like me? My romancing days are long gone. I have only to be concerned about my niece, Mavis. She's the darling who sent that bouquet. I love her dearly. She deserves every bit of happiness that comes her way. You know she's had a difficult time for so many years. I can't tell you how I've prayed that one day she would meet someone nice—like you."

"You're saying her marriage to Larry Johnson was unhappy?"

She closed her eyes and nodded slowly. "Larry was not a very nice person, but I would never have wished him dead at such an early age."

"You say he was not a very nice person. Why?"

"Mavis should explain all that to you."

"But you didn't like him either, did you?"

"Not really. He was not unkind to me, and yet I could not warm up to him—knowing what he was really like."

I waited for her to continue, but she became reticent. "What was there about him you didn't like?"

"I expect men to act like men. Larry was kind of—oh, I don't know—more like a sissy than a real man."

"Can you explain that?"

"I think he preferred the company of gossipy women and, well, maybe I shouldn't say this, but I think he liked young boys."

That startled me. "You think he was a homosexual?"

She looked puzzled. "I'm not sure I know what that is."

"A homosexual is one who's gay, who prefers his own kind sexually." I was embarrassed explaining the term to a seventy-something woman, but among the citizens in this relatively isolated community, social, sexual, and psychological abnormalities were not frequent topics of conversation or understanding.

Mrs. Brown looked at me with sudden understanding. "Why, yes! I think you're right. He must have been a *homo*. Oh, how dreadful."

"And yet, he fathered a son," I said.

She pursed her lips and responded slowly. "Yes, that's what we were led to believe." She turned to touch the petals of a rose in the bouquet.

I leaned forward, eager to continue the discussion when a physical therapist barged in and announced for all to hear, "Time for exercising, and no balking and no squawking."

Puzzled and intrigued by what Mrs. Brown said, I knew I had to return soon.

CHAPTER 41

Simon took the morning newspaper out of the stand near the drugstore entrance then sat at the fountain for his usual coffee and doughnut.

I had three prescriptions to fill, but I couldn't resist the urge to talk with Simon, if only for a few minutes. I sat next to him and asked Eddie for a cup of coffee, my third for the morning.

Simon hardly acknowledged me as he read the second page of *The Capital Times* where crime reports were listed for Madison and environs.

I nudged him. "Ben, you've been holding out on me. What did you learn from those papers in Streicher's motorcycle pouch?"

He peered down his nose at me. "That's none of your business, pal."

"Well, excuse me. I didn't mean to step on your flat feet. I just didn't want you to miss another opportunity to nail a subversive, that's all."

"What d'ya mean?" he said.

"If Streicher takes off from his hospital bed while you're scratching your butt . . ."

"That won't happen." He turned taciturn, folded the paper, placed it under his arm, threw a quarter tip on the counter, and left.

I called after him. "Are you going to interrogate Streicher now? If you are, I sure would like to go with you."

Simon did not respond until he opened the door. "Okay, junior G-man. Get rid of your white jacket and come with me."

He probably thought I wouldn't accept his offer, but I was more than eager to go with him. I hurried toward Mavis, handed her my jacket, and told her to take my prescription calls and tell customers I'd be back soon if they wanted to talk. I followed Simon to his battered coupe.

He said, "I want to talk to that bastard before the FBI yanks him out and puts him in a federal joint where I can't get to him. I'm curious to know who in this town is part of the Bund."

*   *   *

Three motorcycles were parked in the spaces reserved for doctors. Simon paused to look over the big Harleys and the license plates. He shook his head. "Can you believe this? Three doctors on motorcycles? That would never happen."

The head nurse hurried toward us. "I'm so glad to see you both. Oh, I'm so angry and frustrated, I can't get hold of security to get those three horrible creatures out of the cardiac room. I told them they could not visit Mr. Streicher except during visiting hours, and then only two visitors are permitted at a time. Well, they ignored me, practically laughed in my face, and marched into his room. They're committing all kinds of violations. We can't have that sort of thing. I have strict orders not to allow . . ."

Simon interrupted, asked for directions to Streicher's room, and split before the nurse could complete her complaints. At the doorway, we stopped to look at an unbelievable sight: a smoke-filled room with three galoots in black leather jackets, visor hats, and boots, all smoking cigarettes and laughing raucously while sitting on Streicher's bed where he lay with a cigar in his hand. On the bedside table, an open bottle of whiskey added to the barroom atmosphere. With no other patients in the room, it was a scene of total debauchery—a series of flagrant violations.

"What the hell is going on here?" Simon shouted and bolted toward the three. "Goddammit, put out those cigarettes, and you," he pointed to Streicher, "give me that cigar. There's an oxygen tank at the head of the bed! Do you want to blow up this place? You goddamned stupid ignoramuses. Take your damned whiskey and get the hell out of here before I run all of you in." He threw the cigar in the toilet and flushed it.

Simon continued to yell at the three laggards, each of whom stood a head taller than he. The oldest, the one who looked like a constipated English bulldog, took a step toward him.

"You talk like a big man, but I seen you the other day when Streicher almost whipped your ass, and you dodged him like a fucking coward. Mister, you're nothing without that tin badge."

Simon snarled and poked the galoot's chest. "Get the hell out of here, and take your pinhead buddies with you—now!"

They hesitated momentarily, challenging his order, then left swaggering just as a breathless security guard arrived. "What's going on?" he asked.

I explained briefly what had happened. He listened, then hurried to open the windows and flip a wall switch for the ceiling fan.

Simon got into Streicher's face. "Do yourself a favor—answer my questions." Assuming a pious tone, he beseeched Streicher. "You'll feel better unburdening your tormented soul."

Streicher's brow arched; he lifted his head off the

pillow to stare at Simon. "What the hell are you talking about—unburdening my tormented soul? You some kinda preacher or rabbi? Listen, as soon as the doc gives me the all-clear signal, I'm outta this dump, and that'll be the end of that—no more talking, you hear? Just plain goodbye, adios, auf wiedersehen, Mr. Dick Tracy."

"Uh-uh. You think you'll leave this place and be free to spout your shitty propaganda? You're headed for a long stretch in a federal pen, Mr. Storm Trooper. There's a good chance that your fellow inmates won't be interested in your stupid, hateful harangues. In fact, there's a possibility they might want to change your mind—forcibly."

Streicher glowered. "Fuck you, copper."

Simon gave no response and left the ward with me trailing a step behind. In the parking lot, we spotted the three motorcycles still parked in the doctors' spaces. Simon stopped, looked about like a hound dog tracking.

Clustered around Simon's coupe, the three cyclists with arms folded glared at us as we walked toward them. I felt my pulse pounding on both sides of my head with the anticipated skirmish.

Simon shared my concern. Out of the corner of his mouth, he said, "Don't worry, Kiddo. If they come at us with knives or guns, I'll shoot 'em in self-defense. No problem. Can you defend yourself in a brawl?"

"I'll try. It's been a long time since I've had a course in

self-defense."

"You'll be alright. Don't let 'em know you're worried. Just remember, don't fight fair. First chance you get, kick 'em in the balls."

As we neared the bullies with their sneering battle-scarred faces and their folded arms the size of my upper thighs, I hoped they'd leave when Simon threatened arrest.

Simon quickened his pace. "Hey! Get the hell away from my car before I haul your asses in for obstructing an officer in the line of duty."

I thought I'd cringe, but I remembered Simon warning about not letting them know I was afraid.

The ugliest cyclist jeered, "Well, well, look at Abie Kabibble here with his pet pussycat threatening us." He spat. "You ain't planning to dance away like you did from Streicher, are you?"

Simon opened his jacket, revealing his holster.

Big Ugly's lip curled. "Don't reach for it, copper. We got guns too, and we outnumber you. We're just gonna rough things up in your cutesy little town to even the score before we leave—you and your town with its stinking cheese and weak beer."

As he turned his head toward the other two for approval, Big Ugly was struck by Simon's punch, a battering ram to his midsection. The cyclist doubled up and moaned. Simon kneed his jaw with a force that produced a cracking sound. The oaf stumbled and fell backward, and his head struck the running board of Simon's car. He remained on the ground with blood trickling from his nose. Simon bent down and pulled a .32 automatic out of the ringleader's jacket.

One of the others rushed Simon as he pivoted and executed a chopping blow through his would-be assailant's neck, who stumbled forward, stunned and bewildered. He held his neck and grimaced. Simon gave me handcuffs and told me to put them on the limp slob whose bloody face scraped the asphalt.

When the third member held a gun in his shaking hands and aimed it at Simon, I heard a gunshot, and the cyclist's piece fell to the ground. Blood spurted from his wrist as he gave a primal scream. He paled at the sight of his blood spurting from a gaping wound.

Simon's quick and expert shooting had found its mark.

"Black, pick up Tom Mix's gun, then get on my radio. Have Schultz send out a car out to pick up these two assholes. Limp-wrist here can go back to the hospital unless he'd prefer to stay out here and bleed to death. I'll take his weapon, too. That makes three pieces for our collection of PFPs—pieces from pricks."

I was in awe of Simon's ability to overcome singlehandedly the threat of disaster—even death.

"Simon, I've got to congratulate you . . ."

He wouldn't allow any praise. "They're nothing but

ignorant bullies. We'll let the FBI handle them. They're probably complicit in the Nazi push to convert or subvert—dumb assholes."

He grabbed the lapels of the ugliest of the three, the ringleader whose jaw might have been broken and whose hands were in cuffs behind his back. "Well, Mr. Storm Trooper, how do you like being beaten by Abie Kabibble?"

The galoot spat in Simon's face.

Simon wiped his face with a handkerchief, then glowered at the offender. "Ordinarily, I wouldn't strike a man whose hands are tied behind his back, but you don't deserve consideration because you are scum, that's right, stupid, stinking drech. Tell you what I'm going to do: I'll release your hands from behind you, and you can fight with me. Fair enough?"

The cyclist nodded and said nothing while Simon removed the cuffs. Suddenly the biker swung around, landing a stunning blow to Simon's face. Simon stumbled backward but regained his balance after shaking his head, and in a crouching position he circled his enemy, who began to move more slowly, cautiously. Simon must have sensed the cyclist's fear as he rushed toward him, turned sideways, and kicked him in the groin. The bully collapsed and fell to the ground holding his crotch, moaning.

Simon stood over him, grabbed his jacket lapels,

pulled him up, and shouted, "Apologize, you bastard! Say you're sorry. Say it now, or I'll beat the shit out of you."

Bleeding from his nose and lacerated lip, the cyclist blurted, "Go to hell!"

Simon brought his fist back to strike again when the cyclist pleaded, "Okay, okay, I'm sorry. I'm sorry, Jeezus, don't hit me again."

Officer Schultz brought her police car to a screeching halt then jumped out of the driver's seat. Sizing up the situation and getting a quick report from Simon, she put cuffs on one of the two cyclists. The third, with his bloody wrist, had been escorted by an orderly back to the hospital.

CHAPTER 42

Mavis dropped a handful of mail on my desk, then put her arms around my waist and gave me a gentle squeeze. "Thanks, Zach, for looking in on Aunt Alice. She appreciated your visit. I hope she didn't reveal too many deplorable family secrets. I should have warned you, she exaggerates and creates situations that are nothing more than fairytales. Although I'm quite fond of her, I must turn a deaf ear to many things she says. I'm convinced she's suffering from early dementia. That aside, I'm terribly curious about something."

"Go on."

"In that pile of mail I brought in, there's a letter from the coroner's office in Milwaukee. I'm dying to know what it says. Mail like that always grabs me. It's like getting a letter from the IRS demanding an audit for the last five years. Seriously, why would the coroner be sending you a letter?"

"Bob Cornby, the coroner and I, took a class in toxicology years ago. In fact, we were lab partners and became buddies. We dated together, caroused around town—things like that. Over the years, I've supplied him with hard-to-get medications. I knew he'd honor my request for an autopsy report."

I opened the letter, which revealed autopsy findings on Irma Withers. It concluded death was due to ingested cyanide and described cytological changes affecting major organs.

Mavis said, "I don't understand why anyone would put cyanide in her cough syrup. That's frightening and too evil to contemplate."

*　　*　　*

While I compounded drugs, Mavis approached and disrupted my routine.

"Do you like this watch?" She extended her left wrist with two watches. "It's a new line from Bulova. We should do well with it. I haven't priced it out yet, but the markup should be at least seventy-five to a hundred percent."

"You're wearing two watches. Which one is it?"

"I'll take mine off so you can better judge the new one."

I brought her wrist up and sniffed a delightful

fragrance. "You smell good enough to nibble."

"I'll remind you of that later. For now, look at the watch, please." While she slipped her own watch off and placed it on my desk, one of the employees appeared and asked Mavis for help on pricing a new watch a customer inquired about. Mavis hurried off with her, leaving her own watch on my desk.

I picked up the attractive watch and studied the small scrolling on the pearlescent dial: "Tiffany, chronograph, Swiss made." The rose-gold bezel had tiny inlaid diamonds. I examined the back and read an engraved message.

It read: "To"—the space for a name had been buffed out, but the message continued in delicate script—"All my love, Earl." Whose name had been removed? And how did Mavis come to possess it? I was curious. The watch and its gold expanding band were exquisite and costly.

She returned, walked directly to my desk, picked up her watch, and slid it onto her wrist.

"That's a nice timepiece. Is it new?" (I knew full well it wasn't.)

"Heavens, no! It was a gift from an admirer." Her provocative smile and her eyes glinted teasingly. She elbowed my ribs. "Jealous?"

"Should I be? Is someone beating my time?"

"I'll never tell." She was enjoying herself when she sat

at my desk and started opening drawers.

"Looking for something?"

"Earl had a number of photographs on his desk, and I wondered what happened to them."

"I put them in the bottom drawer. I didn't know what to do with them, and Irma didn't want them. Never occurred to me to ask if you wanted them."

"Just a few . . . those taken of our little family with Earl and his wife, Bertha." Mavis rooted around and found several small framed photos and a collection of snapshots bound with a rubber band, some yellowed and creased.

I looked over her shoulder while she made comments about the people and places. She held up one for my inspection. "Can you identify the people—this handsome foursome?"

"This fella on the left . . . looks vaguely familiar. A young Earl Withers?"

"That's right. And the handsome fella at the other end?"

I shrugged. "No idea."

"That's Walt Mason, our handyman. Hard to believe, right? I'd never have guessed if Earl hadn't pointed him out to me years ago."

"Who are the women?"

"The one next to Walt is Annabelle Ainsley, the girl who was killed in that awful car accident years ago."

"And the young lady next to Earl?"

"That's Bertha."

"Earl's first wife?"

"Yes." Mavis paused to study the photo. "Poor thing. She was quite fond of Earl. I'm not sure he was . . ." She stopped.

"Were you about to say he wasn't fond of her?"

"I learned years ago that Bertha, a preacher's daughter, told Earl before they married that she was pregnant. Earl, rather than face the fires of eternal damnation and the wrath of the entire Baptist congregation, had his family make hasty preparations for a wedding."

"Did Bertha have a child?"

"No, and that's a sad and strange story. She never did become pregnant. Whether she honestly thought she was with child or lied to hoodwink Earl into marriage, I'll never know. I think people were inclined to believe Bertha when she claimed to be pregnant. After all, she was a clergyman's daughter."

"In this wedding photo she appears—well, not unattractive, but sort of plain, dowdy, maybe a few pounds heavier than—"

Mavis interrupted. "She became increasingly heavy, less attractive, and less social, kind of withdrawn. Earl, I thought, was embarrassed when they attended gatherings. Bertha always managed to do or say something offensive. My husband and I, however, always welcomed them to our home, and Earl felt at ease in our presence. He would set Bertha in a chair and talk with us while ignoring her."

I said, "I learned she had passed away about two years before I came to town. Earl had already been married to Irma when I arrived. What was the cause of Bertha's death?"

Mavis took a deep breath and sighed. "Bertha had a number of health issues: a heart murmur, chronic pulmonary disease, and diabetes—all aggravated by obesity."

"So, there were reasons enough for her death."

Mavis pursed her lips. "Yes and no."

"What does that mean?"

"Her physician mentioned that she was reasonably well controlled with medications shortly before her death."

"I'm not sure I understand the implications of that. If there were doubts in the doctor's mind, did he suggest an autopsy?"

"Good question. When the doctor asked Earl's permission for an autopsy, Earl refused. He became vehement, insisting that his poor wife had suffered enough pain and indignity. Imagine how silly that sounded—as though an autopsy would be painful to a corpse?"

"What conclusions, if any, did you draw from that?"

"I wouldn't permit myself to have an opinion, not one

that I cared to share. Quite frankly, I liked Earl. He had been very generous to us. I wouldn't badmouth him or say anything that would cast doubt on his relationship with his wife. Now, of course, both are gone, and I feel free to express my thoughts. They were hardly suited to each other from the very start. I thought he tolerated her as though she were a demented child."

"Do you believe Earl was disenchanted enough to—well, hasten her death? Did he hope to marry someone who would make him happy?"

"Earl was unhappy, no doubt about that. I believe he wanted companionship and understanding. After Bertha's death, he lost no time in marrying Irma when she came to town, and that was another totally mismatched relationship."

"Do you think she satisfied Earl's needs?"

"My woman's intuition tells me she satisfied his sexual needs, at least initially, but the two were worlds apart in age, intellectually and culturally, and the differences widened in a short time. They developed a mutual dislike—a hatred that couldn't be resolved. She was greedy and found Earl to be too staid, too conventional." Mavis paused and gave me an accusing look. "When you came along, you satisfied Irma's longing for . . . is intimacy an adequate term?"

"You're embarrassing me, but I can't deny that she and I—well, we found something both of us wanted

291

desperately, a yearning lodged within us. Say, that sounds almost poetic . . . a poor excuse, I suppose, for a tawdry affair."

Mavis looked at me sideways. "You're right about that, Buster, but I forgave you long ago."

"What made you so forgiving?"

"Because you're a handsome scoundrel who is successful and knows how to satisfy the needs of a lonesome widow. Other than that, I don't know why I love you."

I put my arms around her and kissed her eager lips when a harried salesgirl ran toward us. "Excuse me, Mavis. There's a phone call for you. He said it was urgent!"

CHAPTER 43

Mavis, irritated that a moment of flirtation had been interrupted, turned on the girl. "What do you mean urgent? Who called?"

The young salesgirl spoke apologetically. "A sergeant from the Milwaukee Police Department."

Mavis pulled back, spoke quietly, "Police department? What did he want?"

"He didn't say, but he left a number for you to call."

Mavis hurried to the phone at her cosmetics station. I watched as she talked on the phone. Her shoulders sagged; she closed her eyes and shook her head slowly. After replacing the phone, she walked toward me, her expression filled with resignation and anger.

"Zach, I'm sorry. I've got to leave. The police are holding Charles. They won't release him until I arrive."

"Why is he being held?"

"I don't know . . . some scuffle. I can't tell you more. I was told I had to go there for further details. The officer couldn't give me more information." She reached for her purse. After a deep breath, she said, "I don't know what he's done. I'm so aggravated and ashamed. There are times when I could kill him—strangle him with my bare hands."

I reached out to Mavis' arm. "You're in no condition to drive. I'll take you there. My assistant can handle the prescriptions. Maybe we ought to use your car. It's a sedan, and Charles can sit in the back. My coupe seats only two comfortably—"

"My car isn't here," she said.

"Where is it? How did you get to work?"

"Charles took it last night . . . said he had a meeting and would return it before midnight." She hesitated before continuing, "My neighbor gave me a lift this morning."

"Your neighbor? You mean that Helmut Gunz guy? That slob who tried to attack me and practically raped you? You allowed him—"

She cut me off. "Zach, stop exaggerating. Helmut can be very sweet, very helpful at times. Besides, it isn't as though I would ever let him get near me."

"Sitting next to him in a car is near enough. The guy's a moron, a goddammed Nazi. Mavis, I swear there are times when I don't understand you." My remarks distressed her; she wiped tears and her nose with a handkerchief. "Sorry, I didn't intend to hurt you, but when I think about that slob . . ."

She squeezed my hand. "Zach, it isn't you. It's that son of mine. He's going to drive me crazy. He has such potential, and yet he defeats himself with his maddening obsessions, his stupid hatred for people he doesn't even know, and it's killing me."

* * *

The anteroom of the police station, a cold and gloomy place, smelled of disinfectant, which made my skin prickle. A police sergeant stood behind an open sliding glass window. His tired eyes scanned us with indifference, maybe contempt. "How can I help you?"

I volunteered the information. The sergeant nodded, then closed the window while we waited, not knowing what to expect. A side door opened after five minutes, and the sergeant had us follow him down a narrow corridor with closed doors on either side. He stopped, rapped twice on an unmarked door with a frosted window. "Come in," a deep voice sounded from within.

I knew the man in a dark-blue suit who stood behind a desk and greeted us without friendliness and pointed to two chairs in front of his desk. I knew Mavis had hoped Charles would be there. She looked around expectantly, and an expression of disappointment crossed her face.

"Where's my son?" she blurted before the man could

introduce himself.

He extended his hand to shake mine. "We meet again, Mr. Black. Remember me? Jack Miller, FBI. My partner and I called on you several months ago."

I shook his hand. "Sure, I remember you and your partner. Mrs. Johnson is quite worried about her son. Is he here? Is he alright?"

"He's in the building. Before he comes in, I'd like to talk with Mrs. Johnson." He regarded Mavis, then said, "Can I speak to you in Mr. Black's presence?"

"Yes, of course."

Agent Miller turned several pages in a manila folder on his desk. "Mrs. Johnson, your son was involved in a melee between rival groups, one claiming to be super-white nationalists bearing Nazi swastikas and the other an anti-fascist group—mainly college kids. They fought, men in both groups were injured."

Mavis slid forward in her chair. "My son—was he injured? Badly?"

"Not badly. What concerns us is the organization in which he is a member. He's joined a group that has been declared subversive—an enemy of the United States. Membership in this group means he is party to a conspiracy to overthrow our government." Miller paused before continuing, "That constitutes an act of treason. It carries a substantial penalty, and . . ."

Mavis stood abruptly and cut him off. "Mr. Miller, he's

only a boy, for heaven's sake! He doesn't understand what he's doing."

"I'm sorry, ma'am, in the eyes of the law, he is old enough to bear arms and to be inducted into the armed services." Agent Miller leaned forward and in a quieter tone said, "If he confesses to maintaining loyalty to an enemy's ideology, he will be treated as a subversive. That's the law, and as I said, it carries severe penalty. Before we bring in your son, Mrs. Johnson, I want you to understand fully the seriousness of the charges he faces. Unless you convince him to change his thinking, he will face punishing hardships and lose whatever promise the future holds."

Mavis sat back and cried; her shoulders heaved. I placed my arms around her shoulders and gave her my handkerchief to dab her tears. An officer led Charles into the room. He walked tentatively, raised his head, looked around, then hurried to Mavis, who embraced him. They both sobbed. I looked away.

She held Charles at arm's length then put her hands to her mouth. "My God, look at you!" The right side of his face was swelled, his lower lip cut and crusted with dark blood. His blackened right eye was swelled and shut with a laceration on the upper lid. His military-style tunic was torn at the shoulder and collar; one epaulet dangled, and two brass buttons were missing.

Mavis shook her head and looked closely at Charles'

face. "What have they done to you?"

Charles spoke with difficulty but managed to say, "I'm okay. I got a few good licks in, but not enough, I guess. Those guys hit us with baseball bats." He looked at Agent Miller. "Who were they?"

Miller sat back and eyed Charles coldly. "A group called The Sons of Zion. Some of them are being held like the jokers in your outfit for using deadly weapons and inciting a riot." Miller wrote on the papers in front of him, then looked up at Charles. "Consider yourself lucky to have escaped with your life."

"They'll get theirs," Charles said.

"May be a while before you're able to resume your hate tactics," Miller said. "After you spend time in a federal penitentiary, you might lose some of that animosity." He glanced at the guard. "Take Johnson back. Have someone help him clean up while his mother signs a few papers."

After Charles left with the officer, Mavis confronted Agent Miller. "You can't be serious about sending my son to prison. He's not responsible—he's just a boy."

"No, ma'am, we've gone over this. He's an adult and will be charged as such."

"That's preposterous!"

"That group of hoodlums he associates with is a ring of Nazi sympathizers preaching the overthrow of our government. By definition, as I said, that constitutes a treasonous act, especially during wartime. This is no small matter."

"I will not let you imprison my son. He is not a criminal. He is a confused young man who needs counseling, that's all."

"You should consider hiring an attorney, one familiar with acts of sedition. In the meantime, Charles will be questioned further."

CHAPTER 44

Mavis, seated next to me on our return trip to Newbury, twisted her handkerchief and sobbed quietly. She gazed out the side window and said nothing for several miles. I understood her pain caused by Charles' involvement in that Nazi-inspired march and his injuries at the hands of the Zionist gang.

"What are your plans?" I had hoped to get her talking about something—anything.

"Zach, I'm terribly confused. I don't know what to do. Charles' behavior has taken an awful turn." She reached for a cigarette in her purse, lit it, and exhaled a plume through the lowered window. "First thing I'll do is get rid of all that Nazi crap in his room—that swastika banner, those hate pamphlets and books. I'm throwing that garbage into the furnace." Tapping her cigarette ash into the dashboard tray, she turned to look at me. "Zach, can you still love me knowing that my son . . ."

"Our relationship doesn't depend on a kid whose mind has been screwed up by goose-stepping goons."

"That only makes me feel worse."

"I'm only trying to ease your pain."

"Take me home—no, take me to your apartment. I don't want to be alone. Do you mind?"

"Not at all. My assistant can handle ninety percent of the prescriptions until I get back. We'll talk and maybe resolve some issues."

"I need you to hold me. Make love to me—validate my need to live. Can you do that?"

"Try me."

*   *   *

Mavis' physicality during sex bordered on the wildly uninhibited, with forceful movements and cries of ecstasy. At the crescendo of orgasm, I heard the crashing cymbals like the finale of Ravel's "Bolero." She heaved a long sigh and reached for a cigarette on my nightstand while I lay exhausted. My eyes feasted on her nude torso, her pale skin, and enticing contours as she twisted and turned. She gazed at me and smiled.

"Did you enjoy that?" She lay on the covers and placed her hand on my chest, lazily twirling my hairs.

"A penny for your thoughts," I said.

She sat up, stubbed the cigarette, and leaned over to

kiss me. Her firm breasts pressed against my chest, causing further arousal. She rolled away. "Save the hardware," she said as she got out of bed. "I don't want to wear you out—or me."

"Talk to me about our future," I said. "Tell me you'll marry me so we won't have to sneak around like a couple of oversexed high school kids."

Mavis picked up her dress and held it against her body, the first sign of modesty. "Zach, you really know little about me. For all you know, I might be . . ."

"Know little about you? C'mon. How many years and romantic episodes does it take to know you?"

"Zach, dear, this mattress exercise is fine, but it may not be enough to sustain a marriage." She headed for the washroom, exposing her firm buttocks that moved with delightful rhythm.

She emerged wearing a bra and panties and continued conversation as though no time had elapsed. "As I said, you know little or nothing about my past. And if you knew, you might turn tail and run."

I sat up in bed, supported by my elbows. "What could you have possibly done in your past that would turn me off? Don't tell me you made love to a gorilla or worked in a cathouse."

She tossed my shorts at me and made no response to my stupid remarks.

"If you don't tell me about your sordid past, I'll ask

your aunt Alice to tell me all about you."

She laughed. "I'll forbid her to tell you anything about me."

*   *   *

In the car, heading back to town, Mavis' fragrance, like a pheromone, stimulated my animal responses once again. She patted my thigh and said, "You're like a stud coming into the mating season." She smiled, making me feel good.

"I'm starving," I said. "How about dinner at the Lodge?"

"Only if you promise not to nag me about my past."

*   *   *

The dining room at the Newbury Lodge resisted change, clinging to its art nouveau origins, although the original chandeliers had been replaced by neon lights mounted flush to the ceiling and the old satin drapes were now horizontal shutters.

I considered myself to be liberal, tolerant of most people, however my attitude toward some waiters tested my patience; sometimes their fingernails harbored the good earth or dirty motor oil. Apparently, no one had taken the trouble to tell them about proper hand hygiene or underarm deodorant. If my food came with a whiff of unpleasantness, it staunched my appetite.

All that could have been overlooked if menu choices had been more numerous. Truth is, if one ordered anything but a KC steak smothered in onions and mushrooms, chances are he or she could be disappointed. Foods were drenched in butter, lard, or boiled until flavor and essence all but disappeared. Nowhere in town did chefs come with skilled training. There was an absence of real Chinese, Mandarin, or Szechuan restaurants, but a so-called Oriental café featured chow mein in several same-tasting varieties. Rice appeared in a glop like wallpaper paste complete with lumps.

A restaurant with a Gallic menu featured dishes with French-sounding names but served only midwestern foods and sliced white bread. I longed for Italian food with magical herbs and spices and would have gladly settled for Mexican dishes or kosher deli sandwiches, but none were to be found in or around Newbury.

To get any of those options I would travel over an hour to Milwaukee, and even then the pickings weren't always great. We gave our orders for porterhouse steaks after toasting with a red table wine from upper New York State.

Mavis reached out to hold my hands but stopped when she glanced over my shoulder. "Don't look now, but

Lieutenant Simon is sitting with his subordinate, Mary Beth Schultz." Mavis withdrew her hands and continued to stare at the two members of our police force who comprised twenty-five percent of the entire department.

"They make a strange team," I said, looking over my shoulder. "Mary Beth is staring at Simon as though he were an Adonis. He looks bored listening to her chatter that interferes with his veal schnitzel and red cabbage."

Mary Beth possessed a wholesome motherly appearance with blushed cheeks, a double chin, and a twinkle in her eye. Her bosomy chest might have been the envy of every skinny female in the great flatlands of the Midwest—an attribute not lost on Ben Simon.

"Darling, would you want to share a table with them?" Mavis asked.

"I would not." My quick reply took Mavis aback. "Let's enjoy our steaks and wine without—well, you know. We can have an after-dinner drink with them if that's agreeable."

Mavis nodded. "I hoped you'd say that."

I never felt completely at ease in Simon's presence, knowing he still suspected me of involvement in the murders of old man Withers and his wife, Irma.

* * *

At the end of our main course, I caught Simon's

attention. He waved us over to join them. Mavis reached for her handbag and ran a lipstick over her lips.

CHAPTER 45

Simon looked at Mavis as we approached. "Well, well, did the pill pusher finally spring for a decent meal? Or did you get tired of Eddie Polanski's soda fountain hash?"

Simon, forever honing his skills at insulting, continued, "Be careful he doesn't take out a hefty insurance policy on you." Those wiseass remarks irked me, but I refused to respond.

Mary Beth smiled and patted the space next to her for Mavis. "How sweet of you to join us," she said without a trace of insincerity. She went on, "Mavis, you look positively radiant in that dress. How I envy you. With my figure, I have to settle for a Lane Bryant frock."

Surprisingly, Ben Simon, for whatever else he was, championed the cause of women and gave them respect. Several years ago, he had encouraged Mary Beth to apply to the Metropolitan Police Academy. The lone woman in a class of twenty, she placed third and could have gone to any police force in Wisconsin but chose her home city, Newbury, where her children attended school and were cared for by their grandmother.

Simon, exuding confidence, said, "Kiddo, I think I'm closing in on the murderer."

"Good. Does that mean I'm no longer a suspect?"

He lit a cigarette, inhaled, exhaled, studied the burning tip, and turned toward me. "I didn't say that."

Mary Beth shook her head. "Ben, that's not nice."

I was in full agreement. It was just another example of his meanness. "Simon, I think you're playing games . . . trying to sound important. Well, I'm not impressed. Furthermore, I think you're wasting time and screwing the taxpayer." I wouldn't have said that if he weren't a constant source of irritation. Rather than spending more time with him, I motioned Mavis to leave. "Sorry, we've got to go rest up for a big day tomorrow."

Predictably sarcastic, Simon said, "Big day tomorrow? How about tonight? Make the pretty widow an honest woman. Marry her, for Chrissakes."

Eager to leave the obnoxious S.O.B, I hurried Mavis out of the restaurant and into the car where I could finally relax away from Simon and his smartass comments. He had a nerve judging my relationship with Mavis. Did he imagine I thought his familiarity with Mary Beth was platonic? A no-touch casual affair? I couldn't care less about their intimate lifestyle, and I'd be happier if he didn't make snide comments about mine.

Mavis placed her left hand on my right arm and said, "I'm proud of you for not reacting to Simon's provocations. As for me, I'll always think of him as a cheeky, ill-mannered New Yorker."

"He's like any rude, self-centered bigmouth from anywhere. Insecure, a know-it-all jerk needing constant approval."

"You're talking like a social scientist." We laughed and agreed that gossip was more entertaining than business, politics, or the weather.

I slid my right hand onto her thigh and met with immediate rejection. "Keep both hands on the wheel and your mind on driving, please." She turned to face me. "Don't take your eyes off the road, but tell me what makes you so forgiving and not inclined to argue?"

"I'm not aware of that. Maybe something in my past makes me want to avoid confrontation." I was reluctant to talk about my family, but I knew Mavis would insist on knowing everything about me. However, I decided to be selective and omit some unpleasant incidents.

"What were your parents like? You were an only child. Was that difficult?"

"My parents were an interesting pair. I can speak objectively now since one is deceased, and the other . . . my father was known to one and all as Mister Schwartzenpfeffer. His father, my grandfather, was a

German immigrant. My mother was of Irish-English descent. My father's family handed down a moniker that made me the butt of a million laughs, Schwartzenpfeffer. I couldn't wait to change it."

"Were your parents loving?"

"Father, like his father, was an archetypical Prussian with a strong sense of right and wrong and a superiority complex to go with it."

"And your mother?"

"She was the sweetest, most lovable woman in the world. She doted on me; gave me all the love she couldn't give or get from my father. I figured he must have caught her at a time when she was most vulnerable. Of all the mismatched people in the world, those two must have taken the cake. I was four when I became aware that my parents slept in separate rooms. My cradle, and later my bed, was next to mother's."

"What did your father do?"

"He ran a neighborhood bank. I remember him strutting around in a three-piece suit, detachable collar, and a posy in his lapel. He had a shiny limousine, a big black Pierce-Arrow driven by a chauffeur. I remember the chauffeur, Ralph Watkins, in a visor hat and leather puttees. He ate in the kitchen with Helga, the maid."

"Sounds quite affluent. Tell me more about your parents."

"Mother and Father practically lived separate

lives . . . rarely spoke to one another. Even as a youngster, I knew that was unusual. I can recall one day overhearing Mother talking to her sister on the phone. I understood enough to get the gist of what was said. Father, for all his holier-than-thou strictures, had a romp with one of the lady tellers and may have got her pregnant. Fortunately for him, the teller, a married woman, had been trying to get pregnant for several years."

"Oh, how awful. Did your parents divorce after that?"

"Father's misadventure went undiscovered for months. Ironically, he was rewarded when the baby was given his name, Augustus Fillmore. The baby's father, in blissful ignorance, gave Father the first cigar."

"Your mother must have been remarkably tolerant."

"Yes, and as much as I loved and cherished her, I found out she, too had succumbed . . ."

"Oh, I think I'm going to hear juicy gossip."

"I shouldn't be talking about this, but I believe that as a young woman who yearned for loving companionship, which she didn't get from my father . . ."

"Zach, are you hinting that she, too, had an extramarital affair?"

I knew I had said too much, but I couldn't retract my words after opening the floodgates. I had never talked about my family's secrets. As for Mother, how could I condemn the one person I adored?

"In my early teens, the concept of an extramarital affair offended me. I couldn't allow myself to think of Mother bedding another man, and yet I remember her fussing over one caller who brought her gifts, like a bouquet or a bottle of perfume whenever Father left town for a banking convention."

"Did your parents ever resolve their differences?"

"I doubt that they ever did. The crash of 1929 caused a further rift between them and imploded my father's world. His bank, like so many others, went belly-up, and his investments in stocks and bonds bought on margin became less than worthless. When a run on the bank occurred, he couldn't pay the depositors. The disaster was more than he could endure. He committed suicide— a gunshot to the head. As much as Mother and he argued, she was devastated by his death."

"Zach, I'm so sorry. Recalling that must be difficult. Tell me about your mother. Is she alive?"

"She's alive, but unfortunately, she's *non compos mentis*, in a home for the disabled."

"After your father's death, how did you and your mother manage?"

"We moved in with my father's parents in their three-bedroom home in Oak Park, a western suburb of Chicago. The move was hard on Mother, who shared a mutual dislike with her mother-in-law. There was constant tension between them.

"My grandparents were ultra-conservative. Grandfather had invested in depression-resistant corporations like AT&T and Commonwealth Edison. He had cash in safe-deposit boxes. Don't get me wrong. We still didn't live in the lap of luxury.

"Grandmother patrolled the house, made sure we followed penny-pinching practices: lights off when we left a room, heat off at bedtime, bathing once a week, things like that. I vowed if ever I made a decent living, I would enjoy every damn luxury. So far, my income hasn't allowed me to do that."

"You're living well above the poverty level, so you'll get no sympathy from me. Besides, there are too few luxury items with these wartime restrictions. Tell me, how did you decide on a career in pharmacy?"

"Actually, that decision was influenced by Mother, who insisted I become a professional who could earn a decent living. What she had in mind was medicine or law, with dentistry coming in a distant third and accounting as an also-ran.

"As a matter a fact, pharmacy wasn't on her list, but when I suggested it, she got excited . . . said she knew Charlie Walgreen, who would give me a store to manage. From there I could work my way up the corporate ladder. She was still talking about it after I said no.

"That wasn't what I wanted . . . a cushy position in a large corporation. When I told her I wanted to be independent, free of big business, she just about fainted. Said she couldn't understand me. When I think about it, I might have been responsible for pushing her over the edge when I decided to leave Oak Park. She would lose control of the only one who mattered to her."

"Zach, I thought you told me she was sweet and loving."

"Oh, she was, for the most part. I didn't realize until I got older that she was manipulating me . . . at least trying to."

CHAPTER 46

Mavis sidled closer as I said, "In that unfriendly house, I was her only ally, her only confidante."

"So, after graduation, you left Oak Park to strike out on your own. You were bold and adventurous."

"I'm flattered you think so, but after I tell you a few things, you might want to end our relationship."

She gave me a sideways glance. "I doubt that. I've too much emotional energy invested in you. If you tell me you're a child molester or that you go in for bestiality, I'll reconsider. Now, what awful secrets do you have?"

"Not many. One or two."

"Let me guess, you fell in love and . . ."

"Let me tell my own story, please."

"Sorry, just trying to help," she laughed.

"In chemistry lab, I was paired with a cute French gal, Nanette Lapine, a transfer student from the university in Lyon, France. She was what the French might call a *gamin* . . . kind of saucy, a winsome little thing. She had difficulty with some English phrases and idioms. I appointed myself her language tutor, which meant spending evenings studying together in the campus library. After library hours, I would walk with her to her apartment. This went on for about a month, and then she invited me to her room to study for the final exam."

Mavis tilted her head, raised her brow, and said, "This is getting interesting. If you tell me you raped her, I'll beat you over the head."

"No need for that. Nanette's knowledge of chemistry was quite good, and we used our study time well. We would create questions that might appear on the test and go through all the steps to solve them. After three or more hours, I became bone tired. I was about to leave when she took my book out of my hand and placed it on a table. She said, 'Poor boy, you look so tired. Come, lie down on the sofa for an hour. I'll take your shoes off . . .'

"Whether it was the hour or her irresistible face or both, I got an urge to lean over and kiss her. When I did, her eyes widened. She gasped, then held my face and covered it with eager kisses. Like a tiger in heat, she practically ripped off my shirt and pushed me onto the sofa. I swear, I don't know what happened in the minutes that followed, but suddenly we were at it—she took charge—not that I didn't know what to do, but she certainly did.

"When I told her I had no protection, she shook her head saying there was no time and then uttered something rapidly in French. For the next hour or so, we experimented in every way imaginable, and when I attempted to get off the sofa, I fell back, drained. An afghan covered me when I awakened two hours later at 6:15 a.m. The desk light allowed me to see into the bedroom where Nanette lay atop the bed. Her silken nightgown clung to her perky bust line and traced the roundness of her hips and shapely thighs. A manly response recurred, but rather than risk missing the eight o'clock exam, I grabbed my clothes, shook Nanette to get up and get dressed, then rushed to my apartment to freshen up."

"After that tour de force, I would think you'd need a week to recuperate. What happened after that?"

"We creamed our exams—A-plusses. The instructor congratulated both of us. I had learned enough to teach the course."

"Uh-huh. That's nice. Now tell me what I really want to know. What happened between you and Nannette afterward? Don't spare the details."

"She got an offer to teach in Lyon. That thrilled her. She would be back with family and friends, and . . ."

"She didn't mind leaving you?"

"I'm almost too embarrassed to tell you that after the graduation ceremony, she hugged and kissed me over and over in front of my mother and friends. Of course, the French are more demonstrative. Nanette was absolutely radiant as she bounced on her toes and clung to me.

"Mother might have been somewhat annoyed, maybe jealous of Nanette's attentions toward me. At one point, she pulled my head down and whispered that I should accompany her to France. She promised to make me very happy. As much as I loved her, I couldn't see myself living in a foreign land."

"So, your little French paramour left, and so ending a loving relationship?" Mavis' eyes widened as she waited for my response.

I hesitated momentarily before saying, "Not exactly."

Her back straightened. "What do you mean, 'not exactly'?"

I didn't intend to tell Mavis about Nannette in the first place, and now I had to reveal a secret I had lived with for four years. Uncomfortable, I hesitated before continuing, "That one evening we made love—well, Nannette became pregnant."

"Really!" Mavis' voice dripped with malice. "Go on."

"Unfortunately, Nannette couldn't accept the teaching position in Lyon because of severe morning sickness, and she felt awkward explaining the situation to her superiors—even though the French are liberal and less concerned with such formalities."

Mavis stared at me icily, but I continued, "Nannette

delivered a healthy boy and named him Zac, without the H . . . handsome kid . . . resembles me, she said. Her finances were strained since she was unable to work and got little help from family or friends."

"Did she ask for money?" Mavis' voice took on a sharp edge.

"No, but I understood her need, so I began sending a little something every month, and . . ."

Mavis cut me off. "What do you mean by sending her a little something every month? Are you sure you fathered that child, or that it even exists? Have you seen a picture of it? That tramp could have slept with every vagabond from here to Frisco."

"She never traveled west."

"Don't get funny. You really are naïve. I wouldn't give anything to that strumpet. How much do you send her?"

The spate of insults was unlike anything I had heard before from Mavis. Suddenly, I began to feel like a prisoner in our relationship. Was I justified in my thinking based on this one episode? Perhaps silence was the best response, but I was disappointed and confused by her reaction.

I wondered: Should I back off, see her less often before becoming entangled in a marriage with episodes of bitterness? Was I too sensitive? To be fair, she had a right to sound off, to complain about my stupid past behavior.

Moreover, she had been under pressure from her kid who spouted neo-Nazi slogans, gave stiff-armed salutes, and goose-stepped with a bunch of shaved heads. Maybe getting beaten up and charged with inciting a riot would change him, but maybe not. Mavis must have been experiencing shame, anger, and frustration and got some emotional relief in castigating me.

I parked in front of her home and ran around the car to open her door, but she had already stepped out and slammed the door, saying, "Don't bother."

She hurried away. I stood motionless, looking after her, trying to convince myself this was a mere peccadillo and her attitude would change in the morning. I was sure of that— well, almost.

CHAPTER 47

The following morning, the drugstore functioned as usual. I glanced several times at the cosmetic counter to see Mavis attending to customers or arranging beauty products. The events of the previous evening didn't seem to affect her. Men stopped and engaged her in conversation. I hoped they were inquiring about products for their wives or sweethearts, but I couldn't help feeling a little jealousy for fear one might be flirting. Even in this small town, there were indiscreet romances. I, for one, knew about such transgressions.

As I was gathering my thoughts, Ben Simon walked directly to the soda fountain, sat on a stool, opened his folded newspaper, and gave Eddie Polanski a signal which sent the fountain man into motion.

I left my station and found a stool next to Simon. Our friendship, which ran hot and cold (well, never too hot), drew us together to exchange gossip and insults. Truth is, I liked Simon more than I disliked him, and I was reasonably certain he felt that way about me, even though he would remind me from time to time that I remained a suspect in the murders of old man Withers and Irma.

"Well, Kiddo, the pathologist's report on Irma's death is final. I read it last night." He sipped his coffee and broke off a piece of maple bar. "Death was due to cyanide poisoning."

"Simon, that's hardly a revelation. I knew that weeks ago."

Simon placed his coffee mug down. "Yeah, that was the immediate cause of death, but you didn't get all of the information. She had, in addition, a brain tumor the size of a golf ball, a meningioma, he called it, that probably accounted for her screwed-up judgment. Maybe the reason she agreed to marry Earl Withers. No young gal in her right mind would have let that ugly old geezer touch her."

"She knew enough to marry an old guy with a big bank account. What's more, you were the one who introduced her to Withers and insisted she have a prenuptial agreement."

"Don't remind me. There's something else you ought to know." Simon looked around, then spoke in a subdued voice. "I got a call from Dave Lucas this morning. He's a police lieutenant in Milwaukee. He said Mavis' kid is not being charged with treason. Chief Morgan, my boss, put in a call to J. Edgar's office and asked him to pull that hotshot field agent, Miller, off the case and let the kid go. The kid was warned that if he got caught again goose-stepping or shooting his mouth off about Nazi shit, he'd be locked up for life. If the kid has any sense, he'll give up palling around with those fucking morons."

I watched as Simon picked pieces off his maple bar and pushed his mug forward for a refill. He looked toward the fragrance counter where Mavis stood, then turned toward me. "Can we talk a few more minutes?"

I nodded.

"I got to thinking about the background of Mavis' kid, so I did some research at the city hall and hospital and came across a fact or two that might interest you."

I suggested we talk in the pharmacy station for more privacy.

Simon crowded me as I reached for a jar of pills to fill a prescription. His voice lowered to a near whisper.

"Did you know the kid's father, Larry Johnson, was a homosexual?"

I shrugged. "Yeah, I knew. Mavis' aunt Alice told me that in confidence some time ago."

"That didn't bother you?"

"Why should it? Although I must admit, it occurred to me that the kid's screwed-up thinking might be related to that. Maybe he wanted to be more manly, unlike his father, so he joined a bunch of shaved heads with a collective IQ that doesn't register."

Simon's eyes followed me. "So, homosexual tendencies don't bother you? Maybe you approve of queers, fags, and lesbos."

"Look, they are what they are. Why should they bother you? The few I've met have problems like the rest of us so-called normal people."

Simon turned his back and grunted. "Thank you, Dr. Freud. You settled that matter brilliantly." He turned around and pointed at me. "Let me tell you something else you don't know. While looking through hospital records on the kid, I read about the family history—no loonies in the mother or father's background."

"You were looking for familial mental disorders?"

"Listen, Kiddo, in this burg there's a lot of intermarriage. We've got more than our fair share of nutcases. Oscar the Wild, who you met near his cave, is a prime example. His parents were first cousins."

"So, tell me, what else did you discover?"

"Some eager beaver intern did a complete workup on the mother-to-be including a family history . . . must have been a slow day. One item of interest turned up, and damned if it didn't stop the show. The intern caught it and brought it to the attention of the OB chief."

Simon said nothing more, and I waited for him to continue. When he sensed that I wanted to hear more, he said, "You're good at numbers, Black. Listen to this: The kid was born on August 5, 1924. His father, Larry

Johnson, dropped dead on July 7, 1923." Simon looked at me sideways; his brow tented; his lips pursed.

I said nothing and continued to count pills on my board.

"No comment?" Simon sidled next to me, goading me. "Maybe you think she had an exceptionally long pregnancy." He continued, "I asked an obstetrician about that. He said some pregnancies can go nine and a half months, even ten, but that's rare and usually the result of poor timekeeping. Eleven or more months for a pregnancy is simply out of the question." Simon's tongue pushed inside his cheek.

I turned to face him. "How do you expect me to respond? What happened all those years ago to Mavis is none of my business, and I don't know why it should be yours. Have you always been legal, morally correct? Aren't you dipping your wick without benefit of a marriage license?"

Simon nodded slowly. "Listen, Kiddo. I didn't come here for a lesson on morality, ethics, or sanctity. I gave you a few facts. You can do with them what you damn well please."

CHAPTER 48

I may have impressed Simon as being unconcerned about Mavis' delivery after her husband's death. Truth is, I had experienced a multitude of feelings: confusion, disappointment, and skepticism. Did I have the right to judge or condemn a teenager who might have been coerced into intimacy or who had been raped? Should I confront her? What would I gain? Did I love her enough to disregard an ancient sexual encounter and never mention what Simon had told me about the date of the child's birth? Life is complicated enough. I can rise above all that. Besides, I'm understanding and charitable—or am I?

I should have been able to dismiss those niggling questions, but I really couldn't. I rationalized that she could have succumbed to a high school romance or been persuaded by a fast-talking con artist. I would be happier not knowing the facts. I was sorry Simon knew about the birth date discrepancy, but I thought he could be trusted to be discreet.

How ironic—two upstanding citizens, Mavis and I. We had illegitimate children in a disapproving world. Did Mavis' son know Larry Johnson was not his biological father? I doubted it.

Mavis knew I had fathered a son out of wedlock, and she became furious once she learned I had been sending monthly checks to his mother in France. Would Mavis be more forgiving if I told her I knew about her son's birth? Who was I kidding? I needed her love, her emotional support, and her good business sense. She had been handling the business ledgers for years, long before I came into the store. She couldn't be replaced. If she left, I'd probably close the store.

* * *

From my pharmacy section, I watched as Simon came in with a stranger at his side and headed toward the soda fountain. The stranger, a portly man about 5'7", wore a navy-blue double-breasted suit with a jacket that draped like an expensive Italian import. He sat next to Simon, picked up a menu, gave it a cursory glance, then tossed it aside.

As I approached, Simon turned and said, "Zach, meet my cousin Sid Green, personal accountant to the Mayor of New York City. That's right, Mayor Fiorello La

Guardia."

Sid Green shook my hand and handed me a card from a small flat silver box. The card, with a lime-green background, read "Green, Grinberg and Green, Certified Public Accountants."

Sid slid off his seat with some effort. He stood erect, a thick unlit cigar clenched between pudgy fingers of his left hand. His thinning black hair glistened with pomade, and a scent of cologne enveloped him.

"You've got a decent operation here, Black. When I came through here five years ago, old man Withers owned this place. It looked like a relic out of Coolidge's time. You've made improvements." He looked around, nodding, his lower lip protruding as he made further assessments. "Yes, sir, this place has real potential. What's your annual income?"

I couldn't believe what I heard. "I beg your pardon?"

"I'm asking: How much do you make? What's your annual take?"

"That's a personal matter, Mr. Green. I don't think that's any of your business."

"Personal matters are my business, Black. Don't get me wrong. I'm not asking because I'm nosy. I'm here to make you a business proposition." He pulled on his belt buckle and yanked it above his protuberant abdomen. "My firm represents big chains like Rexall, Owl, and Walgreens Drugs. We're always looking for new properties, and we're prepared to pay cash on the barrel head, certified check or stock options."

"Sorry, I'm not interested."

Green nodded and continued, "You've got a good location, but the store could be modernized—maybe double your profits."

He sounded like a blowhard, but I became curious.

The unlit cigar in the corner of his mouth moved up and down, causing his speech to become slurred, but I understood the gist of it.

"My specialty is tax law, but finding new properties is how I make big bucks. When I consummate a deal, my propositions are good for both buyer and seller. That's why we're successful." He looked at me as though I should respond with applause or shout congratulations. I gave him neither.

He walked slowly along the aisles with his hands behind his back, pausing occasionally to pick an item off a shelf, glance at it, then replace it. He returned to the soda fountain and asked Eddie for a cup of coffee.

Simon left him with instructions to meet at the police department in an hour. Looking at me, Simon said, "Listen to his offer, Kiddo. He could make you a rich man."

Talk of a sale was simply out of the question, and I told Green he would be wasting his time trying to convince me otherwise.

"Are you clearing fifty grand a year for yourself?" he asked.

"Of course not! Look, this is a small town . . ."

"That amount is not unreasonable. I can estimate cost and profit by customer traffic and the pricing of your merchandise. Fifteen to twenty-five prescriptions a day and booming retail sales could put you on easy street fast."

His argument intrigued me, but there was a wide gap between his estimate of profit and what I earned. I made less than half of what he projected, and I could not see the business doing much better.

"I can tell you're doubtful," he said. "Let me glance at your books, then I can give you an appraisal of your worth—what you should be making as opposed to what you are making."

That was more intrusion than I wanted. This damn busybody had begun to irritate the hell out of me.

"My employee, Mavis Johnson, has been doing the books for many years. I would want her to discuss profits and expenses with you."

"Fine. I'll be glad to talk with her. Is she here?"

I was happy to tell him that she had to see her lawyer today. "Maybe she'll be in tomorrow."

Green shook his head. "No good. This is a one-day visit. I'll be in Des Moines tonight. Looking at balance sheets is what I've done for over thirty years, and for eight years I was chief of my section for the Internal Revenue Service. In five minutes, I can give you information you may not have been aware of. Don't worry. I'm not going to disclose any information to put you in jeopardy unless you're operating unlawfully." He elbowed me and gave a coarse laugh.

I was too embarrassed to tell him I had not studied the accounts receivable or expenses or made any serious examinations of the books. I trusted Mavis completely since she had been doing the books for over twenty years, long before I owned the store. My two-thousand-dollar-a-month paychecks, which she issued, seemed adequate, and I never had questioned her bookkeeping. However, listening to Green aroused an iota of suspicion and a twinge of discomfort.

"The ledgers are in a top drawer in a file cabinet in my office. I'll get them." He followed me closely.

The steel file cabinet with three drawers was locked. I shrugged. "Sorry, I don't have the key for this." Secretly I was relieved, thinking this would end the investigation.

Green pulled out a pocketknife and inserted the small blade into the lock to open the drawers. He reached into the top drawer, pulled out two ledgers, and placed them on my desk. His eyes scanned a column of figures in one book. "Neat writing," he said. His index finger moved down a row of figures; he turned the page and went through the same movements and nodded.

He left the ledger open as he opened the second ledger. His eye movements quickened, his brow wrinkled, and he turned to look at me. "What the hell is this?" His piercing eyes locked onto mine. You have two sets of books, Black—same dates, different numbers." His finger rested on the column of figures in the second book. "I can tell you sure as hell, this looks like fraud. Out-and-out goddamned fraud, punishable by a heavy fine and possible imprisonment."

"Hey! Wait a minute! I have no idea what you're talking about. This is not my doing—I swear." My heart hammered. I could feel heat rising from my neck into my face. I swallowed hard. My throat went dry.

"I believe you," Green said. "But ignorance is no excuse. Your failure to get involved with your bookkeeping will probably cost you a few thousand bucks—money someone pocketed. Don't look so shocked. These things happen. You can press charges against your bookkeeper or resolve your problem any way you think best, but let me tell you from my experience. That money is gone. There is no way you'll get it back, and Uncle Sam is a voracious money grabber. Better get yourself a tax attorney who'll keep you out of prison."

A burning, twisting pain started in my chest. Jeezus, was I having a heart attack? I reached for a bottle of antacids on the shelf, popped two, and prayed for quick relief. Green must have sensed my distress and said, "Didn't mean to upset you, but you've got a problem—a monster-sized problem."

He placed his hands in his pockets; his double chin rested on his chest. "Look, Black, I'm prepared to make a bona fide offer. I'll give you three times your annual income and dollar for dollar on inventory. That's a damn good offer. One you should consider seriously. Maybe it'll give you enough capital to get yourself out of this mess and enough for you to retire to Florida."

"I don't want to sell. Now, if you'll excuse me, I'll—"

"I'm not through, Black. You might want to listen to the rest of my offer."

"What part of my refusal don't you understand?"

"I understand you, alright. Now try to understand me." He paused momentarily, then pointed his forefinger at my chest. "If you don't sell, we'll squeeze you out."

"What the hell are you talking about?"

"I'm negotiating for two parcels of property with a local attorney, Arnie Teasdale. We could build a store twice the size of yours."

"Good luck," I said with false bravado. "What makes you think you'll drive me out of business?"

"We can undersell you. You won't be able to compete. Simple as that. Now think it over. Give me a yes answer. We'll do the figures, and by next week you'll be a wealthy man. One of the conditions of the sale will bar you from opening another store in Newbury. However, if you want to work for us, we'd be happy to have you."

Green extended his hand as though I would be happy to accept his proposal.

"Sorry, I can't shake on that. I like things just as they are. People have been loyal to me, and I've tried to be fair with them. I'll admit I could lose a few customers to a new store, but most will stay with me. We've become a kind of institution. Our help is familiar with all our customers and . . ."

"You're talking like a sentimental old biddy," he interrupted. "Those cherished employees of yours can be romanced away with a higher salary. No trouble there. We've been at this game too long to fail. Once we invest big dollars in a store, we make it succeed, and the competition dies, shrivels up like a dead rat." He stopped, tilted his head, and looked at me, expecting me once again to accept his offer.

"Every store you acquired is a huge success?" I asked.

"Most have been," he said.

"Tell me about the failures."

"Black, I don't have time for yakking. Think about what I've said, and while you're at it, investigate those double-ledger entries."

"Thanks for the advice," I said. "Coffee's on the house, and anytime you feel the need for a cup, stop by."

CHAPTER 49

The following evening, Mavis left the store without saying goodbye, something she had never done before. Given the contentious meeting we had earlier, I didn't expect a cordial farewell. Nevertheless, I was disappointed.

My world had taken a crazy turn, and I had no one with whom to discuss my problems. The one person I loved, trusted, and shared confidences was now estranged. Confused and angered by what that pompous ass Green had revealed about those double-ledger entries, I had to decide what to do about Mavis.

I was about to shut the lights and leave when the back doorbell rang. The door off the parking lot was intended for the disabled—those in wheelchairs or on crutches and, of course, employees. At 9:30 p.m. the store usually closed, but occasionally a last-minute call came in for digitalis, insulin, or adrenaline, which kept us open later.

I opened the door to find Simon standing there; his

dour expression did nothing to lift my spirits, and yet I wasn't entirely unhappy to see him. During our disagreeable moments, he was predictably unpleasant and suspicious. All the same, I found him interesting.

"You alright, Kiddo?" he grunted while looking over my shoulder.

"Yeah, reasonably so. What brings you here?"

"The light in your prescription section. Wanted to be sure you were alive—no heart attack or suicide."

"That's considerate. Come in. Got a minute to talk?"

Simon tipped the brim of his hat upward. "Giving some thought to the offer Sid made for your store? You could do yourself a lot of good . . ."

"No, Ben. I've got a bigger problem." I sat on a step stool and recounted the events of my meeting with Sid Green, who had discovered Mavis' two-ledger accounting system. Simon did not react as I spoke, but I was sure Green had mentioned the double-entry ledgers to him.

"You confronted Mavis?" he asked.

"We talked, argued, said painful things."

"How the hell did she explain what she did?"

"She was flustered, apologetic, teary-eyed. She began by saying when she started working here, Withers told her he wanted books kept his way."

"What reason did that old bastard give?"

"He convinced her the government was not entitled to

his hard-earned money. He said they took money and squandered it on relief programs for lazy louts, crap like that."

"And she accepted that and did what she was told?"

"He sweetened the deal for her."

"I'm all ears," Simon said.

"Let me back up a bit. Mavis was in her late teens when she came to work here. As I said, she married soon after and became pregnant. Larry Johnson, her husband, fresh out of law school, started a practice but wasn't making much. Truth is, he never made much—the guy was a loser. He gambled and hit the bottle. All this, according to Mavis' aunt Alice. Withers told her that with the money saved by skimming off taxes, he could allow her an extra fifty dollars a month. As business improved, he increased the amount."

"And, of course, she went along with that," Simon said.

"She was the breadwinner, so she gladly accepted all she could get. When her son reached school age, Withers insisted upon having the kid get a private tutor. He didn't want the boy associating with riffraff in public schools. When the kid was old enough, he was sent to a military academy which, as you know, costs a bundle."

Simon's brow furrowed as he stared at me. "The old geezer sure as hell was generous toward the kid and Mavis. She must have done all right for herself to buy a home in that fancy upscale housing development."

"You're right about that. After Larry died, she still lived well. Expensive artwork, first-class furnishings, a new Chrysler, and she dresses smartly."

"All that from undercover bonus money?" Simon asked.

"Remember, Withers had property all around town. He owned some shacks that only squatters would live in. Mavis told me some monthly rentals weren't reported, and others were entered in the two-ledger scheme. Withers gifted her with three of those rentals—rundown shacks."

Simon shook his head. He inhaled deeply and blew out a sigh. "I'm having a hard time believing this. Alright, so she cooked the books for Withers, but why the hell did she screw you out of money? Where was her loyalty? After all, you're having this intimate relationship. Seems to me you're paying through the nose for a piece of ass."

"She told me she had been doing the books that way for so long . . ."

"And you accepted that?"

"Not really. That's when we got into it. I wanted to know what happened to the monies I never received. She said she opened a separate bank account for that. I experienced momentary relief thinking the money was there for me after all, but when I asked her how much was in that account, she buried her head in her hands and said, 'Very little.' Seems every time she made a deposit in that account, a new expense arose, and . . ."

Simon nodded. "Same old bullshit. So, what're you going to do?"

Angry and frustrated, I turned away. "Simon, what the hell can I do? Accuse her of embezzlement and then hope to get what?"

"So, you're not going to press charges? What kind of shmuck are you? You've been fucked royally. While you were playing house, she was taking you for a ride down stupid suckers' alley. Maybe you deserve what you got."

"I wasn't looking for sympathy, but I wasn't expecting humiliation, either. I thought you might have a reasonable solution, that's all. Incidentally, I'd appreciate no publicity. I don't need any shitty notoriety."

"Are you kidding? You and your predecessor with the help of one shifty broad have screwed the local, state, and federal governments, and you want her caper kept quiet? Forget it. Let me give you some advice. Get yourself a mouthpiece who can keep you out of the slammer. As for Miss Wisenheimer with her clever bookkeeping, she could be looking at prison time. There's no way to keep this juicy item under wraps. The whole town will know within twenty-four hours what a schmuck you are. By the way, where are those ledgers?"

"I've taken them to my home for safekeeping."

"Let's get them," he said. "I'll drive. Already, there are

too many people who know they exist. They could be the only evidence to keep you out of the federal pen. The fact that you're surrendering them to the IRS bean counters and pleading ignorant might help."

"That's optimistic. Suppose they rule against me. I could lose everything. They could take over the drugstore, auction it off . . ."

"Hold on. You're getting ahead of yourself. Here's what you do. Get a tax attorney to plead your case since you're a total dummy when it comes to tax problems, and that's a fact. You relied on someone who scammed you. The attorney will arrange for you to make back payments on a reduced obligation."

"Sounds too easy. What do you think will happen to Mavis?"

"She'll hire a shyster lawyer who will tell her to plead innocent since she was coerced into illegal bookkeeping by a crooked boss who is dead, and now she works for one who is a lamebrain."

"Thanks a lot. That's really not fair."

"Life's not fair, Kiddo. Next time you pat yourself on the back for having made steady screwing accommodations, remember there's a price to be paid."

"Simon, your wisdom is exceeded only by the finesse of your elegant language."

"I say what I think."

"Fine. Now, if you don't mind, I'm going to leave. My

head is killing me."

"I'll drive you home, Kiddo. In your condition, you're liable to hit a fire hydrant and drown."

I was reluctant to ride with Simon, but he persisted. Frankly, I disliked his forecast of probable events, but I knew he spoke truthfully.

In the car, Simon kept chattering about my vulnerability to a scheming, unprincipled broad who fleeced and . . .

I had hoped for a quick retrieve from his verbal chastisement as he turned onto Bell, my street. I sat upright, watching flames shooting up from a house.

"Jeezus, that's my house!" I threw open the car door and ran toward the inferno.

Simon barked, "Get the hell away from there!"

I shouted, "The fire's in my den. Jeezus, my books, my papers, every damned thing I value . . ."

Simon got on his walkie-talkie to call the fire department. He jumped out of the car, ran toward me, and grabbed my arm. "Goddamnit! Stay here!" He stopped suddenly and pointed to the house. "Christ! Someone's in there. I bet it's that crazy firebug, Oscar the Wild."

"Oscar, get the hell out of there, now!" I yelled.

The figure who appeared black against the yellow-orange flames scurried back and forth, then disappeared as sirens wailed. Clouds of dense smoke billowed upward through the roof. The acrid smell of burning stuff filled the air, causing me to choke and cough, and my eyes to tear.

Two firemen tugging hoses directed streams into my den after breaking the large window. Ten interminable minutes passed before the flames began to subside; the firemen drew closer to the house, flooding the area, then breaking structures with axes, looking for hotspots. One of the firemen yelled, "Call an ambulance! There's a burned body in here."

I rushed toward the house but the firemen blocked my entry, warning me that it was unsafe and could be the site of arson. Two ambulance attendants hurried with a stretcher and resuscitation equipment. Simon pulled me aside. We waited anxiously.

"I'd strangle the sonofabitch if I could get my hands on him," I said.

"Hope to hell he's not dead," Simon groused. "If he is, his family will find some excuse to blame me . . . not that I give a damn. It's just that they'll cause a stink, and I'll be put on administrative leave."

I was about to pull Simon away when he said, "Hold on. I gotta see Oscar before they haul him off."

A body covered with a blanket on a stretcher passed us.

"Is he dead?" Simon asked one of the attendants.

"No, but he's badly burned on the face, chest, and

abdomen. We'll be taking him to the burn unit at Milwaukee General."

Simon lifted the blanket partially off the victim's face when the attendant stopped him. "Hey! Fella, don't interfere with our protocol."

Simon and I walked back to the car. I asked, "Did you see his face? Did he have whiskers?"

"Couldn't see a damn thing. Saw the skin around his eyes. Didn't see any hair on his blackened face or head—probably seared off." Simon shook his head. "Poor bastard might not make it. I've seen burns like this before. These guys are lucid for a while until the juices seep out, then it's goodbye, Charlie."

"Maybe we ought to question him while he's able to talk," I said.

"That's my job, Kiddo. I'll give the docs time to work on him tonight. Then I'll drop by tomorrow and try to get information—if he's still alive."

"I want to be there."

"This is something I gotta do alone," Simon said.

"Either we go together, or I'll drive there alone. Dammit! I've got to find out why my house was torched. Maybe he's the same bozo who set the store and my car on fire."

Simon wanted to query the guy without me interfering. He turned to look at me. "Where are you sleeping tonight, Kiddo?"

"I hadn't thought about that. In my car, or maybe I can get a room at the hotel . . ."

"You can come to my place and sleep on the sofa. I'll be leaving at 6:00 a.m. sharp. If you can get your tuchas in gear in the morning, you can come along. I'm hoping that crazy Oscar survives. If he doesn't make it, he'll take his arson secrets with him, and we'll be left with circumstantial evidence, which could be as useful as tits on a boar."

CHAPTER 50

I walked quickly behind Simon as he approached the ward station and flashed his badge at the nurse behind the desk. He asked to see the burn victim brought in the night before.

The nurse, a buxom, mid-fifties, officious matronly type in a starched white uniform, looked down her nose at Simon and announced, "That room is off-limits to all but burn-care personnel."

Simon, unaccustomed to being rebuffed, said unpleasantly, "Do me a favor. Just call the doctor in charge and tell him I want to talk with him—will you do that? This is an urgent police matter. By the way, do you have an ID on that patient?"

"All matters regarding burn victims are held in confidence unless the family gives permission."

"Look, lady, this is a police matter that involves theft, arson, and murder, all of which precludes any restrictions."

Looking over Simon's shoulder, the nurse said, "Oh, here comes Dr. Hartman. He's in charge of the burn unit." Her expression shifted gears when her voice turned sweet. "Dr. Hartman, this detective wants to talk with you about the new burn admission."

Simon studied the doctor's face and smiled. "Well, I'll be damned." He extended his hand to shake the doctor's. "Bill Hartman, you old sawbones. You sure as hell changed, but I still recognize you. How the hell are you? Meet Zach Black, pharmacist from Newbury." Turning to me, Simon said, "Bill trained at the Hospital for Bone and Joint Disease in New York where we met over twenty-five years ago. He was a cocky resident, and I was a newly discharged marine with a compound leg fracture. He put me together with hardware, then removed the screws and plates six months later when he had nothing better to do. I know he makes more money than I do, but I've got more hair."

Dr. Hartman, at six feet, wore a white hospital coat with his name embroidered over a breast pocket. He smiled pleasantly. "Ben, we've aged, but you've managed to retain your youthful feistiness. Tell me, did you ever find a girl who would consent to marry you?"

"Not yet."

"Why not?"

"You married her."

The two old friends bantered easily, which meant they

would be comfortable discussing the latest burn patient. Dr. Hartman tilted his head toward the hall, signaling us to follow. "We can talk privately in the doctors' lounge," he said.

The unoccupied room, smelling of cigarette smoke, was furnished with a worn brown leather sofa and four easy chairs, all discolored and nicked. Newspapers and magazines cluttered the room. Hartman quickly gathered the debris and jammed it into the wastebasket.

He sat on the edge of a chair, leaned forward, and directed us to be seated. "You want information on that burn patient from Newbury?"

"That's right," Simon said. "We don't know for sure who he is or how bad his condition is. We think he's been involved in other arsons, but he got caught in his own shit this time. The house he torched is Zach's. He might have been responsible for setting fires in Zach's drugstore and automobile."

Hartman said, "The young man's condition is quite serious. He—"

"Wait a minute," Simon interrupted. "You said young man? Elaborate."

Hartman shrugged. "Early twenties, as I recall."

"Do you know who he is? Did he have identification?" Simon asked.

"Yeah, from his wallet, driver's license—name is Charles Johnson. Someone you know?"

"I'll be damned." Simon turned to look at me. "Zach, you alright? You're pale as a goddamned bedsheet."

I cleared my throat . . . felt lightheaded. "I can't believe this. Has his mother been notified?"

"My secretary tried getting in touch with her several times without luck. My obligation is to treat the patient, keep him alive. I can't wait for legal consent from some judge or family member. If he dies, it won't be because we withheld treatment—not on my watch."

A burning, twisting sensation gripped my gut. "Dr. Hartman, are you able to give us a ballpark figure on his chances for pulling through?"

Hartman took a deep breath and blew it out audibly. "If you mean am I able to tell whether this patient with third-degree burns over three-quarters of his body is going to make it?" He paused and pushed down on his hands over his knees. "I'd say his chances are roughly twenty-five to thirty percent for survival. Frankly, I'm not optimistic."

My mind began spinning. Twenty-five to thirty percent? How was it possible that this young, vigorous kid could lose his life? I blurted, "Why? Why are you so pessimistic? He's getting special care . . ."

"I've been terribly disappointed in patients' responses to burn care. We can't replace his fluid loss adequately— the capillaries, that is, the small vessels in the skin that hold the liquid part of the blood, are burned away, causing a toxic concentration of solid blood elements. Look, there are a lot of bad physiological changes that occur. Suffice it to say we have a hell of a time keeping the circulatory system hydrated, preventing infection, maintaining proper temperatures—all that and more. We're doing our level best. Some new information on burn therapy is coming in from the military, but even so, we're fighting a losing battle."

Simon asked, "Can we talk with him?"

He hesitated, then said, "Alright, but don't interfere with the nurses' work and be sure to observe sterile procedures: mask, gown, and booties. When you're in the room, don't touch anything."

The room smelled of Lysol and iodine. Two nurses in surgical gowns were slathering Vaseline on gauze sheets and applying them to the beet-red skin areas on the neck, chest, and abdomen. The nurses gave our sterile coverups cursory glances then continued their work.

"Can we ask the patient a few questions?" Simon asked.

"After we've finished," one of the nurses said. "Don't get within twelve inches of him, and for heaven's sake, don't touch a thing." The entire personnel chanted the same mantra. I kept my hands behind me.

The nurses left, leaving us with Charles, almost unrecognizable with his disfigured, swollen, scarlet face. His eyes darted from Simon to me.

Simon spoke softly, "Charles, do you know who I am?" He got no answer. Simon waited several seconds before speaking again. "I want to ask a few questions. Just a few, then I'll not bother you."

Charles' eyes shifted toward Simon, but his head remained motionless.

"Why did you start the fire in Mr. Black's house?"

Again, no response. He stared at the ceiling while we waited. The temperature in the room became uncomfortably warm, and the mask began to irritate my nose, as did Charles' reticence.

Simon continued, "Did you set the fire in the drugstore? In Mr. Black's car?" Again, no response, but a flicker in the patient's eyelids suggested that he understood the question.

"I believe you were the one who killed Mr. Withers," Simon said. "That gunshot in his forehead . . . that was the work of a marksman. Someone Withers knew and trusted. Am I right? I think I am. And the poison that killed Withers' wife, Irma. You or your mother took cyanide from the locked cabinet in the drugstore. You had access to your mother's keys and unlocked the cabinet. You also took your mother's keys to Withers' home and poisoned Irma Withers' cough medicine. Yes, sir, it all adds up neatly, wouldn't you say?

"You wanted Irma out of the way because you were hoping your mother would marry Mr. Black. Since that didn't happen, you wanted to destroy everything Black owned: the drugstore, his home, even his car. Then you wanted to kill Mr. Black when he left Walt Mason's home. You shot at him from your car with a shotgun."

Like a mummified pariah, Charles ignored Simon's charges and continued to stare at the ceiling.

I noticed a slight upturn at the corners of his mouth as though he attempted a smile. I whispered to Simon, "Maybe the fire affected his vocal cords and hearing."

One of the nurses returned with a bottle of intravenous fluid and tubing.

"Does he have trouble communicating?" I asked.

"Are you kidding? He can yell like a fishmonger when we start treating him, but of course, I can't blame him for that." She examined his excoriated arms then looked at his legs and located a vein near the right ankle. She looked at her watch. "You fellas have ten minutes. Then you'll have to leave. We have a lot of work to do, and you're in our way."

After she left, Simon resumed his questioning, this time with a hard edge to his voice. "Alright, Charles, let's go again." He listed the criminal acts and paused after each one but got no response.

Simon continued, "Here's my proposition. I'll talk to the state attorney, who will be seeking the death penalty. I know him. He's a hard-ass, unforgiving sonofabitch, but I'll tell him you were cooperative, that you showed remorse during your confession, and because of your age . . . of course, you'll have to give us details about how you killed Mr. Withers and poisoned his wife, Irma."

We waited eagerly for a response but again got nothing. As we left the room, Simon mumbled, "Shit."

We threw our protective gear into a hamper next to the door then walked to the nurses' station where Dr. Hartman stood making notes. He turned toward us. "Did you fellas get the information you wanted?"

Simon said, "No, the bugger wouldn't say a damned thing. Maybe we'll get something later."

With a glum expression, Hartman shook his head. "His lab reports and clinical responses are dismal . . . hemal concentration, rising temperature, poor urinary output. Look, fellas, his prognosis is less than fair. If you're planning to get information, I suggest you get it soon."

"Yeah. How?" Simon asked.

Hartman shrugged.

"I'm going to get that kid to talk if it's the last thing I do. I'll have a smoke then pay him another visit."

Simon and I walked to the visitors' lounge, the solarium, where the sun's rays brightened the already cheerful room with its bold-patterned fabrics and soft, piped-in music. Simon's brooding hadn't improved with the surroundings. He sat heavily, reached for a cigarette, lit it, and took a long drag. He exhaled a plume of smoke upward, closed his eyes, and murmured, "I'd sure as hell like to wrap up this damned case. For almost three years, this kid has been throwing shit in our faces and evaded jail time." Simon stopped, looked around, and jumped up. "She just ran by."

"Who?" I asked.

"The kid's mother, Mavis."

"I've gotta talk to her." I hurried after her as she stopped at the nurses' station.

Angrily, she demanded to see her son and refused to listen to what the nurse was saying.

"I want to see him now! Do you understand? Who's his doctor?"

"Mrs. Johnson, I'll try to get Dr. Hartman. He was here just a moment ago."

The nurse's calm demeanor did little to pacify Mavis, who turned to glare at me with bloodshot eyes and an expression of loathing. She said, "Don't you dare touch me. You're responsible for this—you, you bastard."

I took a step back, not understanding her hatred. Sure, we had talked about her double-ledger entries and her skimming of profits, but she should have known I wouldn't take legal action. We had shared so many memorable experiences. Didn't they mean anything?

Dr. Hartman moved rapidly toward us but gave Mavis his attention. "Mrs. Johnson, let's go into my office where we can talk." Her hysterics were replaced by deep sobbing as Dr. Hartman placed his arm around her shoulders and guided her away. I looked after them, realizing that my world had imploded, becoming a place of hurt and sorrow.

Coming toward me with determination, Simon, along with two uniformed cops, one on each side, said, "Where's Mrs. Johnson?"

"Talking with Dr. Hartman in his office. Why is half the Newbury police force here? You expecting an uprising?"

"Listen, Kiddo, that bed partner of yours is going to answer a few questions along with her closed-mouth son. I've had enough of their evasive bullshit. It's time for straight answers."

*　　*　　*

Simon, with his police escort, waited impatiently at the nurses' station, then moved toward Mavis and Dr. Hartman as they walked along the hall toward Charles' room. Dr. Hartman put up his hand to hold Simon and his cops at bay. "Detective Simon, please allow Mrs. Johnson to visit with her son."

Simon, about to object, relented, then looked at his watch. "I'm giving her ten minutes, that's all. The boys and I will wait in the hall."

CHAPTER 51

Simon's jaw jutted, his mouth turned down; I imagined him grappling with his conscience—straining to nab Mavis, eager to accuse her of crimes he should have solved long ago. He had little choice but to grant her one last visit with her dying son. He looked at me, then pointed to his wristwatch. "Fifteen minutes, then we're taking Lizzie Borden out of there. No more stalling." He signaled his two escorts to walk with him to the visitors' lounge.

I waited outside the patient's room, looking through the door window to watch Mavis as she sat at Charles' bedside, talking to him even though he continued to stare at the ceiling, not saying a word.

Simon, grim, emerged from the lounge with his two uniformed escorts walking in cadence toward me like a death squad.

He looked through the door window, then knocked. After several seconds, he knocked again. "She's ignoring me," he said. Opening the door, he stared at Mavis, then shouted, "Jeezus! What the hell's going on in there?" Charging into the room without sterile paraphernalia, he leaned over to look at Mavis and yelled, "Get a nurse in here, now!"

The head nurse came running into the room, placing a mask on her face and starting to berate Simon for not wearing sterile coverings.

"Never mind that! Look at Mrs. Johnson," he charged.

From the door, I could see Mavis seated at her son's bedside, her head slumped over the bedside rail, motionless, unresponsive to the nurse's attempt at examining her. Another nurse arrived and bent over the motionless Mavis. The head nurse, moving frantically, moved Mavis onto the floor with the other nurse's help and started respiratory movements.

I ran into the room. Mavis' lips were blue, her skin deadly white. Desperate, not knowing what to do but thinking I had to do something, I felt for her wrist and neck pulses. Nothing. I felt again, brushed her eyelids. No response. I broke into a sweat. My heart hammered.

"Call Dr. Hartman," the head nurse spoke softly to her subordinate. She looked around. "Alright, everybody out, now. Go!"

Charles, swathed in moist dressings, kept staring at the ceiling without uttering a sound. I refused to leave and bent over Mavis' lifeless form. How could this beautiful woman be alive one moment then be gone forever? We had shared so much . . . happiness, love, and sorrow. We worked side by side, and I had hoped we would marry soon. Her death was unbelievable.

Dr. Hartman, moving rapidly, straddled me as I leaned over Mavis, who lay on the floor. He placed his hands under my shoulders to help me stand, but I resisted and bent over to kiss her cold lips. There it was—that odor, the odor I had detected in Irma's room after her death. I moved away slowly. The tell-tale odor of cyanide. Why?

Simon, standing next to me, became uncharacteristically compassionate. "Sorry, Kiddo. It's over. C'mon, time to go. Want to stop at the station? I've got some scotch . . . we can talk . . ."

"Yeah. Maybe that'd be a good idea." I wiped my eyes and blew my nose in my handkerchief.

Walking along the hospital corridor, Simon said, "I'll tell you what we found out. We got a search warrant issued by Judge Malloy after we convinced him we had reasonable cause to go through Mavis' home to find evidence linking her and her son to the murders of Earl and Irma Withers."

"If you knew or suspected the kid of murder, why the hell did you wait so long?"

Simon pulled out a cigarette as we walked in the parking lot. "The wheels of justice turn slowly, Kiddo. We had to get all our ducks in a row."

"Your clichés are tiresome."

* * *

Mary Beth sat at the front desk in the dimly lit station, reading a romance novel. She smiled at us like an obedient servant welcoming her master. In this case, her master, Simon, happened to be her lover.

We sat in his dismal office, which was hardly conducive to raising my spirits. I sat opposite him as he reached into his lower desk drawer and brought up a bottle of Johnny Walker Black Label and two cloudy whiskey glasses. He wiped the glasses with a handkerchief from his back pocket and placed them on the desk. After filling each glass, he raised his own and said, "L'chaim," which he explained meant "to life."

I'm not a scotch drinker, but this was relaxing and made Simon's company more tolerable. I was eager to know what Simon and his blue suits found in Mavis' home.

"There are a few incriminating pieces of evidence that I can't tell you about," Simon said. "Arnie Teasdale, Mavis' lawyer, asked me to keep the information under wraps until the estate is settled."

"The estate? Who inherits the estate if her son dies?"

"She has family. An aunt here and a few relatives in West Virginia. But the reason I wanted you here is to give you a sealed envelope addressed to you. It was in a locked desk drawer, which I jimmied open."

"And you didn't read it?"

"Some things are sacrosanct. Truth is, I couldn't get it open without tearing it and having you think I have no class. Besides, I plan to have you read it in my presence."

"Simon, there should be no doubt in your mind about my thinking you have no class, because you really don't. Now give me the letter."

CHAPTER 52

I opened the envelope with my pocketknife and pulled out four light-pink pages with delicate handwriting that I recognized immediately.

Simon leaned forward in his chair. "I'm waiting. Start reading, Kiddo."

"Do you mind if I read it to myself first? I'll be happy to give you a synopsis. The contents could be personal."

"I don't give a damn how personal they are. I want to hear every word—no shortcuts, no omissions. Got that? Now start reading."

"This letter is dated one month ago. It starts: 'Dearest Zach, I think you know that I love you very much. I am hopeful you will never see this letter, but my hopes are fading since Detective Simon has become almost relentless in questioning me. I don't know what the future holds or what misconceptions people have, but I want to set the record straight, and in doing so, ease my conscience.

"'Let me give you some background as to what occurred over the years. Some of the details you may recall from our past conversations. If so, please bear with me.

"'I met Larry Johnson twenty-one years ago. He was a young lawyer who specialized in real estate law and handled Earl Withers' properties. I had just graduated from high school when I was introduced to him. We fell in love and had a whirlwind romance encouraged by his mother, who was eager for us to marry. Larry was handsome, sophisticated, and thoughtful, everything a girl could hope for. I was thrilled at the prospect of becoming his wife.

"'Unfortunately, soon after our wedding, I learned Larry was homosexual. Believe me when I tell you I had no inkling of such things. I was so naïve. I didn't know such things existed. Premarital sex was a strict taboo that had been drilled into my unworldly Baptist head. After days of not having consummated our marriage and listening to all of Larry's excuses—headaches, tiredness, upset stomach—I felt terrible frustration, then anger. Initially, I blamed myself for being unattractive or undesirable. I confided in some of my friends, who identified the problem. I was devastated.

"'After learning the problem was not mine, I became resentful and determined to seek satisfaction. I faced a terrible dilemma since I did not want to do anything to bring open shame upon Larry, myself, or our families. Yet I wished for those experiences all young lovers seek. In retrospect, I should have divorced him, but his mother begged me to remain married. She convinced me that he would change eventually, and to reward me she placed fifty thousand dollars in a private account for me on condition of my staying married for at least five years.

"'To back up a bit, I had been working at Withers' drugstore while I attended high school and became Mr. Withers' favorite employee. He took more than a fatherly interest in me, and after my marriage he began to shower me with costly gifts, things I could never afford. Even our home was purchased from him at mortgage rates much lower than any bank would offer.

"'All that came at a shameful cost. Earl wanted payment in sexual favors. Since I had little or no gratification from my husband, I found giving myself to a generous man was not difficult. I'll confess, I never fell in love with Earl, but he did meet my sexual needs. I think you can rightly assume that my son, Charles, was fathered by him.

"'Yes, that is the truth. Earl was more than proud of Charles, who was his only offspring. He couldn't do enough for him. He paid for a fulltime nanny while I worked at the drugstore, and he bought toys and all of Charles' expensive clothing. As Charles grew older, Earl insisted that he matriculate at the finest military academy.

"'Larry accepted Earl's generosity and thought of him as a doting father to me and grandfather to Charles.

"'My husband believed that he had fathered the boy as a result of one of those rare occasions when he deemed to have intercourse. I could count those times on the fingers of one hand. I knew the evening I conceived, and it wasn't with Larry. Withers and I guarded our secret. Remember, he was married to Bertha at the time and did not have a normal sexual life. Bertha, poor thing, suffered from vague imaginary and real illnesses . . . she was obese and quite unattractive.

"'One evening, Charles overheard Earl and me talking and learned that Earl was his true father. I couldn't convince him that he misunderstood our conversation. He became angry, morose, and hateful. He developed psychological problems when he learned of his own father's abnormal sexuality.

"'When Earl married that horrible floozie, Irma, my son became inconsolable. I had been widowed for several years, and in Charles' mind, Earl should have married me. In his late-teen years, Charles developed more serious emotional problems and suffered from bouts of irrational behavior. That's when he joined that despicable Nazi group.

"'I thought I would die when he came home one night crying, blubbering, banging his head against the wall. I suspected something terrible had happened. He confessed to arguing with Earl at the drugstore, then shooting him in the head. I don't know how I survived that night. I thought of committing suicide. I know I should have reported that to the police, but how could I? My only child would be taken from me. My feelings toward Withers just before Charles killed him, I'm ashamed to admit, were filled with bitterness and hatred. I, too, thought he should have married me rather than that detestable Irma.

"'Before he was murdered, Earl, who had shown signs of early-onset senility, confided that he would get rid of Irma and marry me. He said he planned to prepare a special syrup for her chronic cough. I refused to hear about that and told him not to do anything so stupid. He did not poison Irma. My son did.

"'Earl contemplated getting rid of you, too, Zach, because you made a cuckold of him with his wife, Irma. In fact, Earl asked me to make inquiries about buying an insurance policy on your life with him as the beneficiary. I told him to forget that and never mention it again.

"'I would never let anything happen to you, even though I was terribly resentful of you and your relationship with Irma. I wanted desperately to be your wife, but with my troubled past, I resisted. Firstly, my son is emotionally unstable, and I'm sure he is responsible for the fires in the drugstore and your car. Secondly, the state auditor will hold me responsible for altering the books and withholding taxes. And thirdly, I would be forever remorseful and haunted by the deaths of Earl and Irma at the hands of my son.

"'Detective Simon suspects me in both deaths and has grilled me several times. I dreaded those sessions, but I believe I must have convinced him of my innocence.

"'I gave myself to a married man, one old enough to be my father, but in return I got a son I adored, even with his terrible problems. In addition, I have a beautiful home with lovely furnishings, art treasures, and a fine automobile.

"'"As I wrote initially, I hope you never have occasion to read this letter. I love you with all my heart, but you can see the terrible problems that weigh me down. Despite all that, I will love you to my dying day. You will always be my one true love. Mavis.'"

I refolded the pages, replaced them in the envelope, and was about to put it in my jacket pocket when Simon reached for it.

"Evidence," he said. "I'll make a copy and return the original." He took the pages out of the envelope and started to read. As he neared the end, he said, "You didn't read the postscripts to me."

"They're personal—shouldn't be of interest to you."

His smirk preceded wiseass comments. "Postscript one: 'No one ever made love to me as you did.' Postscript two: 'I love you more than you will ever know, and I eagerly await the next time I can hold and feel all of you.'"

I was grateful Simon made no snide remarks as he stood and placed the letter in his jacket pocket. He said, "C'mon, let me buy you a cup of coffee at your soda fountain. I've gotta tell you; I dislike you less since I know you're no longer a suspect."

"Do me a favor. Don't get chummy. To me, you'll always be a pain in the ass."

"You sell suppositories for that."

"And you are the best argument for a classless society because you've got no class at all."

He shook his head and smiled, a rare occurrence for him. He said, "You're okay, Kiddo, even though two of your former lovers are dead. Be sure to give your next one fair warning."

THE END

ABOUT THE AUTHOR

A.J. Harris M.D. FACS, a graduate of the University of Illinois College of Medicine, served in the Pacific Theatre of Operations during WWII. As an award-winning author, he has written nine novels, four radio broadcast plays, and numerous short stories. He lives in Santa Barbara, California, with his wife, Yetta.

He is the author of *Death Dear Doctor*, *Take Two Tabs Then Die*, *Satan Stalks Sinatra Drive*, *Death in the Saddle*, *Fatal Formula*, *Farewell My Country*, *Revenge/Revancha*, *Lucifer in Celestial Gardens*, and *Murder in a Small Town*.

www.ingramcontent.com/pod-product-compliance
Lightning Source LLC
Chambersburg PA
CBHW021435240626
47153CB00001B/168